Evil
Librarian

Evil
Librarian

Michelle Knudsen

CANDLEWICK PRESS

First edition 2014

Library of Congress Catalog Card Number 2013957277
ISBN 978-0-7636-6038-3

14 15 16 17 18 19 BVG 10 9 8 7 6 5 4 3 2 1

Printed in Berryville, VA, U.S.A.

This book was typeset in Chaparral Pro.

Candlewick Press
99 Dover Street
Somerville, Massachusetts 02144

visit us at www.candlewick.com

For Jen and Steph, who helped me survive high school
and everything that came after

Chapter | 01

Italian class. The shining highlight of my Tuesdays, Wednesdays, and Fridays. Not because I am any good at Italian (I'm not), or because I like the teacher (I don't). It's because Ryan Halsey sits one row over and two rows up from where I sit, which is absolutely perfect for forty-five minutes of semi-shameless staring.

He's one of those boys that you just can't quite believe is actually real. I know how that sounds, and I don't mean to be all pathetic and ridiculous, but — he's *so beautiful*. At least to me. Maybe not, like, French underwear-model beautiful (although I would certainly enjoy seeing him in said underwear — or, you know, without), but definitely worthy of serious visual appreciation. Of course, he has no romantic interest in me whatsoever; he barely knows I exist at all, in fact. I don't even think he knows my name. I have no illusions this will ever change.

I just like to look at him. And think about him. And dream impossible dreams of our future life together as boyfriend and girlfriend, husband and wife, romantic roommates at the old-age home. But I can't speak to him. I can't even be in the same room with him without turning into a mindless drone of longing. I think if I ever touched him I'd just dissolve into a little pool of liquid bliss on the floor, and someone would call the janitor to come and mop me up and I wouldn't even care, because I'd be too happy. Yeah, it's dumb. I *know*, okay? But my brain just sort of vacates the premises when I'm around him.

Anyway, there's nothing wrong with a little pleasant distraction. A girl needs something to get her through Italian (not to mention junior year) without going crazy.

Annie reaches over and slips a piece of paper onto my desk. It's one of her little drawings: me, in all my stick-figure glory (I can tell because of the wavy shape of the hair bunched into a stick-figure ponytail and because there is a little arrow pointing to it labeled YOU), arms out zombie-style, walking toward a stick figure of Ryan, drool streaming from my mouth. (I can tell the drool is drool because there is an arrow labeled DROOL.) Ryan isn't labeled, but he doesn't have to be — even as a stick figure, he's too beautiful to mistake for anyone else. I have a fluffy thought balloon over my head filled with little hearts.

I tuck the paper into my book before Signor De Luca can catch me with it. Then I glance over at Annie, who is looking innocently forward as if today's vocabulary list is the most interesting thing she's seen in months. *Biblioteca?* Really! Fascinating!

"The drool was a nice touch," I whisper at her. "Very classy."

She doesn't look at me but she can't stop herself from grinning. She loves giving me a hard time about Ryan. It's okay. Someday she will be the one with the hopeless crush, and I will mock her mercilessly. I look forward to this with great anticipation.

When the bell rings, I swing around to punch her in the arm and accidentally knock my notebook onto the floor. Before I can get it, four beautiful yet manly fingers and a perfect thumb reach into view and pick it up for me.

"Yours?" Ryan asks.

I take it mutely. Manage to nod. *Yes. Mine. I love you. Let's get married and have a million babies together, right after we both graduate from Ivy League schools on full scholarship and have fulfilling and exciting careers. You are the most perfect creature ever on God's green earth. Love me. Love me right now. Please.*

He walks away.

Annie explodes in peals of laughter. I'd be mad, except she has the best laugh ever, and it's impossible to be mad at someone who can laugh like that.

"Oh, Cyn," she says, when she can speak again. "It's like you're possessed! Seriously. You couldn't even say anything, you just sat there staring and drooling."

"I was not drooling." Oh, God, tell me I wasn't drooling. I can't help it; I rub the back of my hand against my chin. Perfectly dry and respectable. Annie's a jerk. A sweet jerk, whom I love to death, but still.

She's still laughing when we part ways at the second-floor landing.

I can't wait until it's her turn. That girl is in for a world of pain.

Or at least a whole lot of relentless good-natured teasing. She is my best friend, after all.

Later. I wait by my locker for Annie to work her way over from the other side of the building. Students pass by; slowly, quickly, alone, in groups. And in pairs.

I try not to stare wistfully. It's clearly been way too long since my last boyfriend. And I don't even know if my last boyfriend was technically my boyfriend at all. The whole thing with Billy at the end of the summer was more awkward than anything else. We ended up kissing that time at Sarah's party and then suddenly we just were sort of *together*, but it had never seemed to be a conscious choice on either of our parts. And it wasn't what I wanted, anyway. *He* wasn't what I wanted. Even while it was good, I wanted . . . more. Different. *Better*.

It would be so nice to have a real boyfriend. Someone who would hold my hand walking down the hallway and not be embarrassed about it. Someone who would text me during the day just to say he was thinking about me. Someone who would be my guaranteed Friday-night date and who couldn't wait to see me and kiss me and introduce me to his parents and do all the cheesy things I would never admit wanting out loud to anyone in a million years. I don't want to be *that* girl, the girl who thinks all she needs to be happy is a boyfriend. And I'm not, not really. I have friends, I have fun, I have varied interests and above-average intelligence and am deeply invested in running the set and backstage crew for this fall's school musical and rarely spend a weekend night at home if I don't want to. I am far from lonely and miserable. But it sure would be nice. To have someone.

And yes, okay, especially if that someone were Ryan Halsey.

At this moment, of course, ridiculously on cue, he suddenly appears from around the corner, and I swear he's moving in slow motion like some stupid sequence in a bad summer movie, one hand reaching up to run through his perfectly tousled brown hair, head turning to smile at something one of his buddies has just said, the sea of students parting automatically before him, the pigeons outside the windows cooing his personal theme song and the team banners on the wall gently waving in time and the sun shining down in targeted rays to illuminate him in a glorious halo of glowing enchantment.

He's going to walk by me, and I don't know what to do with myself. Smiling and saying hello are, of course, out of the question. I want to turn around and hide in my locker but I think it's too late, it would be too obvious. So I peer farther down the hall, pretending to look for Annie, even though I know she will be coming from the opposite direction, and then when I can't stand it one more second I turn my head and he's right there, passing right in front of me, almost close enough to touch. For one second I think maybe our eyes meet but then it's over and he's gone, passed me by, surrounded by his posse and the swirling invisible whirlwind of my longing, lustful thoughts.

For one crazy moment I am tempted to run forward and just tackle him. My legs are perfectly willing to move at my command, I feel them ready and waiting, eager, giving me the enthusiastic all clear. *Let us go to him,* they implore me. *Release us to chase our destiny!* My legs are a bit melodramatic, but I hear what they are saying. I could throw him down and take a big juicy bite of his absolute deliciousness. Straddle him right there in the hallway and then, after a long, smoldering look deep into his eyes, lean down slowly and start kissing him in the way I have imagined (in excruciating detail) ever since the first day I saw him in the cafeteria last year. (September 18, 12:03 p.m., third table from the windows, counting from the wall closest to the lunch counter. He was wearing a faded *Glengarry Glen Ross* T-shirt and eating barbecue potato chips. Or so I vaguely recall.) And at first he would be surprised, but then after a moment I would feel his hand come up behind my head and wrap itself in my hair and pull me closer against him, crushing my mouth to his, and —

I stop before I really do start drooling.

Sigh.

Where the hell is Annie? Not that I really wanted her to witness a second helping of my Ryan-induced stupidity today, but she is usually here by now. I turn back to watch the corner that so recently produced the heavenly vision of my dream-boy, and finally it releases Annie into view.

Something is going on.

She's sort of half walking, half twirling. She is often a rather bouncy girl, but this is different. This is like a *Sound of Music* the-hills-are-alive kind of thing. Her face is flushed and her eyes are shiny and kind of, well, strange. Intense. In a very non-Annie kind of way.

I take a step toward her and she grabs my arm and pulls me against her and spins me around to walk back the way she came.

"What — where —?"

She leans her head close to mine as she propels us along. "New. Librarian." She breathes the words as if they are sacred scripture.

"I'm sorry, what? New *librarian*?"

She nods like this explains everything. I pull her — with some difficulty — to a stop. She turns to me with very uncharacteristic impatience. "Cyn, come on. You have to —" And now her face sort of melts into helpless dreaminess and I start to get it. "You have to see him."

Ohhh.

I feel an evil grin coming on. Maybe Annie's turn at the hopeless crush is going to come sooner than I thought.

She whips us around the next corner and up the stairs and down the hall toward the library. I suppose I'd heard something about a new librarian being hired, but it's not like this is an event I would expect to greatly impact my life in some significant way. And if I'd thought about it, I probably would have assumed that the new librarian would be something like the old librarian. Who was a perfectly nice-seeming middle-aged woman who could help you find whatever you needed for your paper or project or weekend reading but was not someone who inspired breathless words or flushed faces or shining eyes. Unless you happened to be the sort who got really excited about primary-source research materials or something, I guess.

We reach the double doors and now Annie stops, releasing me so she can try to smooth her short dark curls a little and peek in her compact mirror.

"Do I look okay? I look okay, right?"

"Yes, sure. Of course. Jeez, Annie. You realize he's the *librarian*, right?"

She looks at me, her eyes still bright with—something. "Uh-huh," she says. And again she sounds nothing like the Annie I know. The Annie whose previous semi-romantic interests have been nerdy science guys and various unattainable boyish celebrities and whose yearning has always been sort of cute and fluffy and innocent. This Annie in front of me is way more . . . carnal. And it's not like I don't get it; I mean, was I not just daydreaming about taking an almost-literal bite out of my own fantasy crush? It's just so not like her. It's almost alarming, except I can't wait to tease her to the full extent of my ability. She *so* has it coming.

She takes a deep breath and then pulls open the library doors. Together, we step inside.

I have been in the library plenty of times. Shelves of books, rows of computers, a bunch of wooden study tables, the shiny modern circulation desk that got a makeover during holiday break our freshman year. It has inspired occasional feelings of resignation, or indifference, or maybe panic, when I've waited too long to start a project, and sometimes even a modicum of pleasure when I'm actually there to find something to read for fun. It has never made me feel anything like what I feel right now. The air, usually quiet and still and slightly dusty with the smell of books, is now charged with some strange energy. It's like walking into some otherworldly combination of old church and late-night dance club, where the music happens to be silent and pulsing and all of the dancers are invisible.

I stop, confused, trying to figure out where this feeling is coming from. Shapes seem to flicker at the corner of my vision, but when I turn my head, there's nothing there. It's the same library it has always been, nothing has changed . . . and yet everything is very, very different.

Annie seems to have forgotten me. She steps forward, slowly, one step at a time, and again I find myself thinking of an old church, some sacred ritual where a young girl proceeds slowly and significantly toward some life-altering event. I feel like I should be scattering rose petals in her wake. I want to speak, to break this weird sensation of being somewhere else, but it feels wrong and I can't. It's crazy — it's the high-school library, for Pete's sake — but I feel like an outsider, meant to quietly observe and not interfere.

There is a sound from behind a row of bookshelves and Annie lights up.

"Mr. Gabriel?" she calls softly.

Footsteps, and for a second I want to turn and run. My breath catches and I am suddenly terrified, for absolutely no reason except that Annie is being so weird and the library feels so strange and I don't seem to belong here. I want to grab Annie and pull her away and tear down the hall and down the stairs and outside into the sunny afternoon and not look back.

And then he appears, and I feel ridiculous.

He's just a man. A young and, yes, okay, very attractive man. *Of course he is,* my brain says patiently, as if speaking to a small and not very bright child. *What on earth did you think he would be?* And I don't know what to say to that. I guess, for a moment, I did think he would be something else. Something — terrible. But that seems very silly now. He's just a nice-looking guy in dark jeans and a white button-down shirt. He could almost pass for a student; he must be right out of library college, or wherever young librarians go to learn about library things.

"Annie? Back so soon?" His voice is deep and low and sort of gently amused, and the sound of it instantly makes me amazed that I ever thought he could pass for a high-school boy. His words carry a weight of age and experience that seem way beyond his apparent years. Those library-school courses must really be something.

"Hi, Mr. Gabriel," Annie says, breathless again. "I'm sorry. I hope I'm not bothering you. I just wanted to introduce my friend Cynthia."

He steps closer to her and looks down kindly. "Of course you're not bothering me, Annie. You are always welcome here." Then he turns his gaze to me. His eyes are a startling dark color, maybe gray, maybe black, maybe even a sort of very deep violet. I have to struggle to blink; part of me seems to want to stand there staring into them for as long as it might take to figure out exactly how to describe them.

"Cynthia. How nice to meet you. I guess Annie has told you I'll be the new librarian." He reaches out his hand, smiling, like I'm a colleague instead of some random student who interrupted his book organizing or whatever he was doing back there in the stacks.

I reach out to take it, and as his fingers close around mine I feel a kind of — spark. Like the kind you get from static electricity sometimes, only different in some fundamental way that I can't really explain. I fumble for a second but then it's gone, whatever it was, and I shake his hand firmly. "It's nice to meet you, too, Mr. Gabriel."

He looks at me for a second, like he's expecting me to say something else. "Um, welcome to our school," I add, and after another second he releases my hand and smiles again. For a moment, though, he looked — odd. Surprised, maybe. Or something.

"Well, I guess we should get going," I say finally. "Come on, Annie."

She comes obediently, looking back at him the whole time we are moving toward the doors. I look back, too, just once, to try to see what she is seeing. He is very attractive, there's no question about that. And for a moment, when I felt that weird spark, he seemed beyond just attractive: movie-star gorgeous, almost breathtaking, like I was suddenly seeing him on his best hair day ever in the most flattering light possible. But then it passed and he was just a regular cute guy again. But Annie and I never had quite the same taste in men. I guess she just sees something in him that I don't. Which is good, probably. It would suck if we ever both fell for the same guy. I like that we seem to fall in different directions.

She leans her head against my shoulder as we move down the hall. "Isn't he something?" she asks dreamily.

I reach up and pat her hair gently. "Yes, Annie. He sure is. I bet you're going to be doing lots and lots of reading this year, aren't you?"

"Uh-huh," she says again in that strange, breathless voice, and again I'm struck by the heat underneath her words, so different from the Annie that I know and love. But lust changes you, I get that. And she deserves her chance to drool helplessly over a guy who makes her heart and loins heat up and dance around like they're on fire.

I feel my evil grin coming back. This is going to be a lot of fun.

Over the weekend we don't talk about the new librarian much. Maybe Annie's already feeling a little foolish about her total swooniness on Friday. I don't push it; I suspect I will have plenty of time to enjoy her enthrallment. I want to savor every moment. And so I wait, and we do our normal weekend things: movies; mall; ice cream; more telephone conversations than are strictly necessary, talking about everything and nothing. I dedicate a few solo hours to trying to save the fall musical set from lame last-minute replacement parts that will completely destroy the show as far as I am concerned. (Operative word: *trying*. As in, not yet succeeding. But I'm on it. I will figure it out. I *have to* figure it out. Somehow.) A pretty average weekend all around.

On Monday morning, Annie rings my doorbell a full half hour earlier than normal. I go to the door, still holding my half-eaten bowl of cereal, and raise my eyebrows at her. She just stands there, bouncing lightly on her toes.

"Hello, early," I say. I open the door to let her in.

Her face falls a little. "Oh, you're not ready? I thought — I thought maybe we could go in a little early today. I want to stop by the library before homeroom."

And so it begins.

"Sorry, still eating." I raise my bowl significantly. She is strange again, like she was on Friday. It's less fun today. But maybe that's just because I'm not exactly a morning person.

She comes in but stops a few feet inside the entryway. "How much longer do you think you'll be?"

"About a half hour. Like always. I didn't know it was go-to-school-early-to-gawk-at-the-librarian day, Annie. Sorry."

She nods but still stands there, bouncing.

I roll my eyes. "Go on without me. I'll see you in English."

"Okay, bye!" She's gone before I can say another word.

I shake my head and walk back to the kitchen with my Lucky Charms. She's got it worse than I ever did. Sure, I could sit and watch Ryan for hours at a time if I had the chance, but you certainly wouldn't catch me getting up early to do it. There are limits.

Okay, *maybe* if he were going to be naked.

But I am pretty sure Mr. Gabriel will be fully clothed, and that he will look pretty much the same at lunchtime as he would at 7:30 a.m. I can't see why Annie couldn't just wait until later to stand around and stare at him.

Now I won't even get to make fun of her, since I won't be there to watch. Oh, well. That wouldn't have been worth getting up early for either.

✳   ✳   ✳

I wait for Annie outside the door to English, but she doesn't show up by the time the bell rings. I linger another few seconds, but then Principal Morse walks by and gives me one of his waggly-eyebrow expressions that somehow always manage to simultaneously make you want to laugh at him a little (because he is not even close to being the stern, scary type) and instantly stop doing whatever you're not supposed to be doing (mostly because you just don't want to hurt his feelings). He's pretty nice for a principal. I go inside the classroom and sit down but keep watching the door. It's a full five more minutes before she finally shows up, handing a late pass to Mrs. McKenna. She catches my eye as she slides into her seat, shrugging sheepishly and mouthing the word "library."

She sits three rows over, tricky for note-passing, so I have to wait until after class to talk to her. As soon as the bell rings she comes over to my desk.

"I know," she says before I can open my mouth. "I know. I'm obsessed. I admit it."

"Hey, it's no fun if you don't deny it." I pick up my bag and we head for the door. "But yes, since you mention it, you're right. You are. Completely obsessed. Did you spend all morning in there, peeking out at him from behind the books? You're going to give the poor man a complex."

"No, it's not like that," she says. "I mean, yeah, I was in there for a while — he gave me a pass to get out of first period."

"You skipped class to make eyes at the new librarian?"

"Well, we were talking, and time sort of got away from me, I guess."

"Talking about what?"

She shrugs again. "I don't know. Just things." She looks up at me, beaming. "He's going to let me be a library monitor instead of going to gym."

I'm getting that uneasy feeling again, like I did on Friday. "Can he do that? Just give you permission not to take gym? Besides, I thought you liked gym!"

"I do, but — oh, Cyn, he's so amazing. I don't just mean to look at, I mean to talk to. He's so smart, and there's all these things he knows about. . . ."

She'd been slowing down as she walked, and now she stops and leans her head against the wall. "I've never felt this way about someone before," she says. "It's not like any of those times I thought I liked a boy. This is different. *He's* different."

Alarm bells are going off all over the inside of my brain. "Annie, you're freaking me out a little bit. He's a teacher, or as good as. He's got to be, like, twelve years older than you. At least. And it's probably illegal for him to date a student. And you don't even know him! Do you hear what you sound like?"

She blushes, but not in her usual cute Annie way. She looks angry. And so *strange*. Like she's suddenly become someone I've never met before. "Yeah, I know just what I sound like. Have you ever heard yourself talking about Ryan?"

"That's different! He's a student, and I've known him for longer —"

Annie huffs a mean little laugh. "Known him? You don't know him. You've never even spoken to him! Have you ever said one word to him? Ever? At least John and I have had a conversation!"

"John? You call him *John*? Annie —"

And suddenly her face changes, and she looks like my best friend again. She also looks confused. "That is weird, isn't it? I didn't — it didn't seem weird before, but now . . ."

She looks away and then back up at me. "I skipped class. I never skip class."

"It's okay. You were just —" I have to search for a word here. *Crazy* comes to mind, but that doesn't seem like the most diplomatic choice. "You were just excited. I mean, he's super cute, and smart, and I guess he just kind of dazzled you, huh?"

"Yeah." She smiles weakly. "Yeah, I guess that's what happened. It's still weird, though. I wouldn't have thought . . ." She shakes her head. "Oh, well. Whatever, right? No real harm done, I guess."

We start walking again. I'm still feeling a little freaked out.

The bell rings for third period; we're both going to be late.

We hurry around the corner and suddenly Mr. Gabriel is standing there in front of us. I almost scream. Right there in the hallway. For a second I am filled with terror like I was on Friday when I first heard the sound of his shoes on the library floor. But then it passes, again, and he's just the attractive new librarian.

"Oh, hi, J — Mr. Gabriel," Annie says.

"Now, Annie," he says mock-sternly, "I thought I asked you to call me John."

"Yes, you did, but —" She looks at me and I try to radiate encouragement. "It just feels weird. I'm sorry."

He nods. Glances at me. Looks back at Annie. "I see. Of

course. Well, I certainly don't want you to feel uncomfortable, Annie." He reaches out and touches her arm.

The hallway shifts suddenly beneath me. At least, that's what it seems like. I'm dizzy and there's that church/nightclub feeling again, and I feel like invisible people are shoving me from twenty different directions. And then it's gone, and everything is normal again.

Except that Annie's face has gone all strange and slack and dreamy. Again.

"Why don't you come by at the end of the day and we'll talk more about the library monitor position," Mr. Gabriel says, like nothing crazy just happened.

"Sure. Okay," Annie says in that breathless voice from Friday. She turns toward her chem class without looking at me. "Bye, Cyn." And then she is gone.

I stand there, in the hallway, staring after her. Then I turn and look at Mr. Gabriel.

He is looking at me, too.

"Why don't you come along, too, Cynthia?"

I feel like a mouse locking eyes with a snake. My legs are itching to move, my brain is shrieking at me: *Run! Run away!* But I don't. Can't.

"No, thanks," I say. "I don't think so."

We stand there another few seconds looking at each other. And then he reaches out to touch my arm like he did Annie's. I see his hand extending and I want to shrink back from it but I seem to be frozen in place. It comes closer and I feel as I might if a very large spider were reaching out to touch me instead of a cute twenty-something high-school librarian. Like I might scream. Or faint. Or die.

His fingers brush my flesh and there's that weird spark feeling again and I wait for something else to happen, but then — nothing.

We both look at his hand for a minute.

"Hm," he says. "Well. Good-bye, Cynthia."

He turns and walks back down the hall.

"What the hell?" I say out loud to myself, staring at his retreating back. "I mean, seriously, what the hell?"

A late student jogs by and gives me a very strange look.

I can't even bring myself to feel embarrassed.

Something is seriously messed up here.

Chapter | 02

I walk the rest of the way down the hall and turn into AP Physics. Mr. Levy is already talking at the board; he gives me a squinty look and a "Nice of you to join us, Cynthia," but I barely notice. I mutter an apology and slide into my seat. Then I sit there, staring at my desk, Mr. Levy's voice a meaningless drone in the background.

What exactly do I think is happening?

If I try to think objectively about this, not trying to rationalize it or explain it away or pretend I did not witness that extreme weirdness in the hallway just now, what is going on seems to be that the new hottie librarian has worked some kind of freaky mojo on my nice best friend. She is normal Annie, and then she sees him and she becomes psycho Annie.

No — not when she sees him. When she touches him.

When *he* touches *her.*

He touched me, too, though, and nothing happened. Or almost nothing. I didn't get weird, anyway. *He* got kind of weird, though, didn't he? Like it was weird that I didn't get weird. Or something.

I hear the crazy sound of my own thoughts and shake my head in disgust.

So . . . what, he's hypnotizing her or something? With his hands? Putting some kind of magic spell on her? Turning her into his zombie minion, only without the whole undead thing?

If I were saying this to Annie right now, she would be laughing her head off at me. As would only be appropriate. Because it is ridiculous. *Snap out of it, crazy brain. Are you even listening to yourself?*

"Hey," someone whispers, interrupting my silent conversation with my own head. I look up. Lisa Rinaldi, who sits next to me, is trying to hand me a stack of papers. Out of habit, I take one and pass the rest. Then I look down at it stupidly.

Quiz.

Huh.

Right.

Physics.

I shake my head again to try to clear some of the insanity from my brain, and I take out a pen. I am obviously being ridiculous. I will stop thinking about crazy theories. I will think about linear momentum and whatever else is on this quiz that I forgot to study for. And then the bell will ring, and I will go to lunch, and I will talk to Annie. And we will . . . we will figure out what is really going on. Somehow. Right? Right. Okay.

But when I get to lunch, Annie is nowhere to be seen.

I text her a quick WHERE ARE YOU? and then stare at my phone for several minutes while she does not respond. Leticia and Diane (our most-of-the-week lunch companions, whom we have both known since first grade) are off doing their usual Monday lunch thing with the yearbook crew, so there's no one here to tell me I'm being stupid and worrying over nothing. We're allowed to text but not to make phone calls in the cafeteria (school rules are dumb), so I have to wait until I can slip into the yard to try to call. And when I do: voice mail. Of course. *If she's in the building she wouldn't be able to pick up even if she wanted to,* I remind myself. But she would see that I called *and* texted and so she would guess that it was important and text me back, wouldn't she? But she doesn't.

I get more and more worried as the day crawls on. Annie does not appear at any of our usual pass-in-the-hall-between-classes spots. I linger outside her history class until the bell rings, but she doesn't show up there either, and my own teacher is beckoning to me from across the hall.

Reluctantly, I go to my class.

I take out my notebook, look at the cover, and sit there frowning at it.

It is becoming clear to me that I will have to go to the library after all.

Dammit, Annie.

This is no fun at all.

History takes forever. I feel the centuries turning as I sit there, ready to bolt. I couldn't think of a good enough reason to ask to leave early, and I'm not ready to take drastic measures, like leaving early without permission. I am ninety-nine percent sure that I am totally overreacting. I have had a great deal of time to think about this while waiting for history class to go by. Eons.

Annie has a crush on the new librarian. This is not a big deal. This is not anything to worry about. She's acting like a goofball, but that is what happens when one has a crush. I am an expert on that particular subject.

And he — maybe he is aware of it and is being a jerk and having a little fun with her, touching her arm and asking her to call him by his first name. For someone like Annie, who's never had anything close to a boyfriend, it wouldn't necessarily take hypnotism or magic powers to send her a little off the deep end. The focused attention of those mesmerizing dark eyes and Mr. Gabriel's overall intelligent, attractive, younger-older-man package would be more than enough to make her swoon. Sure it would. Especially if he's turning on the charm on purpose, enjoying her obvious (and no doubt flattering) reaction.

Or maybe he has no idea and is just trying to be all cool and laid-back so that kids will spend more time in the library. Maybe librarians get points or something for all the books that get checked out, points that can be redeemed for valuable goods and services, like fancy date stamps or maybe those reading posters with the celebrities on them holding books, and he has a master plan to get all the points he can by charming all the charmable kids in the school and getting them to read a lot. Maybe it's not even *his* master plan; maybe it's, like, the American Library Association's master plan, and they are stocking high schools across the country with hot young librarians as part of a massive literacy initiative.

These are all more reasonable ideas than the other ones. The ones I cannot allow myself to really think about. The ones that involve scary creepiness totally beyond anything that is remotely possible.

I'm waiting so hard that I'm not ready for it when the bell finally rings, tearing through the air like an ambulance siren. I yelp and everyone laughs but I don't care, because I'm already halfway out the door and racing down the hall.

I fly around the corner, so ready to be relieved, ready to see Annie and have her ask me what the heck is wrong with me, that I'm practically there already in my head, which is why I don't pay quite enough attention to where my feet are taking me. I slam full force into a large, solid obstacle of fellow student and knock us both sprawling to the ground.

I blink and look to see whom I've accidentally pinned to the floor beneath me, and the apology dies on my lips.

It's Ryan Halsey. Of course it is.

I stare, unable to move. It's my earlier fantasy come to life but in some twisted clumsy version that loses all the sexiness and ends up just being awkward.

He looks up at me, seeming a little dazed. "You okay?"

God, he has the sexiest voice. I remain atop him, still paralyzed by his proximity.

"Nice tackle," someone snickers nearby.

That breaks the spell. I feel my face go fiery as I try to scramble off of him. "Oh, God," I say. "I'm so sorry."

I am the epitome of gracelessness as I try to get both feet under me without landing a knee in his groin. My jeans cling to my legs like evil blue vines, stiff and twiny and apparently determined to slow my extraction from Ryan's accidental embrace. His own jeans are darker, more manly, less twiny. I realize suddenly that for those long awkward moments before the even more awkward moment when I began trying to get up, our jeans were flush against each other, pant leg to pant leg, denim sliding on denim. What if I had been wearing a skirt today, I wonder helplessly. What if I had been wearing a skirt and he was in his gym shorts for some reason and instead of thin layers of denim between our limbs it was only skin, warm and smooth. Well, my skin would be smooth; his legs might be a little furry, I suppose. I realize I have stopped to stare again and quickly move my gaze up to his face instead of his pants.

Ryan waits patiently on the ground below me, a slight smile on his full and tasty-looking lips.

I apologize again, stepping free at last from the confusing tangle of our bodies and my thoughts.

"It's okay," he says. "I'm a pretty tough guy. I think I'll recover."

Oh, God. He's joking with me. He's making the effort to be funny. To me.

Then I notice everyone in the hall staring at us, and I realize he is probably being funny for them.

Well, whatever. He still said it to me. I still got to hear it.

I reach down a hand to help him up and he is nice enough to take it, even though, of course, he does not need my assistance. The touch of his fingers, his hand grasping mine, sucks all the blood from my brain and again I stare wordlessly at him as he gets to his feet. *Don't let go!* my body pleads with me. I begin to worry that I won't be able to. My cells are practically singing with joy at his touch. I'm so ridiculous I can hardly stand myself, but knowing that does nothing to change it. Ryan Halsey turns me into a helpless, mindless zombie girl.

Like Annie around Mr. Gabriel.

See? I tell myself firmly. She is fine. Just crushing. Like me.

I shake my head — *Out! Out, insanity!* — and release his hand.

"Really, I'm so sorry," I say once more, mainly just to be saying something.

"Don't worry about it, Cyn," he says, already stepping forward to move past me, to walk on to whatever happy place is his intended destination. He touches my shoulder as he passes, and it's almost enough to make me sink right back down to the floor.

And also: he said my name. He knows what my name is. He spoke it out loud and used it in a sentence.

I pull myself together and continue toward the library at a normal-person pace, willing the flush I can still feel in my face to cool back down. My sense of urgency has been partially knocked out of me by the impact of my collision with Ryan. And partially eclipsed by my amazement that he does know who I am.

But once I see the library up ahead, my worry about Annie takes over again. I pause at the double doors, and through the little windows I can see Annie inside. Right there, perfectly fine, standing with her back to me in front of the circulation desk. I pull the doors open and step through. She turns at the sound, her face alight with that same new hungry hopefulness from last Friday. Her voice, though, when she speaks, is her normal Annie voice.

"Oh, hi, Cyn. What are you doing here?"

"I came to find you. Are you — is everything okay?"

She looks at me strangely. "Of course."

I am still waiting to feel relieved. I don't quite feel relieved.

"You weren't at lunch," I say. "Didn't you get my texts?" *My millions of texts? And my voice mail?*

"Oh, yeah. Sorry." She shrugs. "I figured you'd guess I came here."

I take a step closer. That feeling of wrongness, of not belonging in this space, is starting to crowd in around me again.

"Did you — did you go to your classes? I didn't see you in the hall, either."

She laughs, but it's not quite her lovely Annie laugh. "What are you, my mother?"

I try to laugh, too, but I can only manage a tight smile.

Mr. Gabriel appears suddenly behind the desk, and once more I fight the urge to scream.

"Hello, Cynthia," he says. "We didn't expect to see you."

He is looking at me intently. I don't quite meet his eyes.

"Yes, well, I just thought I'd come by to meet my friend." I turn back to Annie. "Are you ready to go?"

She looks to the librarian, and I want to shake her. *You don't need his permission!*

He nods, and she smiles. "Sure, let's go. See you tomorrow, Mr. G."

Well, it's better than *John*.

I look at him a moment more. He's still watching me. As we stand there, I feel that shifting again, that sense of bodies, of movement, of something else here in the same space with us. But there's nothing here. Nothing beside me, nothing around me but normal library things and Annie and Mr. Gabriel. What *is* that? I want to ask him. I feel like he knows. But I also feel like asking him would be a very bad idea.

"Yeah, see you tomorrow, Mr. G.," I say, turning away.

Annie is waiting by the door. Just as I reach her, I hear Mr. Gabriel's voice right behind me.

"I'll look forward to it," he says softly, his breath tickling my ear.

I spin around to face him, to push him away, how *dare* he sneak up so close to me like — but he's still standing behind the desk, where we left him.

"Good afternoon, girls," he says. Then he smiles at me. Something in that smile makes me grab Annie's arm and practically drag her out into the hall.

Annie and I both have eighth period free on Mondays. I am more than a little surprised that after apparently cutting most of the day to hang out in the library, she is now willingly leaving when she doesn't actually have to be anywhere else. With some trepidation, I point out this seeming inconsistency in her behavior.

Annie shrugs again. "He said he had things to do during eighth period."

And just like that, she is back to being herself. The world crashes back into place around me, and I feel like an idiot.

We head to study hall to pass the time until the final bell. Leticia and Diane wave us over to their table, and we swerve to join them. After a minute, Billy and Kelly sit down in the last two seats at the far end.

I drop my eyes without meaning to and feel Annie's glance of concern from beside me. I look at her and make a disgusted face, and she gives me a sympathetic smile. Kelly Nolan is the girl Billy started dating about five seconds after he told me that it wasn't "working out." She is lovely and petite with gorgeous red-blond hair that she often wears twisted up in some seemingly quick and casual way that I could never pull off even with a team of professional hairdressers to help me. She is one of those girls who don't ever seem to have a bad hair day or a zit or to even once make a regrettable clothing purchase. One secretly suspects that she never gets her period or goes to the bathroom, either. We hate her on principle, even though she is actually perfectly nice.

And really, I don't even care that they are together. I don't want Billy. I want Ryan Halsey. Ryan is twenty times the boy Billy is. Fifty times. Possibly a hundred. And I am way more interesting and intelligent than Kelly Nolan. But I don't really want to watch them making kissy faces at each other all through study hall, either. It's kind of insulting.

Even though I know she has a test to study for tomorrow, Annie spends the whole period drawing me little stick-figure pictures to distract me from our lovebird tablemates. I end up being shushed twice by the teacher on duty for laughing, and by the time the bell rings I have stopped feeling at all weird or uncomfortable or vaguely and stupidly inferior.

Sometimes I love Annie so much I can hardly stand it.

Usually Annie sticks around on Mondays both to keep me company and to make actual use of study hall, because her house is always filled with small, loud children in the afternoons, her little brother and sister and their seemingly infinite number of small, loud friends who apparently do not have homes of their own to go to after school, and so it's impossible for her to get any studying done there. I stick around because I am tech director for the fall musical this year, which rehearses Monday and Wednesday afternoons.

I love musical theater, have loved it fiercely and unwaveringly ever since my parents took me to see a local community theater production of *Pippin* when I was five. I've experimented with being onstage a few times over the years (most memorably as Teresa the Turkey in our fourth-grade Thanksgiving assembly, which I don't think I will ever entirely live down), but as much as I love and appreciate the music and the singing and the acting, my true devotion is for the secret magic that happens behind the scenes. Even at age five, what most captivated me was the seamless shifting of the sets and the mysteries of how what was obviously just an empty wooden floor with some curtains around it could be transformed into another time and place so convincingly that everyone in the audience completely and absolutely believed it.

And since Mary Chang, who was the reigning queen of backstagery for the past three years, is now off enjoying her first year as a college student at Syracuse University, Mr. Henry came to me when this year's show was announced and asked me to be the new tech director. Which (as Mr. H. is fully aware) has been my not-so-secret ambition since freshman year, and I am determined to make him proud.

The set this year is, of course, the most challenging one we've ever attempted. We're doing *Sweeney Todd*, which, in case you are somehow unfamiliar with one of the best Sondheim musicals EVER, is about an insane barber (insane after years spent wrongfully in prison, where he was sent on trumped-up charges so a corrupt judge could steal and destroy his family — mitigating circumstances, people!) who returns to wreak revenge upon those who wronged him. And on pretty much everyone else, too, eventually. There is an equally insane pie shop mistress (Mrs. Lovett) who had been secretly in love with Sweeney from before and who helps him (but also deceives him horribly and is pretty much responsible for eviscerating what little shreds of sanity he had left, to the detriment of all) *and* who comes up with the brilliant idea of cooking the dead bodies of his victims into her meat pies, and there is a young, innocent sailor who falls in love with Sweeney's daughter, who is being raised in captivity by the very bad judge, and there is love and pain and humor and darkness and awesomeness all around.

If you think the plot is complex, you should see the set design. It includes a rotating two-story structure that serves as Sweeney's tonsorial parlor over the pie shop as well as the pie shop itself and Mrs. Lovett's apartment and also occasional other scenes. And one of the key elements is ultimately the barber chair that Sweeney rigs up to be able to dump his victims conveniently down a trapdoor to the lower level, where they can wait to be ground up into pies. Some high-school productions forego the special chair and come up with some far less impressive method of getting the dead bodies offstage. We are not going to be one of those high schools. Just because there was a *little* mishap with the prototype and a couple of people got *very slightly* injured . . . Well, I am going to fix everything and we are going to have a totally kick-ass chair and it will all be amazing. It's still two weeks till the start of tech week (i.e., the week leading up to the dress rehearsal and then the actual performances), which is the deadline that Mr. Henry laid down, and I will figure it out.

And in related news, there is an extra, added bonus to this year's production.

After Ryan Halsey's extraordinary scene-stealing turn as the Pharaoh in *Joseph and the Amazing Technicolor Dreamcoat* last year, which, incidentally, positively sealed the deal for me in terms of my hopeless crush, there was no question that Mr. Henry would be casting him again this time around. And what better way to get to know someone than hanging out in the auditorium together between scenes, freed from the constraints of assigned classroom seating and Ryan's usual intimidating group of friends, who, fortunately, do not seem to share his love of the theater? I only wish I had some talent for sewing, so that I could have volunteered to do costumes on the side and thereby have maneuvered myself to be alone in a corner some evening with Ryan Halsey and some measuring tape and a long list of necessary and intimate measurements that needed taking. But you can't have everything, I suppose.

Of course, thus far I have not worked up my nerve to do more than stare at him whenever he is onstage and then look down in embarrassment and panic whenever he actually glances my way. But as I may have mentioned, there are two weeks until tech Monday, which means nearly three weeks until opening night. Plenty of time. For everything. I will make my move eventually. I just have to work up the courage. Which might be sooner now that he has demonstrated knowledge of my name. My heart leaps painfully upward in pointless hope as I remember this wondrous fact, but I smush the feeling back down firmly. It doesn't mean anything. He just has a good memory, like he has a good everything else, and has heard Mr. Henry calling out tech notes to me during rehearsals or heard someone say my name in Italian class. That's all.

Annie would smack me for thinking that way, I know. But she has an occasional tendency toward optimism beyond all reason.

Ryan, of course, is playing Sweeney, and as he stands up there, holding the pen that is standing in for the razor, which we still need to procure, singing and exuding demonic barberness with a beautiful mix of sex appeal and insanity, all of my problems seem to melt away and I listen raptly, watch helplessly, and let myself temporarily forget that Ryan and I will probably never really be together in some kind of romantically connected way. That's one of the things I've always loved most about musical theater. The way it makes anything, even the most unlikely turn of events, seem absolutely possible.

When Mr. Henry lets us go for the evening, I slip my set notebook back into my bag and then sit for a moment, thinking, as the other students begin to make their way toward the various doors. I am thinking I might swing by the library on my way out, because even though I was right there when Annie said "See you tomorrow, Mr. G.," I have a very strong suspicion that she ended up back there again anyway. And even though I have nearly convinced myself that nothing sinister is going on outside of my own overactive imagination, it will make me feel better to stop by. And then if she is there, we can walk home together, which would be infinitely more fun than me walking home alone with my thoughts.

I stand up and suddenly notice that Ryan is standing in front of me.

"Uh," I say eloquently, looking up into his face from this unexpected and surprisingly close vantage.

"Hey," he says back, as though I had said something similarly standard and comprehensible. "I just wanted to make sure you were okay. I realized I took off pretty fast after our little mid-corridor collision today. I have Marchansky eighth period; you know how he is about people being late to class."

"Oh," I say, which, while significantly better than my first statement, still doesn't exactly register on the charming-and-clever scale. I mentally slap myself across the face. *Wake up and be interesting, you idiot!* "Um, thanks. Although, I'm the one who slammed into you; I should be asking if you're okay. But you seem to have made a pretty speedy recovery as far as I can tell."

Better. Not great, but at least all the words make sentences and things.

He smiles. I manage to stay upright. "Yeah, I think I'll make it. Anyway, I gotta run, but glad you're okay. That was a pretty serious full-on tackle. I can't remember the last time I was taken out like that quite so efficiently."

I smile back. The way he says *efficiently* makes me a little light-headed. "Anytime you want a rematch, you let me know." Crap. Too much? Am I flirting, or threatening him with further bodily harm?

His smile tilts up a bit on one side. "Maybe I will," he says. He gives me one of those chin-first nods that guys seem to use to communicate various forms of hello and good-bye and acknowledgment. I feel like it is all three, in the best of ways. "See you tomorrow."

"Sure, yeah. Yeah, okay. See you tomorrow, Ryan."

I watch him turn and jog toward the door and through the door, savoring the taste of his name on my lips. I tilt my head a little to the side and let myself take in the extremely pleasant rear view of him until he is out of sight.

Oh. Oh, sweet *Jesus Christ Superstar.*

It takes me a second to start moving again; my brain insists on a few instant replays first. Of my *conversation* with *Ryan Halsey.* The one I just had, right here, in which both of us said things to each other, and there was mutual smiling, and no one ended up on the floor or otherwise demonstrated embarrassing behavior of any kind.

I glance up and catch Mr. Henry watching me in obvious amusement from the stage. He raises his eyebrows at me. "Nice boy, that Ryan," he says, grinning.

I grin back, unable to help myself. "No kidding," I tell him. I can hear the wistfulness clearly in my voice.

He laughs, but not in a mean way. Mr. Henry is a pretty cool guy. "You should go for it. Bass-baritones that good looking are few and far between."

"Ha." I shake my head. "Out of my league, Mr. H. Unfortunately."

"Now, Cyn. Come on. How do you know until you try?"

I just shake my head again and give him a wave as I head out of the auditorium. Mr. Henry is a little too far removed from being a teenager to really get it, I think. It's okay. While I am certainly not in any sense of the phrase going to "go for it" with Ryan, that doesn't mean I'm not going to be excited about our new level of interaction. It's not . . . *impossible,* after all, that we could get to know each other better. Maybe we could even become friends, and then eventually he would start to see how awesome I am, deep down. . . .

Now I am actively hoping to find Annie at the library. Screw the creepy librarian. I can't wait to tell her what happened. Okay, it's not a marriage proposal or anything, but now that we've had one conversation, a real one that's not just me staring at him in stupid speechlessness or me apologizing for knocking him over, it is highly likely that we could, you know, have another. And another. Which could be the start of really getting to know him. Which could be the start of . . . all kinds of things. My heart makes a few small twitches of tentative hopefulness and I let it, just this once.

Anything really is possible in musical theater. Even if the music at the moment is only playing in my mind.

Chapter | 03

By the time I reach the third floor, all inner reserve has failed me and there is a full-scale production of "A Heart Full of Love" from *Les Misérables* going in my head. It is taking place in Italian class and began with Ryan turning to me in the middle of a vocabulary quiz and bursting into song. Ryan and I are Marius and Cosette, *obviously,* and I have cast Kelly as Éponine, and Signor De Luca as Javert (despite that character not actually appearing in this number), and the whole scenario brings me great pleasure, even though the voice parts are all wrong and Kelly takes French, not Italian, and as far as I know she is not secretly and hopelessly in love with Ryan to any great degree. But that's the nice thing about fantasies; everything can be completely and nonsensically rearranged to the suit the fantasist. It is why I often prefer them to real life. Still, I stop short of envisioning Kelly's death-scene rendition of "A Little Fall of Rain." I'm not evil, after all.

I do make her dirty and dressed in rags with noticeably unshaven legs and underarms, though.

Also, there may be some lice.

As the song ends I suddenly notice how dim and silent the school is. Every other fluorescent light along the ceiling has been turned off, and the hallway stretches out ahead of me in creepy partial darkness, and I become uncomfortably aware that it is very late. Even if Annie did come back here after study hall, she probably wouldn't have stayed this long. I pause, thinking of the stairway just a few steps behind me, thinking how I could just turn right around and go back downstairs. There's probably no reason for me to even bother checking the library. I can see the big double doors up ahead, flickering a little as one of the ceiling lights nearby struggles and falters. It's probably locked up for the night anyway. I can leave, right now, without opening those doors. *Yes,* my brain agrees. *That is very logical thinking you have going on there. Let's just go. Let's go right now.* The urge to flee is nearly overwhelming.

"Oh, just stop it already," I mutter at myself in irritation. I make myself start walking again. Seriously, delicious Ryan-centered fantasies aside, I need to quit letting myself get so carried away with ridiculous ideas. Even if there is little chance Annie is in there, I will make myself go inside just to prove that there is no reason not to. He's just a librarian. I am not afraid of a *librarian,* for crissakes.

I grasp the door handles and pull, firmly ignoring the twinge of anxious disappointment I feel when they swing open instead of turning out to be safely locked and unopenable. I step inside, and the sound of my shoes against the floor tiles seems way too loud in the silence. Every other row of overhead lights has been turned off in here, too, throwing everything into half shadow and making the far corners of the room seem dark and threatening. There's a light on in the back office, though. But maybe they just leave that on for the janitors. It doesn't mean that anyone is actually here.

I clear my throat awkwardly. "Hello?" I call out.

Mr. Gabriel materializes in the office doorway and I nearly jump out of my skin, a tiny cutoff scream escaping me before I can stop it.

"Cynthia!" he says, smiling. "I didn't expect to see you here at this hour. What can I do for you?"

I ignore my pounding, racing heart and make myself take another step forward. "I was looking for Annie. I thought she might have come back after eighth period. But she's — I guess she's not here. I'm sorry I bothered you."

"Not at all, not at all." He comes forward and rests his arms on the circulation desk. One of the lights illuminates his face as he does, and I have to acknowledge that he really is amazingly attractive. "Annie was here earlier, but she left a little while ago." His smile turns slightly apologetic, then brightens again. "She's a lovely girl, isn't she? Finding good library monitors is harder than you might think, you know. And being new to the school, I find that it makes my job so much easier when I have students I can rely on. You two seem to be very good friends. I'm glad to have met you both."

We watch each other, and I am struck again by how young he looks, and how not-young he seems. "You sound so much older than you look," I say without thinking, then realize how inappropriate a thing that was to say out loud. My face floods with heat. "Oh, I'm sorry. I didn't mean —"

He chuckles and makes a small dismissive gesture with one hand. "It's all right, Cynthia. Actually, I'm glad to hear it. I get a little flak sometimes for my, ah, youthful appearance. From teachers and students both. I guess I make an effort to at least sound like I'm old enough to be doing what I'm doing."

He smiles again, and I find myself smiling back. Maybe that's all I've been feeling — the reason behind his seeming out-of-placeness. It must be hard for him, looking the way he does. I wonder if anyone takes him seriously without him having to prove himself first. You always hear older people wishing they could keep looking young, but I guess there's a limit to *how* young. Especially if you work in a high school.

"Is this your first library job?" I ask, moving up a little closer to the desk.

"Oh, I've been around," he says, his smile twisting a little. I realize maybe that's not an okay thing for me to be asking about, either. Are adults weird about their job histories? Or maybe it's simply none of my business. I don't even know why I'm still here. I hadn't been planning to stay. I had been about to leave, once he said Annie had gone home. But I feel all right just standing here, talking to him. Why did I think he was so creepy? He's not at all creepy. I feel bad for even thinking that about him. He's nice. Just a little awkward, maybe. It's not like I don't understand awkward.

I take another step, and then I'm close enough to lean my own arms on the circulation desk across from him. That's better, I realize. Kind of relaxing. It's nice in the library. Quiet. And there's something very interesting about Mr. Gabriel. And he really is very attractive. He's no Ryan Halsey, but —

Thinking of Ryan distracts me for a moment, and suddenly I feel like Mr. Gabriel is a little too close, right there on the other side of the desk. What was I saying? Was he saying something? I'm confused, like I just missed part of the conversation. Mr. Gabriel is looking at me intently.

"I — I should go, I guess," I tell him. "I only came by to look for Annie." He doesn't say anything, and I feel like more explanation is required. "I was still here because of rehearsal. Fall musical. We're doing *Sweeney Todd*."

"Ah," he says, looking genuinely interested. "The demon barber of Fleet Street! I've always loved that one."

I see a flicker in the corner of my eye and turn my head to catch it. Nothing's there. Of course not. Except then one of the shadows by the computers moves.

My breath catches.

"Cynthia?"

"Is that —?" I look back at him. "I thought I saw —" What? I have no idea what I thought I saw. "Something moved, over by the computers."

"Hmm." He peers in the direction I indicate. "I don't see anything."

I look again, and this time I'm sure I see the shadow of something skitter across one of the tables. "Right there! You didn't see it?" He had been looking right at it. "Maybe — maybe it was a mouse or something."

He looks at me. "I certainly hope not. Bad for the books,

you know. And I'm sure I haven't seen any evidence of mice. But I'll mention it to the janitorial staff, though. Ask them to keep an eye out."

"Yeah, okay." Somehow this plan feels inadequate. I don't know what else I expect him to do, though. Or why I'm so concerned about possible library mice.

Another flicker, this time on the other side, near the closest row of bookshelves. I whip my head around, but again there's no sign of the source of motion. *What...?*

"Another mouse?" He sounds amused. I don't think it's funny, though.

I glance up to meet his eyes again, and now I remember why I thought he was creepy. Because he *is* creepy. He's just standing there, staring at me with those intense eyes, a little half smile on his face. Waiting, watching, something. For what? What is he doing? Why is he even here this late in the day? And why I am still here with him, dammit?

I push back from the desk, clutching my bag. "I should go," I say.

"All right," he says genially. His hand twitches slightly on the desk, and I step back in sudden terror that he might try to touch me again.

I take two steps backward before I can make myself turn around. I don't like having my back to him. I want to run for the doors, but I resist. I walk calmly. Well, I pretend to walk calmly. My heart is hammering inside me, and I'm afraid to let my gaze stray from where I have it firmly fixed on the doors. I don't want to see anything else from the corner of my eye.

That last shadow was very large. I do not think there is any way it could have been a mouse.

I reach the doors, which has seemed to take entirely too long, and with great relief I place one hand out to push them open. They give an inch and then catch.

Locked.

I stare at them. I give them another tentative push. Then a stronger one. A slightly panicked one. Why are they locked? How can they be locked when they weren't before?

"Oh." I hear Mr. Gabriel's soft voice from the desk behind me. "Let me get that for you."

I don't turn around. I can't seem to make myself turn around. I keep staring at the doors, silently begging them to open on their own, as I listen to his footsteps slowly approach. At his final step, the one that brings him right up behind me, I feel all the hair on the back of my neck and arms stand at prickly attention.

"Here," he says, and he places one hand on my arm to gently move me aside. There is one of those strange sparks, one of those I-want-to-pretend-it-is-static-electricity-but-I-know-it's-really-not sensations, and I cannot help it, I turn to look at his hand on my skin and then up at his face, which is too close, again, looking back at me.

He doesn't look away as he turns the key in the lock. His eyes are dark and strange and he still seems to be looking for something in my own eyes, something he does not appear to be finding. I hear the doors click open, but I cannot seem to move. *Run! Run away!* My whole body is in agreement regarding this proposed course of action. But nothing happens, not even when Mr. Gabriel's eyes finally release me. He steps back and pushes open the left-hand door. I stare longingly at the portal to freedom, still not quite able to walk through it.

"Good night, Cynthia. I'm sure I'll see you again soon."

"Yes," I whisper. And then I can move, and I am gone, through the doorway and down the hall, as fast as I can go. I imagine I hear Mr. Gabriel's soft laughter floating after me.

I don't love walking home by myself at night, but compared to the library, the dark streets feel perfectly safe and non-threatening. The little squares of light in the windows of the houses I pass all seem to call out their absolute normalcy, proclaiming themselves evidence of the nice regular world of homework and dinner and shadows that are only where they belong and do not move all on their own in strange and frightening ways.

I stopped running when I got a block away from the school, and I refuse to start again, not even to jog up the steps to my house. Once inside, with the door firmly closed and locked behind me, I am finally able to breathe again.

"Cyn? That you?" My dad's voice, calling over the sound of the TV.

"Yeah," I call back. I walk down the hall and peek into the den. "Where's Mom?"

"Still at the office." He's flipping through various news shows he's recorded, catching up on whatever seems important to catch up on. He's obsessive about staying informed. About some things, anyway. He glances over at me, smiles distractedly. "There's Chinese food in the fridge. I wasn't sure when you were coming home."

"I had *Sweeney Todd* tonight," I remind him, as I remind him every time, but he's already back in information-land, soaking it all in from every source he can find. I head to the kitchen to heat myself up some dinner.

Armed with a heaping plate of chicken lo mein and sautéed string beans, I head up to my room to call Annie. Her little brother answers, and it takes me several tries to convince him to go tell her she has a phone call. I don't know why she lets him answer her phone in the first place.

"I don't *let* him," she says when I ask her this directly, after a long wait during which it sounds like Peter is kicking the phone across the floor as he moves from room to room. "He just takes it when I'm not looking, and I usually don't even realize until somebody calls."

"Well, make him stop. It's annoying."

She sighs. "I'll try. Sometimes it's easier to just let him do stuff like this. You'd understand if you had brothers and sisters. Some things just aren't worth the fight."

"Hmph." I know I'm being unreasonably grouchy, but I still haven't quite recovered from the librarian thing. It seems silly now, the way I got so freaked out over a couple of spooky shadows, but I still can't quite shake the feeling of being scared and trapped. I take a bite of lo mein while I think about how to try to talk to Annie about it.

"Chinese food?" she asks.

I swallow hastily. "How can you always tell?"

"I don't know. It sounds different from when you're eating other things. Plus, it's like a fifty-fifty chance most nights, isn't it? Your mom working late again?"

"Yeah. Big case, I guess."

"Hmm."

We're both quiet for a minute. "I stopped by the library after rehearsal," I say finally. "I had a feeling you might still be around."

"Oh, you probably just missed me! I was tagging books for Mr. G. We got to talking and I hung around later than I'd planned to. How was rehearsal? Did you see your secret love?"

I hesitate, torn. I want to talk to her about Mr. Gabriel, about how weird and creepy he is and how worried I am about the way she has become so infatuated with him. But I'm afraid she'll only get defensive about it again, and I don't want to make her mad at me. And I really, really want to tell her about Ryan.

So I let it go. For now.

I tell her about how I slammed into him in the hallway, leaving out the detail that I had been running to see her, and she goes smoothly from yelling at me for not telling her about it during study hall to commiserating about the humiliation of it while still pointing out the not-so-slight upside of having been in full bodily contact with him for at least several seconds. That's my Annie, always right there with me.

"I know, I can't believe I didn't tell you earlier," I say, setting my plate down beside me. "I guess the Billy and Kelly show kind of took over my head for a little while."

"Yeah, although, you know that's crazy — you have to stop letting them get to you."

"Yeah, well, whatever. Listen, I still haven't told you the *other* upside from the whole Ryan tackling thing!" I relate the post-rehearsal conversation, line by line, with moment-to-moment descriptions of his facial expressions and my thoughts and internal physical reactions, repeating sections as requested, and I can tell that Annie is literally jumping around on the other side of the phone as she squeals excitement for me.

"Oh, my *God,* Cyn! You guys are, like, talking! For real! Finally!"

I can't help grinning, her enthusiasm on my behalf making me even more excited about everything. "And all I had to do was knock him down in the hallway. Who knew?"

We discuss what I should wear tomorrow in order to look my best for Italian, and how I should say hello when I see him, and whether I should make myself not stare at him quite so much as usual if I can possibly help it. By the time we hang up I can hardly remember what my library freak-out was really all about. I bring my dishes downstairs and then return to my room to start trying on potential clothing items for tomorrow's Ryan-ready ensemble.

Annie texts me in the morning to say she's going early to the library to "do some stuff" for Mr. Gabriel, and so she'll just see me in Italian. I am somewhat disappointed that she won't be here to approve my outfit before we head to school, but I guess it was considerate of her not to show up half an hour early again. She doesn't need my permission, after all. Of course she can go early to school if she wants to. It's not like there's some law that says we have to walk together every day. Except, we always have, unless one of us is sick or on vacation. She's certainly never ditched me for a librarian before.

I hear how whiny my thoughts are becoming and force myself to cut it out. Annie has always been there for me, one hundred percent, and it's incredibly selfish of me to want to keep her all to myself when she's got something else she wants to do. I can pretend it's only that I'm worried about this librarian thing, and I *am* worried . . . but that's not what's bothering me now. It's that she's putting something else first, someone else before me. And that's not okay. Is this how I'd be if she had a boyfriend? Selfish and self-centered? *But he's not a boyfriend,* my brain reminds me. *He's the librarian. The very creepy librarian.* Okay, yes, it's weird and wrong and I still need to talk to her about it. But I can do that later, and I can certainly walk to school all by myself like a big girl.

I pass by the library between homeroom and first period, and without quite meaning to I drift over to the double doors to peek inside as I go by. There are several students lingering in there, or maybe they're early for a class session. But something looks off to me. I stand there, trying to figure out what it is. Three girls are sitting at one of the long tables, but they're not really doing anything—just sitting there. One has her elbows on the table and her head leaning forward against her hands, as though she is really tired, or maybe has a headache or is upset about something. The other two are sort of staring into space, one with her head tilted a little to one side.

Mr. Gabriel is standing near the circulation desk, and a small group of students surrounds him. They all appear to be listening raptly to whatever he is saying, and as he speaks he reaches out to touch first one, then another, moving his hands from arms to shoulders and even once to pat some guy on the head. No — not just some guy. I squint to make sure I am seeing this correctly. Richie Donovan, a senior on the football team and a huge, foulmouthed kid who is infamous for his temper getting him into trouble in class. I've seen him swat teachers' hands away for daring to touch his notebook without permission; I cannot quite believe I have just witnessed him allowing the librarian to pat him on the head like a small dog.

As I continue to stand there staring, perplexed, Mr. Gabriel shifts position slightly and his eyes meet mine through the glass of the library door windows. His expression doesn't change, but there is something different in his eyes themselves. *He knows*, I think senselessly. I don't even know what I mean by that. Knows what?

That I know. That I know he's up to something.

I pull back from the window, turning aside and away, pressing my back against the wall beside the door, suddenly afraid. And then I feel an immediate temptation to look again, to keep trying to puzzle out what exactly he's doing or saying, but I am filled with the certainty that if I look back through the window he will be right there on the other side, pressed up against the glass like that gremlin thing from that old *Twilight Zone* episode with William Shatner and the plane, and I can't bring myself to do it. Instead I start to edge away, reminding myself that I should be hurrying toward Italian so I can say hello to Ryan now that we're all friendly and everything and see Annie and not just keep standing here feeling scared and alone. The doors swing open and I almost scream, but it's only the students finally filing out into the hall. They walk slowly, not speaking, apparently all lost in thought. I take off before the last of them emerges, just in case Mr. Gabriel is following them out.

I make it to Italian about two seconds after the bell rings, and Signor De Luca gives me a reproachful look as I slide into my seat. I mouth the word "sorry" at him and busy myself with taking out my notebook. When I next glance up, Ryan is looking back at me. He gives me a dead-on replica of the De Luca Look of Lateness and I have to bite my fist to keep from laughing out loud. It's better than the hello I'd been imagining would have been, way better, like a million times better. When Ryan winks at me and turns back around, I look over at Annie to make sure she has witnessed this exhilarating exchange, but she isn't looking back at me. She's just sitting there, staring into space.

"Hey," I whisper at her. When that doesn't get her attention, I tear off a sheet of notebook paper and crumple it up into a tiny ball. When De Luca is safely engrossed in writing today's vocabulary list on the board, I throw it at her. It hits her arm and bounces silently onto the floor. It takes her a second too long to notice it, but finally she sort of shakes her head and looks down at her arm, then up at me.

Her face seems weirdly slack, and my first thought is that she must be getting sick or something. Some vibrancy is gone from her expression, some essential Annie-ness that makes her look like her normal bouncy self.

"Are you okay?" I mouth at her.

She looks slightly confused, then slowly nods. Then nods again more quickly, seeming to come a little bit back to herself.

"Yeah," she whispers. "Yeah, sorry. Kind of spaced out there for a minute, or something."

"*Yeah* you did," I whisper back. Before I can say anything else, Signor De Luca's deep voice booms warningly at us from the front of the room.

"*Attenzione,*" he says meaningfully, and we both turn around and start copying down vocabulary words in our books. I steal glances at her throughout the rest of class. She seems okay, mostly, but still a little out of it. I want the bell to ring so I can ask her what's going on. But when it does, she gets up before I can say anything and walks to the teacher's desk in the front of the room. Students are standing up around me and my view is partly blocked, but it looks like, as she speaks, she reaches forward and touches Signor De Luca on the back of the hand. He jerks a little, as though — as though he's felt one of those little static electricity shocks. Or maybe just because it's a little awkward to have one of your cute young female students touch your hand while she talks to you. Or maybe I didn't quite see what I thought I saw, and it's just my stupid imagination going crazy on me again.

I stand up to try to see better, but then Ryan walks by and gives me another smile and a chin-nod on his way out, and I stand there grinning like an idiot until Annie comes back over to my desk.

"Did I just see what I thought I saw?" she says, bouncing a little on her toes. "Was that a smile and a nod I observed? An acknowledgment of your existence with a simultaneous expression of pleasure across the lovely face of one Ryan Halsey?"

"Hey, shut up," I say, glancing around to make sure no one else was close enough to hear her. But she's smiling her Annie smile and is so suddenly and completely back to herself that I don't spend too much time being nervous about it. "That's nothing. I can't believe you missed what he did before that," I tell her as she falls in beside me on our way out into the hall.

"When?"

"Right when I came in. When you were still lost inside your head, or whatever was going on with you before. What was that, anyway? Are you sure you're okay?" She seems okay now, though. Like nothing ever happened.

"Oh, yeah, I'm fine." She brushes off my concern and grabs my arm, pulling me along with her down the hall. "Tell me what I missed!"

I swallow my misgivings and give in, since I'm dying to replay it for myself, anyway. Annie is duly appreciative, and I begin to feel that happy excitement of potential with a much-liked boy bubbling up inside me, that lightness and frenetic hopefulness that I haven't allowed myself to feel in what seems like a very long time.

For some reason the hallway seems especially clogged with students, and it takes forever to make it down to the stairwell at the far end of the hall.

"What's *up* with everyone today?" Annie asks, pushing past another group of students partially blocking our way.

I look around, searching for the explanation. It's not like there's a fight or something going on, because we'd hear it, and no one seems to be selling candy or hanging up flyers or spreading loud gossip or any other obvious thing that would account for all the slow-moving hallway blockiness that seems to be happening. In fact, the more I look around, it seems like nothing is happening. At all. People are just sort of standing around, looking a little lost.

Kind of like those kids looked in the library before first period.

Kind of like Annie looked at the beginning of Italian.

I look at her now, and her face is as animated and excited as ever, even in her frustration at having to push past people every few steps who are standing in her way for no particular reason.

Without really consciously deciding to do so, I turn around to look back down the hall, toward the classroom we just left.

Signor De Luca is standing in the doorway, looking after us. His face is slack and a little confused.

"Annie!" I turn back around as I call her name, wanting her to see, to confirm that I'm not imagining things. But she's already in the stairway entrance, too far away.

"I gotta run, Cyn!" she calls back to me before she disappears. "I'll see you later!"

I stand there, watching the space where she was standing. The students around me continue to mill about, not making much progress toward wherever they should be going.

The bell rings, and all of us are late, but no one seems to even notice this but me.

Chapter | 04

If I were to make a little list of all the things I most want to do at this moment, I can pretty much guarantee that this would not be on it: walking back down the hall toward Signor De Luca's classroom.

I don't like him. He never smiles and he wears strangely irritating ties and he always grades me just a little lower than I think I deserve. I shouldn't care that he's standing there looking as lost and vacant as the students who still remain in the hall. Plenty of kids moved from class to class just like normal between the bells, talking and laughing and walking and running and dropping things and picking them up and pushing each other playfully, and less playfully, and whispering and wishing and everything else. It's not like *no one* was doing what they're supposed to be doing. But you rarely saw even one or two students standing around after the bell. There have to be at least fifteen or so that I can see. And something is wrong with them. That is clear. And I know what it is. Or at least, I know who is responsible. My brain makes little noises of objection at this thought, but I don't listen. I know what I know. Not that I have the faintest idea how or why.

But Signor De Luca had not been anywhere near the librarian when he became wrong. Signor De Luca had seemed totally fine until Annie went up to talk to him after class. And then *Annie* had been fine, and Signor De Luca had been — like he is now. Not fine.

I take a breath and walk back toward the classroom. Around me, most of the lingering students seem to be drifting slowly off, beginning to move with a slightly more purposeful sense about them. But only slightly. Signor De Luca is still looking down the hall, toward the stairwell where Annie disappeared.

"Signore?"

He doesn't seem to hear me. I think for a moment, and then I say, slowly and clearly, "Hey! Mr. De Luca!"

Now he blinks and turns toward me, seeming to notice me for the first time. "*Signor* De Luca," he says, but without his usual snarkiness. Usually he bites our heads off if we forget to use the Italian form of address.

"Yes, sorry, signore. Um, are you okay?"

"I don't —" He peers at me as though he's trying to make out some cryptic message written across my face. "Yes. I'm — I'm fine. For a second, I just —"

He looks around at the now nearly empty hallway, then

back at me. His eyes narrow into suspicious slits. "Shouldn't you be in class, signorina?"

I sigh and walk away. He seems to be recovering.

Without giving myself too much time to think about it, I march downstairs to Annie's economics class. I can see her through the open doorway, sitting attentively, notebook open before her on her desk. Before I can chicken out, I knock on the door and step inside. The teacher turns to look at me, eyebrows raised.

"I'm sorry to interrupt, Ms. Bennett, but Principal Morse sent me to ask Annie Gibson to come to the office. She —" I pause for the slightest instant. "She has a phone call."

Ms. Bennett looks instantly concerned. Her worry about what sort of emergency might involve a phone call in the middle of class conveniently distracts her from asking if I have a pass from the principal's secretary, or anything like that. Annie gives me a *what are you doing?* kind of look but obediently gathers up her things and follows me out.

I lead us down the hall toward the office but then continue past it, ducking into the first empty classroom we come to. I close the door as soon as Annie comes in behind me.

"Cyn, what —?"

"Annie, what is going on?"

"What are you talking about? *You* just dragged *me* out of class, remember? I'm assuming I don't actually have a phone call. Unless it's from the insane asylum, warning me that my best friend is a crazy person." She looks at me expectantly.

Not letting myself think too much about getting to this

moment has had the unfortunate side effect of leaving me somewhat unprepared in terms of what to say next. Annie's not really mad, not yet, but she's going to be.

I hate when she's mad at me.

I force myself to take another deep breath and look her in the eyes.

"Annie, what happened with De Luca after class?"

She stares at me like I've just asked her why the ceiling is made of bees. "What?"

"What did you go up to talk to him about?"

"I had to ask him about the homework assignment for tomorrow. Why?"

"Ask him what, exactly?"

She crosses her arms and continues to stare at me incredulously. "Cyn, what is this about?"

"Do you remember touching him?"

"*What?*"

"You touched his hand, when you were talking, and then —"

She laughs, a mean *I can't even believe you* laugh. "What are you, spying on me now? Are you suggesting I have a thing for icky Italian teachers? I don't know what's up with you lately, Cyn, but I don't like it."

"Annie, listen to me. Please." I then proceed to not say anything for several seconds while she stares at me with growing impatience. How the hell do I say this? *The evil librarian did something bad to you! I think he's made you a danger to yourself and others!* "Okay. This is going to sound a little, uh, nuts."

"I believe you."

I take yet another deep breath. "Mr. Gabriel—"

She practically explodes. "I *knew* it! I knew this had something to do with him! You can't stand that I'm spending time with someone other than you, and now you're making up excuses to get me out of class and accuse me of—of—of whatever it is you're trying to accuse me of—I don't even *know*—!"

"*Annie, shut up and listen to me!*" That was actual screaming just then. We both glance nervously at the door. Then she crosses her arms again and goes back to staring at me, but at least she's staring at me silently. Her face is blotchy with anger.

"There is something going on with Mr. Gabriel. It's not about me being jealous. I mean, yes, I miss having more of you to myself, and I get that that makes me a selfish jerk, and I will work on that, but that's not why I'm worried. You're different around him. He makes you—weird. And whenever you start to realize how weird, he touches you and you forget. You've been skipping class and going in early and staying late and acting so *strange* . . . What was wrong with you in Italian today? You were all spacey and not-there, just like those other kids in the hall afterward, and then—"

Annie holds up her hands and shakes her head, apparently unable to even speak to me. Her face has gotten even redder and blotchier.

"Stop it," she whispers finally. "Just stop it. You *are* crazy. I don't know what you're talking about. I'm going back to class."

I grab her arm before she can open the door.

"Get *off* me!" She tries to pull away but I don't let go. I can't try to start this conversation over again some other time. This is it, right now. I have to make her listen.

"No, Annie. Goddammit, listen to me. You did something to De Luca, do you even know that? You touched him and he got that same spacey thing that you'd had earlier. You touched him and then *you* were fine and he was messed up. What was that? Do you even know? Did you even know you did it?"

She keeps shaking her head at me, not saying anything. She backs into the door and I move with her, not releasing her arm.

"And all those kids in the hall, just standing around? I *saw* him, Annie. I saw Mr. Gabriel doing that to other kids in the library. He's *doing* something. I don't understand it, but I know it's something bad. And you spend all that time with him, and now he's got you doing things I don't even think you know that you're doing, and I'm so *scared* —"

Annie finally manages to rip her arm free and then uses it to push me away from her. I stumble back, looking at her helplessly. She's not listening. She's not hearing me at all.

"Fuck you, Cyn," she says, which is kind of a shock because Annie hardly ever swears like that. And never at me. "I can't believe you. I really can't. For once I have something good happening, something fun and exciting, and you have to try to mess it up for me. You suck as a friend sometimes, you know that? I'm always there for you, *always*, and you —"

I realize suddenly that she is close to crying. I reach out to her. "Annie, no, I'm not —"

She smacks my hand away. "Don't talk to me. Just leave me alone."

This time when she goes for the door, I let her.

At lunch, I find Leticia and Diane at our usual table near the last set of windows. They move their stuff to make room, then look behind me for Annie.

"Where's your better half, Cyn?" Diane asks.

"She's probably at the *liiibrary*," Leticia drawls, rolling her eyes. "That girl is crazy."

"Yeah," I say. Although they don't know the half of it.

"Mr. Gabriel is pretty damn hot," Diane says. Leticia rolls her eyes again, and Diane leans forward across the table. "No, really—have you seen that man close up? Seriously L, he's like, *amazing* looking. Like once you start looking it's hard to stop. We went to the library in English today to start working on thesis outlines, and I don't think any of us managed to get anything done."

I am on this instantly. "You went to the library? Are you okay?"

Leticia and Diane both turn to stare at me with identical *what the hell are you talking about?* expressions.

"I mean, did anything weird happen? I heard—I heard some weird stuff about him, that's all. The librarian."

"Oooh, like what?" Leticia's eyes go wide. "Is he a *naughty* librarian? Has he been reading aloud from the sexy parts of the books or something?"

Diane snickers. "He could read the frickin' dictionary and make it sound sexy. He makes me want to do lots and lots of research. I think I'm going to write my paper on sex scenes. Do you think Mrs. Stiller would go for that?"

Leticia pretends to think about this. "You'd have to include a lot of footnotes with explanations. She probably wouldn't understand a lot of it."

"I could include some helpful diagrams."

"Maybe you could get your sexy librarian to help you."

"Ha! Annie would scratch my eyes out. You know she wants him all for herself."

They're both laughing now, but it's not funny.

Leticia finally notices my lack of amusement. "What's up, Cyn? You okay?"

No, I want to tell her. I'm not okay. And neither is Annie. And Mr. Gabriel is . . . is . . . what? How can I try to explain when I don't even know what I mean myself?

"It's just—Annie and I had a fight. She's really pissed at me."

Leticia and Diane exchange a startled glance. They know Annie and I hardly ever fight. "What happened?"

"I—I tried to talk to her about Mr. Gabriel. I mean, I think she's going a little too far with all the time she's spending with him, you know? Having a harmless crush is one thing, but she's skipping classes to go to the library, and she's acting all—different. Haven't you noticed it?"

Diane picks at the crust of her sandwich. "You don't really think she'd—you know—do anything, do you? Or that he would? I mean, I don't think it's such a big deal if he flirts with her a little, but he wouldn't . . ."

"I don't know. It just seems . . . wrong. I'm worried about

her. And when I tried to finally talk to her about it, she went totally nuts. She won't even talk to me now."

"That is kind of weird for Annie," Diane allows. "She never stays mad like that."

Leticia pulls out her phone. "Here. Let me text her and see if she wants to meet up after school today. Maybe we can try to talk to her together."

She sends her text and we wait, watching her phone. When it finally chimes, she picks it up and reads it. Her mouth twists to the side, and then she reads aloud, "Can't. Library. And tell Cyn to mind her own fucking business."

There's an awkward pause, and then Diane touches my arm. "She'll calm down again, Cyn. You'll see."

"Yeah," Leticia says, pocketing her phone. "She probably only got so mad because deep down, she knows you're right to be worried. She just needs a little time to realize it."

I nod, trying to hope that this might be true. Maybe Annie's insanity is only temporary. Maybe she'll come to her senses once she has a chance to think about things. Maybe we'll be okay again by the end of the day.

But the honest part of me inside my brain knows all of that is crap.

Something has changed in her, and she's not going to suddenly snap back to herself. I know that nothing has really happened that I can point to. I know that I have nothing other than my own creeped-out feelings about Mr. Gabriel to go on. But I also know, I *know,* that there is something wrong about him. And that he's doing something to my friend.

I look for Annie in the halls between each class for the rest of the day, but it's not until after eighth that I see her, standing by her locker with Leticia. I steel myself and decide to go over; maybe she won't flip out at me with Leticia standing right there. I wonder if Leticia tried to talk to her about the Mr. Gabriel thing herself. I hope so. Maybe it will carry more weight coming from someone else.

I walk down the hall, pushing past the occasional slow-moving or not-moving student standing in my way. I'm still maybe twenty feet away when I see Annie reach out to touch Leticia's hand. I stop, something inside me going small and cold and terrified. After one further agonized moment of paralysis, I throw myself forward, calling Leticia's name, trying to run toward them, but now it seems like every student in the school is suddenly standing in that hallway, blocking my progress and obscuring my view of Annie and Leticia. It feels like forever before I shove the last person out of my way and stumble out of the throng toward Annie's locker. Annie turns to look at me. Her eyes are cold and hard, and her mouth turns up in a tiny smile that is not a smile at all.

Leticia is leaning back against the locker, staring blankly at nothing.

I grab Annie, digging my fingertips into her arms. "What did you do?" I shout at her.

Her expression goes cloudy and then clears to reveal shock and anger. "Get off, you freak!" she shouts back, pulling at my hands.

"What did you do?" I shout again, slamming her back against the lockers behind her. Her hands drop away and she stares defiantly back at me. I search her eyes, trying to see if she's really there. "Do you even know?"

"What are you *talking* about?"

"Look!" I let go with one hand and point at Leticia. Annie shifts her eyes to where I'm pointing, and I can *see* her making herself not understand me. She knows, but she won't let herself know. She looks back at me and then pushes me so hard that I stumble backward, tripping over my own feet and landing hard on my ass on the floor.

"Stay away from me!" She spits the words and then takes off down the hall, the students parting before her like the Red Sea and closing up again behind her.

I stay on the floor for a few minutes, not really letting myself think about anything. Then I look up to where Leticia is still standing there, oblivious to what just happened. I swallow and climb back to my feet.

"L? Leticia? You okay?"

Her eyes turn to track across my face, but she doesn't seem to be able to focus.

"Hey," I say. "Hey. Leticia, come on. Come back." I'm not sure what I mean by that, exactly. But I'm remembering that when Signor De Luca was all spacey after Annie touched him, he came back to himself after a few minutes. He didn't seem quite as gone as Leticia does right now, though. But, surely, whatever . . . whatever the hell Annie did to her, it's just temporary. She's not going to *stay* this way. . . .

"Leticia!" I scream suddenly into her face, and she blinks and jerks back.

"What . . . ?" She shakes her head and then she seems to be there again. Mostly. "Cyn? What happened?"

Annie made you go away. My best friend sucked something out of you like a goddamn vampire, only it wasn't blood, it was something else, and I don't understand how any of this can really be happening.

"You—uh, I think you fainted. Standing up. You're okay now, though." *Be okay now. Please please please be okay now.*

"I did? Huh. That's . . . weird. I don't . . ." She looks around. "Okay. I guess . . . I guess I'll go home now."

"Are you sure you're okay? Maybe you should sit down."

"Okay," she says agreeably, not sitting down. I do my best to guide her gently down to the floor. We sit there in the emptying hallway for a minute.

"Leticia?"

"Yeah?"

"Are you really okay?"

"Sure," she says. "I feel a little tired, though. I probably should go home now." Her voice is kind of listless, not anything like her usual vivacious, teasing, energetic self. Slowly, she pushes herself back up to her feet.

I stand up, too. I feel like I should stop her, but I don't know what to say. And maybe she should go home. Maybe she just needs to sleep it off or something.

She gives me a vague kind of smile. "See you tomorrow, Cyn."

"Are you really—?"

"Yeah," she says, waving her hand listlessly toward me. "I'm

65

fine." She smiles again and walks off down the hall. I watch her go. I do not feel fine at all.

I walk outside and drop onto one of the benches that line the scraggly front lawn of the school's main entrance. It seems like maybe two of every ten kids who pass by me are walking slowly, not talking, sort of drifting along. I watch them, trying to think. Assuming for the moment that I haven't actually lost my mind, and that Mr. Gabriel really is doing this to everyone, what would be the point? What could he possibly get out of it? Does he just like being surrounded by mindless zombie types? It doesn't really make any sense.

A thought occurs to me, and I sit up a little straighter, staring intently at nothing in that way that people do when they are thinking very hard about something.

Maybe the zombie-ness isn't the point. Maybe it's just a side effect of something else. When I watched him earlier, he was touching people, seeming to take something out of them. Maybe *that's* the point — whatever he's taking. Which is . . . ? Whatever makes people not like zombies most of the time.

But say that's true. (I know. I know. But let's just go with it.) He's doing something else to Annie. Or something additional, I guess, since she was also kind of zombie-like in Italian. But she's not usually like that. She's altered around him, and a little starry-eyed, but not lethargic and sort of *gone*. Usually. Until today. And then she did to De Luca what Mr. Gabriel was doing to those students before first period. And then she did it again, to Leticia.

Is he turning her into whatever he is?

I want to skitter away from my own thoughts. I get up

from the bench, too agitated to sit still. This is all very nuts. None of it makes any sense. What do I think he is? How could he possibly turn Annie into anything? And why? And how can I ignore the fact that all of this is absolutely *not actually possible*?

There's a shout nearby, and I jerk out of my spirally reverie. I look up to see Ryan and one of his friends. Ryan's the one shouting. At the friend. Who is kind of just drifting along, not paying attention to him. As I watch, he grabs Jorge's arm — I think that's his name — and spins him around to face him. Jorge stands there, looking at Ryan but not really seeming to see him. Like Leticia hadn't really seemed to see me. Ryan drops his books and pushes Jorge. Jorge stumbles back and shakes his head a little. Then he starts drifting forward again like nothing happened, right past Ryan. Ryan shouts after him but doesn't try to grab him again. Was Jorge one of the students I saw in the library earlier? I think maybe he was. He doesn't seem to be snapping out of it as easily as De Luca did. *Because the librarian got Jorge, and only Annie got De Luca, and Annie's effect is only a shadow of what Mr. Gabriel's is.*

I think that must be true.

At least for now, my mind whispers relentlessly.

Shut up! I scream at it. *You don't even know what you're talking about! None of this makes any goddamn sense!*

My mind shuts up.

Ryan stands there for another minute, staring unhappily after his friend. Then he turns and sees me. For a moment we just stand there looking at each other. Then he picks up his books and walks over to me.

"Hey," he says.

"Hey," I say back. "So, um . . . that was weird, huh? With Jorge?"

"You saw that, huh? Yeah. I don't know what's wrong with him today."

I sit back down on the bench, making sure to leave plenty of inviting empty space beside me. The sun is shining down behind Ryan, giving him a backlit Greek-god quality. I squint up at him. "You know it's not just Jorge, right?"

He stands there a moment more, then sits beside me. His leg is mere inches from my own. He scratches at a corner of a textbook.

"Yeah," he says after a minute. "I guess a lot of people were acting strange today. What do you think is going on?"

He turns to look at me. There are so many things I want to say. *An evil librarian is taking over the school. He appears to be making my best friend his special evil library monitor. I am afraid that he knows that I suspect him. I am also afraid that if this craziness continues, the school community will never get to experience your portrayal of Sweeney Todd, which I think would be a terrible crime. Also, I would like to kiss you.*

Instead I say, "You mean the whole thing with everyone spacing out and wandering around like zombies?"

For a second Ryan seems about to laugh, but then he doesn't.

"Yeah," he says. "What's that about?"

In that moment, I know I am going to try to tell him. I say a silent apology to my future self, since I'm fairly certain the tenuous connection Ryan and I have established between us since my hallway tackle is about to crumble into sad and tattered bits of broken dreams.

"I have a theory," I say hesitantly.

"You do?"

"It's going to sound crazy."

"Okay."

"But I'm going to tell you anyway."

He nods encouragingly. "Bring it."

"Have you, um, met the new librarian?"

Ryan's eyebrows seem to climb very high up onto his forehead. "Is he . . . very boring? Do you think he is boring everyone into this permanently glassy-eyed state?"

I smile uncertainly. He thinks I am kidding. "Um, not exactly."

He waits. I take yet another deep breath.

"I don't think he's exactly, um, a regular kind of person."

Ryan takes this in for a moment. "I'm not sure I know where you're going with this, Cyn. Maybe you should just come out and say it, whatever it is."

I bite my lip, look away, look back at him, look at the distant horizon. Finally I look down and say, "I think he's some kind of monster or demon or psychic vampire or something, and he's slowly sucking the life force out of all of the students in the school. Or, you know, something like that."

I risk a glance up at Ryan's face. His expression is carefully blank. "That is definitely not where I imagined you were going."

"I told you it would sound crazy."

"Yeah," he says. "You weren't kidding."

"You don't believe me."

He runs a hand through his perfectly imperfect hair. "Well, no. I mean, a demon? A—what did you say, a psychic vampire? I don't even know what that means."

"I know. Not really possible. Right?"

"Seriously? That's more than a little crazy. I thought you were going to say maybe he was poisoning the school lunches or something."

"Jorge was there in the library with him today. I saw, through the door. Mr. Gabriel did something to all the students. Made them . . . well, like Jorge was. All spacey and out of it and not right. I'm not making this up. I swear it."

His face is kind of closing before me, his desire to have an explanation eclipsed by his desire to not believe in crazy things. I am watching him slipping away. I can't let that happen.

"Ryan, I swear, I know how it sounds. But I *saw* him—"

"Saw him what? Sprout wings and fangs and dance around in the middle of a giant pentagram?"

I wince at his sarcasm. "Okay, yes, I get it. A demon librarian is not exactly something you talk about as being a real thing. But just bear with me here, just for a second. He did something to Annie, too. He's practically brainwashed her!"

"You mean your friend who's in Italian with us, right? That girl?"

"Yes. She's started skipping classes, and hanging out in the library all day, and after school, and today, she—"

"Cyn, come on. Stop it." He looks slightly concerned. And maybe a little annoyed. "I know you're upset about this, your friend acting all different and everything, and the other kids, too, but this isn't funny, okay? There's got to be a rational explanation for what's happening. What you're doing, pretending there's this . . . this demon stuff, it's not helping."

He can't back away from our moment of shared understanding quickly enough, apparently. He was right there with me, knowing something beyond standard strangeness was going on. Right there, and then suddenly not.

"Look," I tell him as calmly as I can. "I know how all this sounds. Do you think I don't know how all this sounds?"

"Well, then, stop it, okay? Let's try to think about what might *really* be going on."

Suddenly I am very mad at him.

"Dammit, Ryan, open your eyes. What kind of rational explanation could possibly account for what's happening to everyone? What do you think was wrong with Jorge just now? Do you think all the other students are involved in some elaborate prank, that they're all just faking?"

He is taken aback by my outburst. "Well, no. And it's not, I mean, it's not like it's *everyone* . . ."

"Not yet."

"Cyn, come on. You can't really expect me to believe —"

I get up off the bench. He's right, of course. Why should I expect him to believe this? To believe me? He doesn't know me. I'm just the awkward girl who tackles him in hallways and stares at him in Italian and at rehearsal.

"Come with me. Right now. I'll prove it." I hold out my hand.

He stares up at me, bewildered. "Prove what? How? What are you talking about?"

I'm getting so sick of that question.

"Just come with me. You'll be able to tell, I'm sure of it. There's something wrong with him."

"Him who?"

I want to shake him. "The *librarian*. Just come up and talk to him and you'll see." I suddenly realize that Annie is probably up there right now, too. "My friend — Annie — she's been spending a lot of time with him. I know that he's been doing something to her. Something really bad. I thought I could talk to her, make her see it, but she won't listen to reason anymore. Maybe, if you came with me, together, we could . . ."

He shakes his head. "I'm sorry, this is just too — I think I should just go. I need to go check on Jorge and the other guys, see how they're doing."

"Fine. Go do that. See how much good it does you. In the meantime, I'm going to go try to save my best friend." Again. I grab my bag and stalk off toward the school's main entrance.

"Cyn, wait! Come on, don't be like that." On any other day I would be doing little cartwheels in my head to have Ryan Halsey calling after me. But right now I'm just sad and angry and frustrated and disappointed. I didn't realize how desperately I wanted him to believe me until he didn't.

I push through the doors and take off down the hall, going fast so I won't have time to stop and think. Suddenly I'm extra worried about Annie. What if she told Mr. Gabriel what I said? What if he decides to step up the pace on whatever he's doing to her? What if he's doing it to her right now? I try to conjure brave images of me dragging her out of there by force. It doesn't matter if she's pissed at me. She can forgive me later, after I save her.

I take the stairs two at a time. I emerge on the third floor breathing a little heavily and make myself slow to a walk. I don't want to be all out of breath when I burst in there to save Annie. It would kind of ruin the effect.

The sound of someone coming up the stairs behind me makes me stop and turn around. It's Ryan, looking angry and apologetic and confused, all together.

"Cyn, wait." He's not at all out of breath from the stairs, of course.

I try to get my breathing in check. I try to resist being filled with terrible hope.

"All right," he says. "I'm coming with you, okay? I don't know what you expect me to see, and I'm telling you straight out that I do not believe there's some kind of evil demon librarian taking over the school. But —"

I start to walk again but then he touches my arm. I stop instantly, chills radiating from where his fingers rest lightly on my skin, still not immune to ridiculous swooniness, apparently. Not even now. He steps in front of me, blocking my path, looking down at me. I remind myself to breathe. God, he's still so lovely to look at. Even when I'm mad at him.

"Look," he says seriously. "I don't want you to be mad. And I do want to know what's going on with everyone. And if you think the librarian has something to do with it . . . well, I'm coming with you. But don't be pissed at me if I'm not instantly convinced."

I blink several times and make myself speak. "Okay," I say. He doesn't want me to be mad. He cares about how I feel about him. He cares enough to run after me to try to make me not-mad even when he thinks I'm crazy. Why couldn't this be happening when I didn't have to be distracted by evil-librarian zombie-student insanity?

Life is so unfair.

We resume our walk to the library. Just as we approach the doors, I feel Ryan's eyes on me and turn to look at him. He looks uncertain and kind of nervous and embarrassed but he's coming with me anyway, and then he gives me one of those delicious half smiles, and I don't even glance at the doors as I reach out and pull them open.

And then we stop right there, staring.

Mr. Gabriel is standing in the center of the room, facing slightly away from us. The tables have been cleared away against the bookshelves, and a giant and disturbing shape has been drawn in chalk on the floor. Its unpleasant lines and angles form a kind of frame around the librarian, who seems to have sprouted large black bat-like wings. Also, long twisty black horns of some kind are now spiraling out of the top of his head. He is bending slightly forward, looking at the floor, muttering something incomprehensible in a low, guttural voice.

He's not dancing around, at least. So that's something.

After an eternity of standing there in the doorway, trying to take this in, I hear Ryan's voice speaking from what seems a great distance.

"You were right. I was able to tell right away."

Mr. Gabriel slowly turns, raising his head. The amount of blood spattered across his light-blue button-down shirt makes me gasp. Whose blood is that? Where did it come from? There is blood on the floor, too, I realize. A lot of it. There is so much that I think there cannot be very much left at all inside whomever it came out of.

"Oops," Mr. Gabriel says. "Thought I locked those." Then he grins. It is not a comforting expression. Especially because of the fangs.

"You're—" Ryan appears to be trying to think of something appropriate to say.

"John Gabriel, the new librarian," Mr. Gabriel says brightly. "Pleased to meet you!"

"But you're—you're not—" Ryan stops, swallows, starts again. "You're not *human*," he says. He seems to feel it is very important to point this out. Perhaps in case Mr. Gabriel was not aware.

Mr. Gabriel's terrifying grin grows even larger, stretching impossibly across his face. He begins to laugh. Then he stops laughing and winks at us.

"Strangely, the job description did not specify that as a requirement."

Chapter | 05

"Time to go," I hear myself say. My hand reaches out for Ryan's and grips it tightly. "Time to go right now."

For some reason Mr. Gabriel has not moved from where he is standing. Something about this fact seems significant, but the most immediate thing it seems to suggest is that we should run away, very fast, while we still have the chance.

Ryan is still staring in horrified fascination. I pull on his hand as hard as I can, trying to make the running away start happening. He stumbles, looks at my hand holding his, looks up at my face. Then he looks once more back at the librarian.

That is a mistake.

Mr. Gabriel's eyes go big and dark and Ryan freezes, staring back into those eyes with a suddenly slack expression. I yank again on his hand, but it's like I'm not even there.

Then Mr. Gabriel turns to look at me and I forget everything else.

His *eyes.* His eyes are enormous, they are impossible black holes of nothing, they are so big that I start to fall into them. I can feel the floor shifting and tilting and I am going to plummet right into those gaping holes filled with darkness and disappear forever and I can still feel Ryan's fingers laced with mine and —

wait

what?

I shake my head, blinking, stumbling a step backward and trying to clear the fog that seems to be filling my head. When I'm able to focus again I see that Mr. Gabriel is still staring at me, but the giant black holes are gone and he just looks — surprised.

Then his eyebrows draw down with renewed determination, and his eyes start to go black again.

I rip my gaze away. "Stop that!"

There is a moment of silence in which I keep my eyes firmly fixed upon the New Fiction shelf.

"Huh," Mr. Gabriel says finally. Then something in his voice suddenly changes. "Oh. Oh, wow. *That* explains — wow."

My gaze flicks back to him before I can stop it, and I see that his giant evil eyes of blackness are gone. He's still looking at me, but now he just seems kind of — fascinated. I wait for whatever he is going to do next, but he just keeps standing there, staring at me.

"What?" I ask finally, starting to feel uncomfortable.

"You're —" He shakes his head. "Huh."

"*What?* I'm what? What are you talking about?"

"You're a —" He says a word here that isn't a word,

just a jumble of harsh syllables and consonants that hurt my ears.

He sees me flinch and shrugs. "Sorry. There's not really a word for it in English. Or any human language. It translates roughly as *super-roach*."

This is such an unexpected thing to hear that when I try to respond, it takes me a moment to make words come out. Finally I manage: "I — excuse me?"

He smiles. "I know. Not the most flattering of terms. Don't take it personally. All humans are like insects, really — there are so *many* of you, and you get everywhere, crawling busily all about, intent on your tiny insect goals. Annoying and plentiful and easy to kill, at least in reasonably sized batches. But there are some of you, a very small number, who have an extra . . . resistance. Who don't succumb to the usual methods of pest control. *Super-roach* is kind of the shorthand. It doesn't come up that often, because there aren't too many. You're actually the first one I've ever encountered."

I hold up my free hand. "Wait. Just — wait. What —?" There are *so many questions* that could go here. I pick the most obvious. "What *are* you? I mean . . ." I gesture helplessly at his leathery black wings. "Seriously?"

He stands up a little straighter, stretching his wings to their full impressive width behind him. "You like?" His expression is somehow both proud and a little sheepish.

I stare at him, standing there with his gigantic goddamn *wings* in the middle of the library, shelves of books and desks and computers and other completely and totally normal everyday pieces of high-school existence all around him. "No! No, I don't frickin' *like!* What — Why —" My hands try to go up to my forehead, perhaps to try to soothe my struggling brains and convince them to stay inside my skull and not explode with the impossibleness of everything that is happening here, and I realize I'm still holding Ryan's hand, and that he is still staring vacantly at Mr. Gabriel. "What did you *do* to him?"

"Oh, he's fine," Mr. Gabriel says dismissively. "Just mesmerized. You would be, too, except for the whole super-roach thing."

"Stop calling me that!" I know it is ridiculous to feel insulted when there are far more important things going on, but I can't help it.

"You should be glad," he goes on. "It makes you much harder to kill than the other bugs. Although, of course, still squashable when one puts his mind to it." Something in his playful expression shifts here, and he gives me a level and considering look that makes my stomach try to crawl out through my spine. I remember that we need to run away. That whatever Mr. Gabriel is, he is obviously not filled with happy good intentions toward my companion and myself.

And Annie? What are his intentions toward her?

Dammit.

"Where's Annie? Is she here?"

He smiles again, a disgusting, knowing smile that my fingers ache to scratch right off his face. "Ah, Annie," he says, speaking her name like a caress. It makes me want to throw up. "No, no. She's safe at home. My task here was not one that required her assistance. Not yet."

His task. His task, which is — what? I stare at him, at the

chalk symbol, at the blood on his shirt and all around the floor. *Whose blood is that?* my brain whispers again. He must have killed someone. He's doing some kind of demony witchcraft (demoncraft?), and there is someone's blood all over the place, and do evil murdering demon librarians generally let witnesses to their crimes go running off into the late afternoon to tattle to the world? No. No, they do not. Why hasn't Mr. Gabriel killed us already?

Oh, right. Because I'm a super-roach, and it's not so easy.

But still possible, my brain reminds me.

Right. Thanks. Shut up. But Ryan —

"Aaaaanyway," Mr. Gabriel says, breaking into my spiraling thoughts. "I'm kind of in the middle of something. So I'm afraid I'm going to have to —" He takes a step forward.

I take a step back, but Ryan doesn't step with me.

Dammit!

I yank *again* on his hand, but he's clearly still lost in the paralyzing memory of Mr. Gabriel's gaping black-hole eyes. He's not here with me, not able to help or even to move. I pull my hand from his and step in front of him. I am horribly conscious of Mr. Gabriel still standing a few feet away, but at the same time I finally register that his step forward was only a single step. I think about the chalk-drawn symbol on the floor. A million half-remembered movies and TV shows and horror novels race through my mind, and I think about pentagrams and portals and containment fields, and I start to believe that Mr. Gabriel can't actually leave the lines of the shape he's standing inside. Not right now. Which is why he went for the mesmerizing thing. Possibly to keep us standing there oblivious and helpless until he was able to move more freely and kill us at his leisure.

"Ryan!" I scream at him, the same way I did to Leticia earlier. Then I raise my hand and slap him across the face as hard as I can.

He staggers backward. He blinks and shakes his head and seems to be coming back to himself, finally. He looks at me, confused. "Cyn? What the hell—?" His eyes go wide and I see him start to remember, and then I see him start to shift his gaze over my shoulder to where Mr. Gabriel is and I grab his head with both hands.

"Hey!" I shout. "Eyes on me. Do not look anywhere else. I mean it."

"But—"

"*Ryan goddammit just do what I say and keep your eyes right here on mine or I will kill you!*" He is a little startled by this rather harsh directive, but it does the trick. For the moment. Slowly I start to move to the side, drawing Ryan's gaze with me, making him turn as I do, until he is facing the door.

"Okay," I say. "Okay. Listen. I am going to let go of your head, and you are going to keep looking right there at the door, okay? *Okay?*"

He nods. "Okay. Yes, okay."

"Okay. I don't know what you remember, but I will explain it all later. We just need to get out of here."

There is a dark chuckle from behind Ryan, and I see him wanting to turn around.

"Hey!" I shout at him. "Don't you dare turn around. What did I say?"

"Okay," he says again. He looks scared. I don't blame him. I am feeling somewhat terrified myself. Except there's no time for that now, and so I will just have to be terrified later.

"Okay," I say. "Here we go." I take a breath and then I move, simultaneously releasing Ryan's head and turning around to face the door and grabbing his hand again and pulling him forward with me toward the exit. I am certain as I reach for them that the doors will suddenly be locked as they were the other night, but they push open instantly, releasing us into the dim hallway. Mr. Gabriel is letting us go. For now.

With every step Ryan seems to come more back to himself, and together we tear down the hall and the stairs and outside and away, away, away, away, away, running and running and not looking back.

Before too long he is the one pulling me forward, and I curse myself for not having had the foresight to start doing track or something years ago so that I'd be ready for situations like this. But terror is a pretty good substitute for athletic fitness, it turns out, and I'm able to keep going even though my lungs are about to disintegrate and my legs feel like they weigh a million pounds each.

Eventually Ryan slows down, looks behind us, and finally stops.

"Oh, thank God," I say, stopping beside him and bending over with my hands on my thighs. I am trying to remember how to breathe.

Ryan whips out his phone.

"Who—are you—calling?" I manage between gasps.

"911," he says, his tone suggesting that this should be obvious.

I straighten and snatch the phone from his hand.

"Hey!"

"And what are you going to tell them, exactly?"

"The librarian is a demon! We have to tell someone!"

"And how well do you think that will go?"

"I—" Ryan frowns at me. "Well, maybe I could say something else, like that we saw blood in the library, and then they can go and see for themselves."

"Ryan, think about it. Mr. Gabriel will probably be long gone. The police will show up and find all that blood, and they'll want to ask us all kinds of questions, and we won't have any answers, and for all you know they'll think *we* did it! And we don't have time to be murder suspects right now. We have to—have to—"

"Have to what?"

"Stop him! We have to find a way to stop him."

Ryan runs his hand through his hair and lets out a strange, shaky sound that's part laugh, part sigh, with maybe a touch of barely suppressed scream. "Jesus, Cyn. What . . . what *was* that? What did we just see? I mean, he actually was some kind of demon, wasn't he? For real. That's . . . not possible."

Right. I've already had a nice slow buildup to this confirmation of my suspicions. Ryan is only just joining us.

He's holding up rather well, I think, all things considered.

"Yeah. Not possible, I know. Except," I add carefully, "I guess it must be, because that's what he is. You saw it."

"Did I? Maybe we just . . . imagined it. Or, I don't know, maybe we're having hallucinations." He begins to get excited at this possible out. "Maybe it's related to what's been happening to everyone else, and there's, like, some kind of chemical in the air or something, and it makes some kids into zombies and gives some of us crazy hallucinations . . ."

"No. Ryan, you are not going to talk yourself out of what's going on. We saw it. It's real."

"But—"

"No!" I yell at him. He blinks and tries to take a step back from me, but I clutch the front of his shirt and hold him there, looking up at him. "Ryan, please. Please don't. You can't leave me alone with this thing. I can't handle it all by myself. I need you to help me."

His eyes dart up, around, seeking escape. I dig my fingers even more deeply into the fabric of his shirt.

"Ryan. We have to stop whatever he's doing to Annie and everyone else before anything else terrible happens!" *Please, please don't let anything else terrible have happened already. Where is Annie right now? Is she okay? Is she really safe at home like he said? Or is she still there, in the library somewhere, with him? I can hardly bear to even think it.*

Maybe that was her blood you saw, my brain suggests quietly.

For a second my heart just stops. But no, that can't be— he's clearly interested in her for some reason. He wouldn't— I'm sure he wouldn't just kill her. He couldn't.

Ryan looks back at me, clearly not wanting to give up on the possibility that none of this is real.

I force myself to focus on convincing him. *Annie is okay. He wouldn't kill her. He wouldn't.* "Think about Jorge," I say. "Think about your other friends. Not to mention all the teachers and everyone else. Think about all that blood, Ryan. He must have killed someone! Who knows what else he's capable of!"

"But — but what can we even do? How can we possibly…?"

That is, I have to admit, a valid question. I hand him back his phone. "I don't know. We need to . . . we need to think."

Ryan nods, tucking his phone back into his jeans. "Okay. But not here, out in the street. Let's go to my house." He looks back toward the school, mutters something about getting his car tomorrow, then starts off down the street in the other direction. I hurry along beside him.

On the way, I call Annie. The call goes to voice mail the first two times, which could be because she's busy or because her brother stole her phone again or because she's not speaking to me or because she's lying dead or dying in the school library. I try again. The third time her stupid brother picks up. When I ask to speak to Annie, he says she's not home. Which could be true, or could be what she told him to say to me. But the fact that he has her phone means that she must have come home after school, at least. She's probably still there. She probably just still hates me right now and doesn't want to talk to me. Which is okay. I mean, it's not *okay,* it sucks, but I'll take it over that being her blood splattered all over the library and the librarian. I try to ask him where she is but he hangs up on me midsentence. I hate that kid.

Ryan's house is one of three well-kept two-story houses arranged around the end of a cul-de-sac about two miles from school. Neither of us said much on the walk over, lost in our own impossible thoughts, but I pull myself out of my brain as we approach and try to come back to the present so I can look around properly. It seems like a nice place to live. Large leafy trees cast friendly shade over everything, and the mailboxes are uniformly white and shiny with recent painting. The houses aren't as close together as they are in my neighborhood, where most of the homes are attached on one side and share a yard fence on the other. There's a basketball hoop in a small paved area between two of the houses, and Ryan steers us toward the one on the right of it.

We go up to the porch and then he unlocks the door and steps inside, holding it open for me behind him. The house is dark and quiet. I follow him down a short hallway into the kitchen. Ryan grabs a plate and two pieces of what looks like banana bread from the counter and tucks two bottles of water under his arm and then leads me up the stairs. We pass an open door that gives me a glimpse of a neatly made bed and a poster of some sports figure I don't recognize. ("My brother's room," Ryan explains over his shoulder. "He's at college.") And then Ryan opens the door at the end of the hall and we step inside. My heart does a stupid little fluttery thing inside me as my brain needlessly whispers with barely contained excitement: *We're in Ryan Halsey's bedroom! His bedroom! Where his bed is! The room where he sleeps and does his homework and surfs the Internet and does whatever else boys do in their bedrooms!* And then it tries to start calling up a very non-PG collection of images of what boys might do in their bedrooms, and I cut it off before it makes me blush uncontrollably.

Yes, thanks, I almost didn't realize, I tell my brain. *Now shut up.*

Ryan's bedroom is both like and unlike the few other boys' bedrooms I have seen thus far. It falls somewhere happily toward the neater end of the spectrum, but there's still plenty of stuff everywhere; stuff that gives a very full and abundant sense of *Ryan-ness,* complete with all his lovely contradictions.

Like his brother, he's got a poster of some sports figure I don't recognize, but he's also got a framed *Empire Strikes Back* movie poster over his bed and a series of *Playbill* covers from various Broadway shows tacked to one wall. A program from last fall's school musical — signed across the front by the other cast members — occupies a place of honor on a shelf above his desk, flanked by rugby trophies and a couple of photos of Ryan and his brother, one of them when they were little kids, the other taken two or three years ago at what appears to be his brother's graduation. (His brother is kind of hot, too, but in a different, distant way that doesn't really do anything for me.) There's a flat-screen TV mounted on the wall and some nice-looking speakers hung in the corners of the room and a pile of dirty laundry in the corner near the closet, and I have to forcibly remove my eyes from a pair of cherry-red boxer briefs tossed atop the white T-shirts and jeans and gray sweatpants and socks and whatever else he's worn in the past few days.

And now I have to forcibly prevent my eyes from darting to his general pelvic region and trying to see through his jeans to whatever tantalizing color boxer briefs he might be wearing today.

Maybe he's going commando today, my brain whispers, and I walk abruptly over to stare at the *Playbill* collection.

"Have you seen all of these?" I ask.

"Yeah." He comes over to stand beside me. "My aunt takes me to a show every year for my birthday. It's kind of our thing."

"That's awesome," I say, because it is. My aunt doesn't even send me a card on my birthday.

"Yeah, she's pretty cool." He walks back over to the door and closes it, and then he sits on the floor, setting the plate of banana bread and bottles of water in front of him. I notice the lack of chairs, notice that he did not invite me to sit on his bed, and plant myself on the floor a little ways away, facing him. I arrange myself so I can lean back against the edge of his bed, though.

I can't be in his bedroom and not touch his bed. I mean, come on.

One edge of a dark-blue sheet barely brushes the back of my neck as I settle into place. I allow my brain exactly two seconds of thinking about what parts of Ryan that edge of sheet might have come into contact with while he was last wrapped up in it. Then I force myself to focus on what we're supposed to be doing.

"So, uh . . ." Ryan looks at the floor, looks around, meets my eyes.

Right. Time to get down to business.

"Okay," I say. "So . . . the new librarian is some kind of evil demon, huh?"

Ryan looks at me a second longer and then laughs suddenly. And briefly. He rubs the back of his hand against his forehead. "Jesus, Cyn. This is really happening, isn't it?"

"Yeah." I take in the room around me, which seems perfectly real and there and normal. The navy-and-crimson sisal rug beneath me is rough and gritty where my hand rests on it, and I can tell it is in severe need of vacuuming. Ryan's chemistry textbook is propped open on his desk. There's a crumpled-up energy bar wrapper lying on the floor next to a small wastebasket bearing a sticker that says RYAN in bright-green puffy letters that looks like something he stuck there when he was about six years old. This is clearly the real world we're in.

And yet.

Ryan nods. Then he blows out his breath, sits up and leans forward, and grabs one of the banana bread pieces.

"All right, then," he says. "What are we going to do about it?"

I could kiss him.

Well, okay, yes, this is not a new desire, the kissing. But in this moment, I feel my lust and longing and liking swirl themselves together into something much more like love. He's not running away from this crazy and terrible impossible thing. He's still here. He's going to help me. We're going to do this together.

I hadn't realized how afraid I was of facing this alone, afraid that Ryan would find a way to deny what was happening after all. But he's not, he didn't, he's sitting right there ripping off giant, boy-size bites of banana bread with his almost-perfect teeth and looking at me expectantly, ready to go, ready to make a plan and take action and get things done.

My relief is immense.

Except, of course, I still have no idea what we can do.

"Okay," I say for about the millionth time. "What do we know so far? We know that Mr. Gabriel is some kind of demon."

"Check."

"We know that he killed someone. Or at least, he probably killed someone. I don't know where else all that blood could have come from." Ryan nods. I think we're both trying not to think too much about whom he might have killed. Someone from school? Someone we know? I keep talking. "We know that he was at least temporarily stuck inside that shape he'd drawn on the floor, or he would have killed us."

"What — what *did* he do to us? He did something . . . I remember . . . and you, uh —" He blinks and looks at me with sudden surprise. "Did you slap me?"

"Oh. Yeah. Sorry. I had to! He was hypnotizing you or something."

"With his crazy giant eyes," Ryan says.

"Yeah."

"But why didn't it work on you, too?"

I explain what Mr. Gabriel said about the super-roach thing. Ryan listens with fascinated interest.

"Cool," he says. "So he can't hurt you?"

"No, he can, just not — not so easily, I guess. I mean, if

he was even telling the truth. Because, you know, evil demon librarians, not so much known for the honesty policy, I bet."

Ryan waves this away. "He obviously was trying to hypnotize you, or whatever, and not managing to. And I can't really think of why he'd bother to lie to you about it. I mean, it would make more sense to lie in the other direction. You know, *not* tell you that you had this resistance thing."

"That's a good point." I consider this. "I guess he figures it won't matter. He'll be able to kill me anyway. It will just be a little harder."

Ryan jumps on this. "But why hasn't he killed us already? Surely he could have gotten out of his chalk thing by now, right? How come he's not here right now, slicing our throats open or whatever?"

I turn involuntarily to look at the window, sure that I'm going to see Mr. Gabriel's leering face hanging there outside the glass, just waiting for the perfect cue to pounce. But there's nothing. Just trees and sky and houses and normal everyday world.

"I don't know," I say. I pick up the other piece of banana bread and take a bite. (It's really good.) I chew, swallow, then go on, thinking out loud: "Maybe he can't just go wherever he wants?" I'm just throwing things out there, but as soon as I say this, it feels right. "Maybe he's stuck in the library. Well, no, not the library. I've seen him in the halls. But maybe the school. I've never seen him out in the parking lot or anything like that. And he seems to be at school all the time, no matter what time it is. . . ."

"Maybe," Ryan says. "We can use that as a working hypothesis, anyway."

I feel the smallest tinge of hope. "So, if we assume that's true, then as long as we don't go back to school —"

He stares at me. "What? We have to go back."

I stare back. "*What?* Hello? Evil demon librarian wants to *kill us . . . ?*"

"But — we have rehearsal tomorrow."

And my heart contorts into even greater paroxysms of love, while my brain tries to convince my hands, which are still full of banana bread, to shake some sense into his idiotic head.

"But we will never *make* it to rehearsal, because we will be dead on the library floor by first period!"

His idiotic head shakes itself back and forth. "No. Think about it, Cyn. He's not going to kill us with everyone there. He's obviously got some kind of limits on what he can do and not do. Otherwise, what's he doing pretending to be a librarian? He might as well just walk right in and suck everyone's souls out, or whatever, and then be on his way. There must be, like, rules or something."

This actually does seem to make some sense. If he were all-powerful and able to just do whatever he wanted, surely he would be just doing whatever he wanted, not seducing Annie in gradual increments and stealing whatever he is stealing from students in small doses, a few at a time, in secret. The need for secrecy means that there must be consequences if the secret is revealed. Maybe — maybe if he is discovered too soon, it is possible he could be stopped.

"I wish there were someone we could tell," I say. "I mean,

someone who would believe us. And who other people would believe."

"A teacher or someone."

"Right. A responsible adult, who other adults would take seriously." Only, any adult who would believe us, if any exist, could hardly be someone that other adults would take seriously.

But Ryan is nodding as though I have put forth a plausible next step. "Okay, so that's our goal for tomorrow. Find a teacher or some other adult who will believe us."

"Do you really think that's going to happen?" I do not think so, myself. My tiny tinge of hope has abandoned me again. I want to console myself with more banana bread, but I seem to have eaten it all.

But Ryan is nodding again. "We'll find someone. Adults aren't incapable of believing things that are hard to believe. I mean, most people our age wouldn't believe this either, right? But we believe it. I mean, you convinced me, right?"

I laugh. "I did not. Do you not remember how it actually went down? You told me I was nuts."

"I didn't say that."

I give him my best raised eyebrows and skeptical twist of the lips. "It was certainly implied, if not stated outright. You only ran after me because I got mad, and you"— *you cared that I was mad and wanted to fix it* —"I don't know, you wanted to be there to show me that I was being ridiculous."

He shrugs. "Maybe. Okay, yes. I did not believe you. But then I *saw* him. I mean, there's no not believing something like that when you see it, right in front of you." He shakes his head, and

I suspect some part of him is still trying to find a way to not believe it. "I have never been that terrified in my entire life."

He looks at me again, and I can't quite decipher his expression. "You didn't seem scared at all."

"What? Are you *crazy*?"

"I don't know, Cyn. I was frozen —"

"You were *mesmerized* —"

"But first I froze," he insists. "I just stood there staring at him like an idiot. And you — you got me out of there."

"Only by smacking you around until you came back to your senses. . . ."

"You could have left me. You could have run while he was distracted."

"I would *never* —!"

He rolls his eyes. "I know. That's my point, moron." I am somewhat taken aback by being called a moron by the object of my affection, but also disarmed by the actual content of his words, which, upon reflection, I suppose are true. It never occurred to me to run away without him. Could anyone really do something like that? Just run off and leave someone else to die?

His eyes stay on mine for another second, and I want to say something back but my brain refuses to cooperate. Then he shakes his head again and pushes himself up off the floor.

"So, okay. Tomorrow we find an ally. A respectable, serious-minded, one-hundred-percent-credible, and ideally over-age-forty person to believe our story and help us mobilize forces, or whatever. Deal?" He reaches down and I take his hand, which is large and warm and feels *really nice* wrapped around mine, and I simultaneously seal the deal and let him pull me away from the touch of his sheet and up from his gritty rug.

This appears to be my cue to go away. We exchange cell numbers. I manage (I think) to not grin like an idiot while I type "Ryan Halsey!!!!" into my contacts, and then he walks me to the door and I head home.

It has been a very, very strange day.

Back at my house, I grab some of tonight's takeout feast from the refrigerator and head upstairs to work some more on the design adjustments for Sweeney's chair. Well, what am I supposed to do? Just sit here freaking out about Mr. Gabriel? And anyway, if we're going back to school, that means the show will (as they say) go on, and that means I have to figure out this chair situation. (And if I don't focus on *something*, I really am going to just sit here freaking out, and I don't think I can handle that right now.)

So: the chair. The problem is that I don't just want it to be functional; I want it to be the best *Sweeney Todd* chair *ever*, and that has turned out to be difficult to manage while still upholding certain safety considerations that are apparently nonnegotiable. I know we could fairly easily do the upside-down flip that they did in the movie version with Johnny Depp, which does look impressive, but (a) I have a lot of issues with the movie and so don't really want to use that chair design, and (b) I want to do something different and special that people won't forget. Something I can point to on my upcoming college applications and use to help me get positions doing set design for whatever student or community theater I can get involved with after graduation.

Later that evening, while I am brushing my teeth for bed and not-thinking about Mr. Gabriel by envisioning very impractical chair designs with moving robotic arms that wouldn't even make sense in the context of the play but would otherwise be very cool, my dad calls up to me. I go downstairs and find him watching a local special report that has interrupted whatever other news show he has been watching. I sit beside him on the couch, alarmed by his expression. I'm even more alarmed when he puts his arm around my shoulders. Then I start to watch and listen, and my alarm blossoms into horrified shock and dismay.

Principal Morse is dead.

A reporter wearing an appropriately sympathetic expression is interviewing Assistant Principal Jensen on the street outside the school. Jensen is insisting in a tear-choked voice that school will be open tomorrow and all clubs in session as usual, because "that's what Principal Morse would have wanted."

He'd been found by a janitor. In his office, slumped over his desk. Heart attack, they are saying. There is no mention of the library, or the librarian, or chalk symbols or possible witnesses or a suspicious absence of blood in the principal's body. But I know. It can't be a coincidence. Mr. Gabriel must have done this.

My dad looks over at me, takes in my expression, looks concerned. "Did you know him well? The principal?"

"No. Not really. I mean, he was always around and stuff,

you know. He was nice." He *was* nice. I think of his waggly eyebrows. He didn't deserve to die.

"You can stay home tomorrow if you want to, honey," Dad says. "Do you want to?"

Yes. Yes yes yes yes yes.

"No, that's okay," I say softly. I can't look at him, can't take my eyes off the screen. The camera has pulled back to show the whole school, which seems alien and unfamiliar from this angle and at this time of night. "I want to go. I think I'd feel worse staying home, by myself, you know?"

He says this is fine, says it's also fine if I change my mind later, or tomorrow, whatever I want. Anything I need is okay with him. I nod and make noises of assent and keep my eyes on the television.

For a second, I was sure I saw the flash of a face in one of the third-floor windows.

Chapter | 06

It is very hard to walk through the front doors of the school the next morning. I can feel the wrongness of what has happened all around.

High school has always felt like a relatively safe place to me. I know it's not that way for everyone; I know some kids have to deal with all kinds of awful things in high school— sadistic bullies and mean girls and abusive teachers and unspeakably bad experiences in gym locker rooms and bathrooms and worse, things that make them dread coming to school each and every day, things that maybe make them stop coming altogether. I've been lucky; not enough on any of the mean kids' radars to be a target, a large enough circle of friends and acquaintances that I'm rarely stuck completely on my own when I don't want to be, not even any truly horrible teacher experiences. Signor De Luca is a pain, but he's not mean like some teachers can be, doesn't have it in for me in that relentless way that I have seen some teachers go after students they don't like. No one has ever jumped me in the stairwell or started a vicious rumor about me or even stolen my lunch money. School has always just been the place where I go every day to see my friends and go to my classes and get out of my house and, in recent times, stare at Ryan and indulge in delightful distracting imaginings.

Obviously, it does not feel like a very safe place anymore.

I expect Mr. Gabriel to jump out from behind every corner, to be lurking in every shadow. I am careful to stay in areas where there are other people, lots of people, but still my pulse is pounding and my eyes cannot stop darting in all directions, trying to see the danger I am sure is going to come flying at me any moment.

Everywhere, students are gathered in little groups, talking about what happened. Principal Morse was a relatively young guy, really. And seemed to be in pretty decent shape and stuff. Not what you would think of as heart-attack material. And he really was nice. Everyone liked him. Teachers are standing together in doorways, hushed voices absolutely failing to hide how freaked out they are. Some of them are teary eyed. Two sophomore girls sit on the floor by their lockers, holding hands and crying outright.

And here and there, leaning against a wall or walking slowly along the thick black line that bisects the hallway floor, there are other, less-expressive expressions. Students who don't seem to be thinking about Principal Morse or sudden unexpected deaths or really much of anything at all. It almost could pass for shock, those empty eyes and vacant faces.

Almost.

Annie, of course, did not come over this morning to walk to school with me. She shows up in Italian, but I can feel her anger like a physical barrier, pushing me away. She won't look at me, let alone talk to me.

Ryan looks at me when he comes in, though, looks at me *and* gives me a little wave hello, giving me the first spot of non-awfulness so far today. We both made it to first period, at least. That's something.

I texted him last night, once I fled back upstairs to my room. He'd seen the news, too. He agreed that it could not be a coincidence. But he also agreed that it shouldn't affect our plan. It just made it even more important for us to stick to it.

Signor De Luca clears his throat and steps to the center of the front of the room. For perhaps the first time ever, he begins the class in English.

"I know it's hard to think about your studies today," he says, standing there solemnly, hands at his sides. "What has happened is truly terrible, and it would be foolish to think any of us could simply put our shock and sadness aside. Principal Morse was —" Someone makes a little gasping sound, and De Luca changes tack slightly. "We will be feeling his loss very greatly, for a very long time," he goes on. "But I believe that Assistant Principal Jensen was correct in his assertion that Principal Morse would not want his death to undermine the purpose of our school. Most of the teachers here, including me, have agreed to proceed with classes as usual. But if any of you feel unable to participate, you may go to the nurse's office at any time. Mr. Jensen has brought in special counselors who are available to talk with any students who wish to meet with them, and you may find that talking to someone about what has happened will help get you through these first few days."

He takes a step toward his desk and then stops, turning back to face us again. "I am very proud of all of you for coming to class today," he says.

Then he nods and continues to his desk, opens his copy of the textbook, and in his normal gruff Italian directs us to turn to chapter six. We all exchange wide-eyed glances while obediently turning pages. This is not the Signor De Luca that we know and strongly dislike. Or rather, it wasn't; now that he's perched on the edge of his desk with his book in his hand, his imperious gaze seeking out the uncertain and unprepared, he seems to be returning to normal. But the ghost of the man who addressed us in serious, compassionate English a few seconds ago is still there, and I think it will be hard to unsee him again. It's disconcerting, like De Luca has suddenly become two people, one superimposed upon the other. I don't like it. I like people to be who they are and stay that way and not become different people all of a sudden.

Like Annie has, for instance.

I notice that even though De Luca has reverted pretty much to form, something still seems off, somehow. He's distracted, not quite as barky or intimidating as usual. Maybe it's the lingering effect of his earlier words, or maybe he's going easy on us because of what happened, or maybe his own sadness and surprise over the principal's sudden death is simply keeping his heart from being fully in his lesson plan for the day. That would certainly make sense. They might have been friends, for all I know.

But there is something else, and after a while I am finally able to tease it out. He does not look at Annie all period. When he rises to prowl around the room and look over our shoulders as we struggle to compose competent Italian sentences with proper verb conjugation and creative vocabulary choices, he avoids the aisles near her desk. He usually enjoys calling on Annie; she's almost always paying attention and can often give him the answer he wants, and even when she can't, she appears perky and interested and probably makes him feel that at least one of his students is actually trying to learn something. But today it's like she's not there at all for him. I watch more carefully, and I can actually see his eyes just skip right past her as he looks around for his next victim. And I know, without the slightest doubt, that he is remembering how she touched his hand yesterday, and how it made him not-the-same afterward, at least for a while.

It does seem to only have been for a while; there are no traces of that vacant look that was there when she first touched him. I hope very hard that this means Leticia is back to normal by now, too. She stayed home today, but she texted me to let me know, and her text seemed perfectly regular and Leticia-like. It's not easy to glean a whole lot of reassurance from STAYIN HOME 2DAY MOMS FREAKED ABOUT MORSE ME TOO TALK L8R? but I do my very best.

Not all the students seem to recover so quickly, though. I think about those vacant faces in the hallway this morning. Is Mr. Gabriel getting a whole lot of kids to stop by the library before homeroom every morning? Probably not. Maybe when *he* does . . . whatever it is he does . . . it lasts longer. Maybe Annie doesn't quite have her soul-sucking chops yet. Maybe it's the kind of thing that gets better with practice.

I hate that I'm thinking about my best friend this way.

I want to ask Ryan if he's talked to Jorge and his other friends, if they seemed okay today, and I plan to do this as soon as the bell rings, but about ten minutes before the end of class, a student comes in, hall pass in hand, and announces that Ryan Halsey is wanted in the assistant principal's office.

Ryan turns to look at the messenger in surprise, then turns a little farther and catches my eye. I am trying to will him not to go. I am instantly and completely very certain that the message is actually from the librarian, and that Ryan is being summoned from class to have his throat slit and his lifeless body shoved into a locker or sacrificed to demon gods or fed to rabid squirrels on the front lawn or some other horrible thing.

Ryan seems to correctly interpret the *Luke, don't — it's a trap! It's a trap!* message my eyes are beaming at him, but Signor De Luca is telling him impatiently to gather his things and go, and finally Ryan only shrugs a little helplessly and gets up. I watch him walk toward the door. I watch him walk out through the doorway. At the last second he glances back at me but he doesn't stop. He keeps walking and is gone.

Signor De Luca returns to the lesson, but I can barely pretend to listen because I am busy imagining Ryan being led to his doom like some fairy-tale urchin following a will-o'-the-wisp, forgetting the danger, walking blithely into the evil librarian's clutches. In remarkably quick succession, my tireless brain is able to concoct all kinds of terrifying scenarios. Their one common element is Ryan's painful and horrible death at Mr. Gabriel's hands.

Before I really understand what it is doing, my hand raises itself and then my mouth is calling out, "Signore? I'm sorry — I think I need to go to the nurse." The other kids turn to look at me, but De Luca hesitates only a second before nodding and gesturing toward the door. I grab my books and my bag, and via monumental effort, I am able to walk, not run, for the hall.

But the second I am out of sight of the classroom I launch into a sprint, noticing but not caring about the students who gape at me from open classroom doorways, caring about nothing but getting to the library in time to stop Mr. Gabriel from whatever he is about to do (*about to do, still about to do, not done, not finished, please, not too late*) to the boy of my dreams who also happens to be the only person who is awake and aware of being in this nightmare with me. I tear up the stairs in giant, superhero-size leaps, and the third-floor hallway is so long, it's never been this long before, he's made it longer somehow, he's pushed the library farther away so that I will get there just too late, will only be in time to see Ryan's bloodied body dropping to the floor at the monster's feet.

Finally the impossible distance is covered and the doors are there before me and I burst through them screaming Ryan's name.

And skid to a halt as thirty pairs of startled freshman eyes turn to stare at me. A completely human-looking Mr. Gabriel is standing in front of a screen displaying examples of proper MLA citation style. He does not seem startled. While the students begin to titter and whisper and generally try to figure out what to make of me and my sudden dramatic entrance into their obligatory pre–research paper library visit, Mr. Gabriel pins me with his laughing eyes and his terrible, knowing smile.

"Can we help you, Cynthia?" he asks, sounding even to my knowing-better ears absolutely sympathetic and concerned, a kindhearted adult worried about a student in distress. "Are you — are you all right, my dear?"

Ryan is obviously not here.

"No. No, I'm — I'm sorry, I —" I give up and turn around and walk back out into the hall. The racing and the terror and the relief and the humiliation have all suddenly caught up with me and I'm finding it hard to catch my breath. I want to take a moment to lean against the wall and allow the world to realign itself around me, but I don't. I keep walking, back to the stairs, down and around, until I reach the AP's office on the first floor.

From the hall, peeking, I can see Ryan in the guest chair. Ryan, perfectly fine and alive and apparently being reprimanded for too many late homeroom arrivals or something. I want to march in there and punch Jensen in the face. Really? Today? *Today* you had to call him to your office to threaten him with detention? I want to scream at him for scaring the hell out of me when I'm clearly already at the edge of my tattered sanity as it is. I want to cry and fall into Ryan's arms and have him reassure me that he's fine and that everything is going to be okay.

I don't do these things. I turn away and walk back down

the hall. The bell rings and students pour out into the space around me, and I ignore them as I make my way to gym.

I text with Ryan between every class for the rest of the day, but Mr. Gabriel never makes a move.

At rehearsal, Ryan finds me as soon as he enters the auditorium. I had just gotten his latest STILL ALIVE, YOU? text a few minutes before, but it is still a relief to see him standing whole and breathing before me.

"Do you think he's just torturing us?" Ryan asks. I'd told him that I saw Mr. Gabriel moving freely about the library (not the other humiliating details of my crazed and panicky library visit, thank you, just the facts, ma'am), and so we are pretty certain that he could have done something violent and deadly to us by now if he'd wanted to.

"Maybe. Probably. I don't know." I'm happy to not be dead, don't get me wrong, but the waiting and the not knowing is maddening. Around us, the other theater kids are arriving, dropping off stuff on chairs, getting onstage or heading backstage or sitting down and opening notebooks to get started on homework until their scenes come up. No one here seems zombie-ish so far. Mr. Henry is consulting his notes in his favorite eighth-row-center seat.

"Well," Ryan says, dropping his stuff off next to mine, "we're safe for the next couple of hours, at least. He's not going to show up here and kill us in front of all these people, right?"

"Right." Right? I find it hard to feel sure about anything.

Ryan gives me one of those yummy lopsided smiles before turning and loping toward the stage. I almost (almost) wish

I could ask him to turn down the charm a little; I can't quite handle it in my current fragile state. I sit before my weakening knees betray me. My favored viewing position when I want to see how the set looks from the audience is twenty-third-row-right-center-aisle, and as I settle in with my notebook and my feet up on the arm of the chair in front of me, I let the delicious anticipation of watching Ryan in action push aside my worries about evil librarians and brainwashed best friends and everything else.

Mr. Henry says a few words about Principal Morse and echoes the general consensus that Morse would want us to carry on, so let's honor his memory and carry on, people. He cues Mr. Iverson (musical director and rehearsal accompanist in one) to lead the vocal warm-ups, and then everyone leaves the stage except for Ryan and Mrs. Lovett (played by senior-class hard-core-diva Gina Rosenberg). Today they are doing "Epiphany" for the first time in front of the rest of us. This is the song during which Sweeney pretty much loses it all together and decides that everyone deserves to die and that he will start making that happen. It's one of my favorites. The stage lights dim, and Mr. Henry tells Ryan he can begin whenever he's ready. Ryan nods and then looks down and closes his eyes and takes a second to get into character. I think I am suitably prepared for how awesome this will be. As soon as Ryan lifts his head, I realize I am not prepared at all.

He narrows his eyes and with a voice that is his but different, deeper, full of rage and gravel and despair, he shouts the opening lines of dialogue and the piano starts its soft accompaniment and Gina comes running up and their voices build and the music does, too, and then Ryan launches into the song proper and everything else stops.

In my peripheral vision I can see that everyone — Mr. Henry, the other cast members, my minions painting flats in the wings — is motionless, watching, listening, unable to do anything else. Only Mr. Iverson on the piano manages to keep doing what he is doing, and I imagine that this is only because he is part of it, that he is swept up in Ryan's song like the rest of us even as his fingers unerringly perform their key-striking choreography despite him. Ryan has absolutely become Sweeney on the stage before us. He stands there, eyes blazing, singing about darkness and loss and regret and revenge and we are all locked together in this moment with him, overcome, feeling this toxic, enthralling, undeniable combination of love and madness swallow us whole.

When he begins the part where he addresses the audience, razor thrust out before him, I am pinned to my seat with pity and horror and a weird, twisted affection laced with longing and traces of lust. And awe. I am unaware that my mouth has fallen open until the final exquisitely discordant notes of his last words fade along with the final piano chords into the absolute silence of the auditorium. For several seconds no one moves or speaks or, as far as I can tell, breathes. Finally, Gina, after a gentle and somewhat hoarse-sounding prompt from Mr. Henry, comes back to herself and says her next line, and the show goes on.

I close my mouth, still experiencing residual tingly feelings in all of my nerve endings, and try to shake it off. There are probably some set notes I should be making. Which would be easier if I had remembered to take out my pen. I turn to rummage through my bag and Mr. Gabriel is sitting there beside me.

I scream. I can't help it. The complete and total shock of him there would have knocked me flat to the ground if I'd been standing up. As it is, I can only shrink back against my seat in terror. Which is followed, stupidly and quickly, by horrified embarrassment, because in a second Mr. Henry will ask me why I have interrupted the rehearsal with my inexplicable screaming, and I will turn to see everyone staring at me and what will I be able to say?

Except—he doesn't, and they aren't. Somehow I am able to look away from Mr. Gabriel and notice that the rest of the auditorium seems to not be quite there in the same way it was a second ago. I can still see it, but it's like watching through a thick wall of glass. Like we are slightly somewhere else. I look back at my uninvited companion, fear and confusion fighting a horrible little battle inside me.

"Wow," Mr. Gabriel says, eyes wide. "He is *amazing*. I had no idea." He laughs a rueful little laugh. "I'm so relieved you stopped me from killing him before I had a chance to see this. I know you said Mr. Henry was doing *Sweeney* this year, but it never occurred to me that your boyfriend might be involved. I had him pegged for more of a sports type."

"He plays rugby, too," I say before I can help myself. "And he's not my boyfriend."

"Ah." Mr. Gabriel tilts his head and regards me with that hateful knowing expression. "But you wish he were, don't you? Don't bother denying it. It was obvious enough yesterday, but today . . . well. I saw the way you were watching him just now. Wanting him. It was all over you, all around you, wafting from your skin, oozing from your pores. That sense of wanting something more than anything else you've ever wanted. The kind of wanting that makes you willing to let everything else go if only you can have your heart's desire."

The way Mr. Gabriel purrs the word *wanting* creeps me out. Also the part about my pores. "You're — I don't —"

"I can give you that, if you want." He smiles his charming, awful smile. "Let's make a deal, dear Cynthia."

This is confusing. In several ways. The top two are (1) what does he mean, he can give me that? and (2) why would he possibly need to make a deal?

"I don't understand you," I say. "Why haven't you just killed us both already?"

Mr. Gabriel sighs. "Sadly, it's not quite that easy. It would take a lot of effort to kill you right now, and I don't have unlimited resources. But it is becoming clear that you could make things annoying for me, and I don't like to be annoyed. And now you have your friend buzzing about along with you. It's one thing to squash a single bug, if necessary, but if enough of them start swarming around, it can get very tiresome to keep swatting them all away. I'd rather settle this with you right now." He leans back, stretching, and puts his feet up on the back of the seat in front of him. "So: back the hell off, and your sexy singing heartthrob can be yours forever. What do you say?"

He waits for my response, watching me, sitting there

beside me in the creaky wooden auditorium seat just like he was some normal kind of person with every right to be here.

"What are you *doing* here?" I ask.

"Right now, what I'm doing is offering you a chance to save yourself and your dream-boy."

"No, I mean —"

"I know what you mean." He appears to be studying the ceiling tiles. The playfulness is dropping from his voice. "You haven't answered my question. Do we have a deal?"

"What about Annie?"

"No." And now he faces me again, and the playfulness is gone entirely. "Annie is mine. Annie is nonnegotiable."

"No deal." The words are out before I really consider them, but I know that I mean them. Really I know that I'm not actually thinking about any of this: about what Mr. Gabriel is truly offering, about the wisdom of making deals with demons, about what moral and ethical implications might be involved in making some under-the-table arrangement to spare myself and get to be with Ryan while letting this monster continue to do whatever he wants to do to the rest of the school. None of these things have been evaluated or decided upon or anything, mostly because I'm still not quite believing that I am even sitting here having this conversation at all. But none of that really matters, because I can't even begin to consider considering any kind of deal if it doesn't involve saving Annie. I just can't. No matter what he's starting to turn her into, she's still my best friend. I can't just walk away.

Mr. Gabriel looks at me steadily for a moment, then turns

to look at Ryan, who is now, along with the apparently mostly recovered Gina, entertaining everyone else with "A Little Priest," in which they sing about all the delicious flavors of meat pies one might bake using people of various (former) professions as ingredients.

I notice the intensity of Mr. Gabriel's gaze and my heart lurches to a stop.

"Please," I whisper, knowing it is stupid, and pointless, and that there's no way I can stop him from doing anything he wants to do. "Please don't hurt him."

Mr. Gabriel swings his head back around to look at me in surprise. "Are you kidding? He's incredible. Oh, sweetheart, I'm not touching him until the show is over, no matter how much you piss me off. All demons love *Sweeney Todd,* you know. It's kind of a given. And your Ryan may be one of the best Sweeneys I've ever seen, high-school production values notwithstanding."

I gape at him. I can't even get past my surprise enough to feel insulted by his dig at high-school production values.

"No, seriously," he goes on, apparently entirely in earnest. "The whole cast and crew is safe, at least through opening night. I expect that will be all the time I need, in any case."

"Time for *what*?" I shout at him, infuriated and starting to completely lose my grip on the whole conversation. "What are you *doing*? What do you want?"

"I want a lot of things," he says, and his eyes go dark and huge but not in the same swirly-black-hole way from yesterday in the library. He is somehow looking at something far away and elsewhere but also at me and *through* me. The force of his gaze is like a knife in my gut and I can't breathe and his eyes are kind of burning deep inside the pupils with black and twisty flames and suddenly I am very sure that I don't want to know what most of those things that he wants actually are. But he keeps talking. "There are some things here that I need in order to get what I want. And I am going to have them. And one of them is your lovely friend Annie, and one of them involves the souls of pretty much all the students in the school."

He looks at me again and the flames vanish and the knife is gone and his voice goes light and breezy and all coffee-shop conversational, as if he wasn't just one second ago impaling me with fiery eyes and discussing the dark fate of my best friend and the souls of all my classmates. "I tried a women's gym first, you know. I thought that would be an excellent place to find a bride. I mean, right? It seems so logical. Someone lithe and flexible with good strong thighs and nice triceps. And while I was looking, I would have all those other souls to taste." He leans in as if about to impart some valuable words of wisdom. "The souls of women are more — more exquisite than the souls of men. Like the best wine you've ever tasted. Or for you, my underage friend, maybe melted chocolate. The best melted chocolate you've ever had, warm and thick and so unbelievably sweet as it slides slowly down inside you, filling you with syrupy hot delicious goodness as you suck out every last . . ." He blinks and clears his throat.

I say nothing. This is clearly a monologue, not a conversation, and I'm too appalled and freaked out to even attempt to try to speak. Also: *bride?* He wants Annie to be his *bride?*

"Anyway, it didn't work out as I'd hoped. I set myself up as a personal trainer, and the ladies all flocked to me like flies to honey because they could not possibly do otherwise, but . . ." He shakes his head, still apparently dismayed by his miscalculation. "They were all too hard, too tired; they came before work or after work or to escape their husbands and children and their stunted frustrating lives, and they channeled all their heat and fire into the elliptical machines and there was nothing left for me. It was very disappointing. But then I got this one girl, a teenage client, young and hungry and so full of life and energy . . ." His face brightens horribly at the memory. "I drained her little by little, mostly while stretching her out after a session, and while I was savoring the final remnants of her on what became my last night there, I thanked her for reminding me. Teenagers have more fire than anyone. Their souls are burning with life and youth and hormones and desire and all the things they want and need and hate and love. And no one would miss those pieces of them that I took away at first; no one pays attention to teenagers except other teenagers, who of course don't matter either. And I knew I'd be able to take my fill, take my time, gathering what I needed . . . and by the time enough people finally caught on, it would be too late."

He looks at me then, looks at me stricken into silence with my horror at what he is describing, and for a second flickers of black flames dance again in his eyes. "I didn't expect someone like you, dear Cynthia. You are very . . . inconvenient. If you are smart, and I think you can be, you will not push me. If you stay out of my way, I may decide to let you live at the end of things. You and your Sweeney both. Think about it."

And then he is gone, and the world rushes back in around

me. "A Little Priest" is just finishing and everyone is applauding and shouting out compliments, and Mr. Henry struggles to make himself heard long enough to call a break before we start the next scene. Mr. Gabriel is clearly insane, evil and dangerous and insane (and, let's not forget, you know, a *demon*), and even though I still really have no idea what he's doing and why, it is all the more evident that we have to find a way to stop him.

But how?

Chapter | 07

Ryan accepts the congratulations of everyone near enough to say something or smile or high-five him as he goes by. Mr. Henry beams radiantly at him, then goes back to scribbling enthusiastically on his legal pad. Ryan is glowing when he reaches me. The stage lights have made him kind of sweaty in (of course) a very sexy way, and he's breathing a little hard, and despite everything, I feel an extra surge of *want* as I take in the sight of him. But then I hear Mr. Gabriel's voice in my head, observing my wanting in that gross and disturbing way he did, and most of the pleasure drains out of it.

Something must show in my face, because Ryan's smile fades as he looks at me. "What?" he asks.

I tell him. As well as I can, anyway; some of it is kind of hard to explain, and I don't want to repeat the part about Mr. Gabriel calling Ryan my boyfriend and certain related statements. But I tell him the rest, modifying the deal offer slightly to be just about letting me and Ryan survive, not letting me "have that" in the sense that Mr. Gabriel seemed to mean, and by the end of it Ryan is sitting on the dirty carpet of the aisle beside my seat, looking up at me with evident and reasonable dismay.

"Jesus," he says.

"Yeah."

Mr. Henry calls five minutes. Ryan and I look at each other.

"I think the fact that he wanted to make a deal means something," Ryan says finally. "He's obviously got some limits on his abilities, and if he was trying to bribe you to back off, that must mean that you are capable of messing up his plans somehow."

"Do you think . . ." Visions of swarming insects fill my mind. "Maybe if we really can find someone who will believe us, that could be the start of, I don't know, some kind of formal resistance. If we got enough people to fight him . . ."

Ryan is nodding. "I think that's still the best plan. If we can find someone." He looks over his shoulder, then back. "What about Mr. Henry?"

"Maybe," I say doubtfully. Mr. Henry would seem to be a great choice; he's pretty laid-back as far as teachers go, and he likes me, and he *loves* Ryan. But somehow I'm not feeling it. Maybe just because I don't want Mr. Henry to think we're crazy. Or morons. Or that we're trying to play some mean trick on him or something. Mr. Henry has always struck me as kind of the tenderhearted type. And he's not . . . I try to put my feelings into words. "I don't know if Mr. Henry is — powerful enough." I look beseechingly at Ryan. "Do you know what I mean? He's super nice, and everyone likes him, but he's not the guy I would necessarily pick out to follow into battle. He's more dreamy than deadly. I think we need someone a little . . . meaner. Capable of serious ass-kicking."

"Which is probably exactly the kind of person who would never believe us in a million years." Ryan sighs. "*I* can still hardly believe us. I know, I know—" He puts up a hand defensively. "I know it's really happening. I get it. I'm in. I'm not trying to jump ship. But still . . . it's *nuts*. You know that, right?"

I give him my best eyebrow raise. "What do you mean? This kind of thing happens to me *all the time*. It's getting so old I can hardly stand it."

"Okay, okay. You are equally as freaked out as I am. You just seem to be handling it so much better."

I laugh. "I'm not handling it better. I'm just—I'm just not letting myself fall apart. Because then we automatically lose, right? And you seem to be in about the same place, I thought. Are you not? How are you not handling it?"

"I'm *terrified*, Cyn. All day I was so sure he was just going to jump out and rip my throat open or something. And yesterday—when he had me frozen there, hypnotized . . . that was awful. I mean, once I realized what was happening, after you shook me out of it. To be trapped there, helpless, just waiting for him to kill me . . ."

"You do a good job of hiding it," I say. "I screamed so loud when he showed up here next to me; I swear my heart stopped completely. And all day, waiting and wondering . . . it was horrible. And, oh, my God, when that kid came to get you in Italian, and you just sauntered out, like nothing was wrong . . ."

"What else could I do? Tell De Luca I just didn't feel like talking to the AP?"

"Well, still. You didn't look scared. And you didn't seem at all distracted just now on stage — my God, Ryan, you were so amazing. . . ." I feel the *want* suffusing my voice and clamp my jaw closed, but it is too late. Ryan's mouth has curved up in a very pleased-looking twisty half smile, his expression suddenly focused in a way it hadn't been a moment before.

"Oh, yeah? *Amazing,* you say?" He's looking at me very intently, eyes unblinking.

My face flushes with heat. "Shut up," I mutter, looking down, then back up, unable to resist soaking up more of the way he's looking at me. I can't help twisty-smiling back. My lips have gone rogue and will no longer obey my commands. "You know you're amazing. Jesus, even the evil librarian was impressed."

That kills the moment a little, which is probably for the best. *Must. Focus.*

"He really said the whole cast and crew was safe?"

I shrug. "Yeah. But . . ." I leave the rest unsaid. It's obvious we can't actually trust anything he tells us.

Mr. Henry calls time, and Ryan rises lithely from the floor and jogs back to the stage. Rehearsal resumes, and Ryan continues to be awesome, and I head backstage to supervise what remains of set construction (other than the chair, of course, which no one is working on because I have yet to come up with a new plan, and I absolutely must figure out said new plan *very seriously soon,* because tech week starts in a *week and a half, dammit*) in between sneaking little glances sidewise to make sure that Mr. Gabriel has not appeared again beside me.

After, Ryan walks out with me into the nearly empty parking lot. We are still trying to think of teachers we might be able to talk to. Suddenly Ryan nudges me and points.

A few rows over, a solitary navy-blue Nissan Sentra sits beneath one of the parking lot's dim streetlights. Signor De Luca is sitting in the driver's seat. He hasn't started the ignition or turned on the interior lights. He's just sitting there, hands on the steering wheel, talking. To himself. At least, his mouth is moving, and no one else is in the car.

"What's he doing?" Ryan asks me.

"Preparing tomorrow's lesson?" I have no idea.

As we watch, he nods, then shakes his head, then takes one fist and pounds it against the dashboard.

"Is he having an argument with himself?" I ask.

"I think he is."

"That's — weird."

"Yeah. I wonder who's winning."

We continue to watch him. He continues to argue with himself. I can't tell for sure, but I think he is arguing with himself in Italian. I remember how he was in class today, surprisingly decent and temporarily not an asshole. I remember how he avoided looking at Annie.

"I think he knows that something is going on in the school," I say.

"Really?"

I start to tell him how De Luca had been acting, then realize that I never told him what I'd seen Annie do to him. And to Leticia. Quickly, I fill him in.

"Wait." Ryan holds his hands up in front of him as if to ward off the new crazy of this additional information. "Annie was doing—doing whatever Mr. Gabriel can do? He's, like, turned her? Into . . . ?"

He doesn't quite say it. I hurry on. "No. At least, not all the way. He's done *something* to her, obviously, but De Luca and Leticia seemed to recover faster than the students Mr. Gabriel got to. Annie's not like him. She's still human." I say this very firmly, to make sure I believe it. It can't be too late already. It can't.

"What is it that she—that he is taking, anyway? Souls? I mean, for real?"

"I don't know. He mentioned souls, but—can you take part of a soul? Isn't it kind of all or nothing? He seems to be siphoning off little amounts of whatever he's taking at a time. Life force? Psychic energy? Internal battery power?" I suddenly remember that I never did ask Ryan about his friends. "Is Jorge okay? Does he seem back to normal?"

Ryan shrugs. "Seems to be. Normal as he ever is, anyway."

"Do you think—would he believe us if we tried to tell him what's going on?"

Ryan looks startled for a moment, then shakes his head. "I don't think so. I'm trying to imagine how that conversation might go, and I just—can't. And . . . I'm not sure I want to drag him into this. I mean, if Mr. Gabriel found out that Jorge knew about him, that would probably be very bad. And

Jorge wouldn't have the *Sweeney Todd* thing to protect him. Assuming that's even true."

"I could give him a job painting or something," I offer half-heartedly. But really, I know he's right. It's the same reason I haven't thought seriously about trying to tell Diane or Leticia. Either they'd think I was crazy, which at best would make them avoid me and at worst would lead them to try to get me committed for psychological evaluation, or they *would* believe me, which at best would force them to face the horrible things going on at school and, at worst, would get them killed.

"We do need help," Ryan says. "But I still think finding a teacher or something is the best option."

The sound of a car engine starting up cuts through the quiet parking lot, making us both jump. Signor De Luca has concluded his private debate, it appears.

"Quick! Get in the car!" I say.

"You really want to —"

I give him a little push. "We can discuss on the way. But unless you happen to know where he lives, we need to follow him. Now."

"Now?" But he obediently breaks into a run beside me. We reach his car and he digs out the keys and drops into the driver's seat, leaning over to unlock the passenger door just as I reach it.

"Go, go, go!" I shout as I pull the door shut.

He goes, peeling out of the spot like a maniac. And then slams on the brakes to avoid hitting the Sentra, which has paused at the parking lot exit. We wait, breath caught, for the

Italian teacher to come storming out of the car to scream at us for nearly denting his shiny back bumper.

But nothing happens. After a moment, he turns right out of the lot and drives off down the street. Ryan waits what seems like a reasonable amount of time, then follows cautiously after.

The caution, it turns out, is not really necessary. Following Signor De Luca proves to be ridiculously easy. He drives slowly, and we can see that he has not, in fact, concluded his argument after all. It rages on, clearly distracting, as evidenced by the way he sits at every stop sign and forgets to start driving again for several minutes.

"Are you sure you don't want to wait until the morning?" Ryan asks for at least the third time as we wait behind the Sentra at another intersection.

I don't bother answering him again. I'm sure. Maybe De Luca is struggling with whether or not to leave his wife or quit his job or give someone an A- or something else that has nothing at all to do with Annie and Mr. Gabriel. But I don't think so. I watch his movements in the car up ahead. It's getting harder to see him; the sky is dark, but it's that incomplete evening-dark of midautumn, and the world has that in-between feeling like it's holding its breath, almost but not quite ready to give up the last remnants of day to the darkness. This seems like a much better time to try to convince someone of something hard to believe. It's easy to pretend that things are okay in the morning, with the bright, shiny sun winking happily down at everything and birds chirping and people heading off to work and dropping off kids at school and radiating normalcy in every direction. At night, impossible things are a lot easier to swallow.

Signor De Luca turns onto a side street and then another, and we stop at the corner, headlights off, and watch him pull into the driveway of a very regular-looking yellow house with a neat little rectangle of lawn out front and a wooden slat fence marking off the edge of a small backyard.

He turns off the ignition but doesn't get out of the car.

Ryan looks at me. "Should we go over there now, catch him in the driveway? Or do you want to wait until he goes inside?"

Both options have their drawbacks. And I haven't really figured out what we're going to say, exactly. This strikes me as one of those situations where making a plan is just going to bite you in the ass, anyway. Everything depends on everything else. There's no way to predict what his reactions are going to be.

He gets out of his car while we sit there debating. We watch him walk slowly up his front steps, unlock the door, go inside.

"Well, that's decided, then," I say. "Ready?"

"Sure." Ryan draws the word out as though trying to put off for as many extra seconds as possible the moment when we actually have to get out of the car.

I open the passenger door. Ryan meets me on the sidewalk.

I am ridiculously nervous as we approach the house. You were directly threatened by a demon today at rehearsal, I remind myself. This is nothing. This is your *Italian teacher*. The worst he can do is fail you. Which won't matter if Mr. Gabriel kills us all, anyway. It's win-win! Or lose-lose. Or something.

I feel Ryan's eyes on me and glance over. He gives me a half-amused, half-terrified grin. "The crazy just keeps on comin', huh?"

I flash him a grateful smile as we climb the steps. Then I ring the doorbell.

After a moment there's a sound on the other side of the door, and then it swings open, back into the house. Signor De Luca looks out at us, little lines of confusion and displeasure crinkling across his forehead.

"Signorina. Signore. Why, exactly, are you on my doorstep?"

"We have to talk to you." I'm shocked by how calm and serious I sound. Like I show up at teachers' houses all the time, delivering important information.

"You may talk to me tomorrow," he says, starting to close the door. *"Buona sera."*

"It's really important," Ryan says. The door stops moving, and Signor De Luca and I both look down to see Ryan's foot stopping it from completing its journey to closed-ness. Signor De Luca's face darkens. More. He looks back up.

"I don't care what—"

"I saw what Annie did to you," I say quickly, before I can think too much about it. De Luca's eyes widen, and for a moment his expression shifts to something else—almost a look of relief—before he gets it back under control and resumes his unpleasant frown.

"Signorina Rothschild, if you do not remove yourself from my property this instant —"

"Please," I say. Ryan has not moved his foot. "Please, just let us talk to you. Five minutes."

De Luca looks back and forth between us. Then back at Ryan's foot. Finally he rolls his eyes and mutters something angry and insulting sounding under his breath. But he steps back and pulls the door the rest of the way open, gesturing us inside.

It feels very strange to be entering Signor De Luca's house. You kind of forget that teachers actually even exist anywhere outside of the school and occasional field trips, unless you have one of those awkward and terrible run-ins at the supermarket or something.

The front hall opens into a softly lit living room: tan couch, coordinating easy chair with matching ottoman, well-used coffee table, moderately sized TV. The chair is currently occupied by a curled-up dark gray cat who opens one eye to regard us sleepily as we walk in. Signor De Luca points to the couch and takes the ottoman for himself. He fixes us both with steely glares, then settles his unsettling eyes on mine.

"So? Start talking. Why are you here?"

Okay, go. "This is going to sound crazy," I say.

De Luca's expression clearly indicates his opinion that the crazy is already well underway with our presence in his living room. I glance at Ryan, who gives me an encouraging nod.

"So, okay. There's something bad happening at our school. Really bad. Like, seriously very terrible and dangerous and kind of not really possible except that it's really happening, so it must be. Possible, I mean." I take a breath, then go on. "And I think . . . I think you already know."

De Luca says nothing. His face is not exactly radiating invitation, but he's still listening. I know I got his attention with my mention of Annie. He does know, even if he's not really aware of it, or admitting it, or whatever, that something is going on. He wouldn't have let us in, otherwise. Right?

Ryan nods at me again. Right. I take another breath.

I say, "It's the new librarian."

De Luca barks a laugh at this, but his expression seems more disappointed than amused. "The librarian," he repeats. "That's what you came to talk to me about?"

"He's not a real librarian —"

"Not a real librarian!" De Luca's voice is scathingly sarcastic. "My God, that *is* bad! Did he forge his MLS documentation? How could we have let this happen?" He starts to get up. "Thank you so much for letting me know. You're right — this could certainly not have waited until a more appropriate time."

"Sit down!" I shout at him.

He stops midmotion, shocked at my tone. Then his eyes narrow, and he finishes standing up so he can glare down at me. "How *dare* you come into my house and speak to me that way? I don't know what you're playing at, but my tolerance is at an end." He points to the door. "Get out."

"I saw what she did to you! But, listen, Annie isn't the real problem, it's —"

"I don't know what you're referring to, but I advise you to stop this nonsense right now if you wish to have any hope of getting out of this with nothing worse than detention."

Ryan and I stand up, looking at each other helplessly.

"Signore," Ryan begins, but De Luca's face is closed and barred, and he only points again to the door.

"Please," I say, taking a step toward him. I reach out to touch his arm in supplication.

He jerks away from my outstretched hand with a cry of abject horror, as though I were trying to set him on fire. He stumbles backward about half a step before the ottoman trips him and he falls, grazing the edge of it and continuing down onto the floor.

There is a moment of very uncomfortable silence. De Luca's face is white.

I bite my lip, careful to keep my hands down at my sides. "I'm not—like Annie is," I say softly. "He's done something to her, something that lets her—lets her do what she did, *take* what she did. I'm trying to save her. Save all of us. I swear, I'm not on his team."

Signor De Luca seems as shocked at his reaction as we are. He's breathing heavily now, but as I finish speaking, his terrified expression slowly transforms into something more like resigned acknowledgment. Ryan reaches down to help him up, and after a tiny hesitation, he lets Ryan do so.

We all sit down again.

"Well," De Luca says finally. "At least this means I'm probably not going crazy."

"What do you think is going on?" I ask him.

He looks at me for a long moment, perhaps still wavering on the whole believing thing. Maybe he thinks there's a hidden camera somewhere, and this is all some elaborate prank that we're going to post on the Internet to try to humiliate him for being such a hard-ass all the time.

But in the end he simply starts talking. "Your friend took something from me. Something she shouldn't have been able to take. I don't know how, or why, but I know that's what happened."

I can't help asking, "Does it come back? What she took? I saw you—that day, in the hall. Do you remember? I saw you go sort of vacant and distant, but then you recovered. You did, right? Recover?"

"I don't know," Signor De Luca says softly. "I recovered from the initial shock of what she did, and I think—I think I will recover completely in time. But how—how can she—?" He looks at me intently. "You believe it has something to do with the librarian?"

I nod. "He's not human."

Ryan leans forward. "He's really not. I mean, I didn't believe it either. But then I saw him. Yesterday. He was absolutely not a human being. He had wings and stuff. And we think he killed Principal Morse."

De Luca stares at us. "The librarian killed Principal Morse?"

We tell him the story of yesterday and today. About all the blood and the very coincidental timing of Principal Morse's "heart attack." We tell him the whole story, including background, including side notes, including all of my suspicions about Annie and about Mr. Gabriel's appearance at *Sweeney Todd* rehearsal, except not the part about not harming the cast and crew, because that part seems even more unbelievable than the rest of it. He listens silently until we finally run out of words.

"*Porca miseria.* I knew something was going on. I didn't really believe it until Annie did — what she did. But I knew. And even then I did not want to believe it."

"What did she do, exactly?" I ask him. "Did she — are they really taking pieces of people's souls?"

De Luca turns his palms up in a gesture of uncertainty. "I don't know if *soul* is the right word. I don't know if there is a word for what they take. It is your . . . essence. The thing inside you that makes you *you.* Some believe that small losses of this essence can be recovered. That we are capable of regenerating, to a point. But only to a point."

"Some believe?" Ryan asks. "This is, uh, a thing that comes up often enough that there's documented opinion polls or something?"

De Luca smiles mirthlessly. "Not so often. And, no, no public surveys. But among certain circles . . ." He glances at the ceiling, or through it, then continues. "My great-grandmother was a — I guess you'd call her a fortune-teller, back in Italy. Not one of your Renaissance-fair charlatans. She was truly gifted. She knew about things under the surface of the world. She told me many stories when I was a small boy, most of which I dismissed as fiction, but they always had the ring of truth to them, no matter what I let myself believe. She had stories of demons, from time to time. Of what they could do and take and how they could make people suffer."

"But *why?*" I cut in. "Why is he doing this? What does he get out of it?"

De Luca gives me a look of what feels uncomfortably like pity. "He likes it," he says. "Maybe he's got some additional motivation, maybe there's a larger story, some ultimate over-arching goal, but in the end, demons do what they do because they want to. I think our essences are like candy to them. Or like drugs. They cannot always come through to our world; that must be true, or else we would all have been wiped out long ago. But some of them come through, and some of them are able to get to us in various ways."

"All right," Ryan says. "So how do we stop him?"

LOVE. Seriously, the way he stays on topic is just incredibly hot.

I look at Signor De Luca. This is it; this is the moment when the official grown-up is going to tell us what needs to happen in order for the bad things to go away. This is where we get to hand over the mantle of responsibility to someone older and wiser and more equipped to deal with these things.

"I don't know," he says again. "I think to start, I will talk to him."

"And say what?" Ryan asks. "Hey, I hear you might be an evil demon?"

De Luca gives him a withering glance. "No. I'm not going to confront him. I'm just going to talk to him. See if I can tell anything more about what he is. Now that I know what to look for . . ."

"But then what?" I ask impatiently. "What will we do? We

have to *do* something. We have to stop him! We have to at least start telling people, warn them about what's going on. . . ."

"We must have more information first," De Luca says firmly. "You don't just confront a demon and try to bash its head in with a dictionary, signorina. There are different ways to deal with different kinds of demons, different tactics that might work. . . ."

He is clearly slipping into teacher mode, wanting to do research and make little lists and graphs and things. I don't want to wait for all of that. I want to stop him now. *Annie* . . .

"But —"

"That's where we start," he says, rising. "And now you should go. I need to do some thinking. Come see me at the end of the school day tomorrow, and we can talk some more."

A tiny thread of hope stretches out inside of me. We have help now. Even if he's moving way too slowly for my taste at the moment . . . we have help. And Signor De Luca seems to have been the right choice after all. He's not a young man, but he's not super old or anything, and he seems to be in reasonably good shape physically and has all of his marbles and stuff. But most important, he's well-known as a take-no-shit kind of guy, someone all the students fear and respect, and I can't imagine he doesn't command respect from his colleagues, as well. He is someone that other people will listen to. That's where it has to start. He'll confirm his suspicions tomorrow, and then he'll start to tell some trusted teacher friends, and that will be the beginning. We'll gather more people, students and teachers and probably the APs and maybe even parents and cops and anyone else we can get to listen, and we'll stop being individual little bothersome insects to Mr. Gabriel. Instead we'll be a giant frickin' swarm of army ants or killer bees or something, and we will take him down. And no one else will die, and no one else's life force will get sucked out, and Annie will go back to being herself, and all will be well with the world again — hallelujah, amen.

We say good-bye and walk out to the car. I feel better than I have in what seems like a very long time. I can see that Ryan does, too. He opens the passenger door for me, and I climb in, letting myself relax into the faded fabric as I wait for him to get in on the other side. He smiles as he turns the key in the ignition, and I smile back.

Everything is going to be okay.

The next morning, Ryan and I can't resist loitering near the parking lot entrance. Both of us want to confirm that we didn't dream the whole De Luca thing, that he really listened and believed. We want to be sure that we're not on our own in this thing anymore.

The blue Sentra pulls up, and Signor De Luca gets out, locks the doors, comes toward the school, briefcase in hand. He looks like he does all the time, like it's just another day. He doesn't wave or smile as he approaches. He doesn't seem like he's going to acknowledge us at all. My heart begins a slow downward slide toward my feet. It didn't happen. Or it did but he doesn't remember. Or won't remember. Or changed his mind. He had an attack of good sense in the night. He's not going to help us after all.

But at the last second, before he passes by us completely,

De Luca turns his head the slightest bit and gives us a teeny-tiny nod. An almost invisible nod. But there.

"You saw that, right?" I breathe when De Luca has passed out of sight into the school.

"Yeah," Ryan breathes back. "Thank God. I thought —"

"I know. Me too." I turn to face him, a smile tugging at my lips. "But it's okay. It's going to be okay. We've got him on our team now."

Ryan smiles back. "The first of many."

"Yes." My relief is so great it almost hurts.

No Italian today, which is probably for the best. I can't imagine being able to sit there all period pretending yesterday's conversation with De Luca didn't happen. It seems ridiculous to go to classes at all, but skipping seems risky. It feels better to act like things are normal, like we're not plotting anything, so Mr. Gabriel won't have any reason to be suspicious. I can't imagine he really thinks we're just going to roll over and let him carry out his evil plans, but as long as he thinks we're on our own, that we're not really capable of stopping him, hopefully he'll leave us alone. For now.

I catch no glimpses of Annie in the hallways. That's also probably for the best. Anything I try to say to her will just make things worse. I should just stay away from her until we're able to take care of the librarian.

At lunch, Diane and Leticia see me coming solo and exchange a silent glance.

"Yes, we're still fighting," I say as I slide onto the bench across from them. I squint at Leticia, searching for signs of lingering wrongness. "Are you okay?" I ask. She'd called my phone last night, but by the time I saw the message it was too late to call or text without violating her parents' very strict no-phone-after-8:00-p.m. rule.

"Yeah. I mean, still really sad about poor Principal Morse, but yeah."

Diane reaches over and pats her head. "No more weirdo fainting spells, okay? Your little brain needs to stay with us."

Leticia rolls her eyes. "I told you, I'm fine. I was just dehydrated or something."

"Okay, well, drink more water, then. You scared us, you jerk." She pushes her unopened bottle of water over toward Leticia's tray. L rolls her eyes again but obediently takes a giant gulp. We laugh, but Diane's eyes catch mine across the table. She's worried, too. And she doesn't even know what really happened.

"Are *you* okay?" I ask her. "It seems like something's going around, you know? Like a virus or something."

"So far. But, um, you can keep the water, L. Just in case. Keep your fainty cooties to yourself."

Leticia is unoffended. "Score! Free water for me and my cooties. Hey, does that mean if I touch your brownie I can have that, too?"

Diane snatches her brownie out of harm's way.

"Anyway," Leticia says, "I believe we have more important things to talk about."

"We do?" I ask, startled. They can't know. Could they have suspicions? Have they seen something, too?

"Yes, Little Miss Innocent. We do. Spill." She leans forward.

"What's going on with you and Ryan? You have been spotted in his company several times over the last couple of days. Talking in the hallways, leaving rehearsal together, getting into his *car* . . . My little spies have seen you."

Diane crosses her arms and leans back. "I can't believe you didn't tell us."

I scramble hastily to switch gears. "There's nothing to tell! I mean, we're not, like, *together*. We're just — talking and stuff."

"*Just* talking and stuff? Hello? I believe there was a time when the idea of talking to Ryan Halsey was enough to send you swooning to the floor, my lovesick friend."

Leticia jumps in with her best Cynthia impression. "Oh, you guys, I can't *stand* it, he's so *amazing*, he's so *beautiful*, I love him *so much*. He is a god who walks among men. I want to kiss him and marry him and have his sexy little babies." She falls backward into Diane's arms. Diane fans her with her math notebook.

I feel my face go red. It's an exaggeration, *obviously*, but it's pretty spot-on all the same.

"Well, yes, okay. I will not pretend that the talking has not been kind of awesome." My mouth stretches up into a grin before I can help it. "It was the hallway tackle that did it, I think. He couldn't ignore me so much after that."

"So?" Leticia sits up. "Has there been kissing? Has there been more than kissing?"

"No," I sigh. They raise their eyebrows at me in unison. "No! Not yet, anyway."

"But there might be kissing?"

"God, I hope so." Once we get past the whole demon-killing thing. "I did — I did get to see his bedroom."

"What?!" they exclaim in unison.

"Nothing *happened*. It was just to talk about stuff for the show." I'm still grinning, though, and they are not satisfied. I look back and forth between them, meeting their eyes in turn. "But. I think maybe he kind of likes me a little."

Diane punches her fists up into the air in victory and Leticia raises the water bottle in a toasting gesture. For a second, I let myself forget everything else and just enjoy the moment. It's so nice to just be here with my friends, talking about boys. Especially, of course, this boy. My grin stretches wider, thinking about him. He does still make me all swoony. I *do* want to have his sexy little babies. And he does kind of like me a little. He must. It's not just the demon thing making him hang around. He started talking to me before that, after all. Right?

I wait for my brain to respond with a resounding, assured *Right!* but it is strangely silent on the matter.

He did start talking to me, I remind my brain. *Remember? He ran after me because he didn't want me to be mad.* Of course, there is liking, and there is *liking*. Maybe he was just being friendly. Maybe he just wants to be friends.

"He probably just wants to be friends," I say out loud. I'm not grinning anymore.

"None of that," Leticia says. "I am pretty sure boys do not bring girls up to their bedrooms when they just want to be friends. Confidence, please, dearest!"

"But —"

Diane cuts me off. "L is right. Even if Mr. Halsey has not yet attempted to get smoochy, I guarantee he has thought about it. You'll see. You just keep being your adorable, charming self, and he will soon be unable to help himself."

I try to believe them. I am probably just being dumb. He obviously kind of likes me. Right? Obviously.

All too soon the period is over, and we go our separate ways. Diane turns back to point a stern finger at me and says, "Keep us posted!" I nod obligingly and try to muster up the minimum necessary motivation to convince my feet to take me to my precalc classroom. *Math is fun!* I tell myself gamely. Even if Mr. Hoffmeister is sometimes a little creepy. But not in an evil librarian kind of way, so that's something, at least. Mr. Hoffmeister is missing most of a finger on his left hand, and sometimes he uses his finger stub to point out incorrect answers in your work. Which is sort of a good motivator to get the right answer, I guess. Unless you enjoy seeing the stub, which some kids clearly do. Some kids have issues.

I trudge wearily up the stairs, still chanting, *Math is fun! Math is fun!* to myself inside my head. Halfway across the landing I am suddenly shoved back hard and fast against the wall. Before I can regain my bearings I hear his voice, low and dark and angry and cold and directly in front of me.

"Do you think this is a *game*?"

I am staring into the handsome and terrifying face of Mr. Gabriel. My stomach clenches so hard that for a second I am certain that I am about to throw up all over his crisp button-down shirt of the day. Faintly, through the vertical blue and white stripes on the fabric, I can see that he's wearing a LOVE YOUR LIBRARY T-shirt underneath.

"What?" I whisper, still fighting with my recently eaten lunch.

"Was I unclear in my stated desire for you to *stay the fuck out of my way*?" His words are short and clipped, like little missiles fired at close range. He doesn't yell, but the soft, quiet rage is worse, somehow. His fingers dig deeply into my upper arms. I stare desperately around, but for some reason, even though the halls were crowded with students a second ago, there is no one else in the stairwell.

He smiles humorlessly. "Nope, it's just you and me, dear Cynthia. You and me and sometimes your beloved Sweeney but it had better end there, it had better stay that way, do you understand? If you send one more teacher sniffing around, you are going to be very, very sorry. And if you make me kill Sweeney Todd before the show goes up, so help me, I swear I will make your death as long and difficult and painful and all-around horrible as I possibly, possibly can."

His last sentence barely registers. Oh, God. Oh, Signor De Luca.

I struggle to find my voice. "What did you do?"

His bright eyes hold mine like a bear trap. No swirly black holes, just clear and focused fury. "I did what I had to do. And it's your fault." He gives me a little shake, and my head smacks painfully against the wall. "Got that, Cynthia? Your fault. He'd be alive right now if you hadn't opened your roachy little mouth. I don't want to be wasting my time and energy on damage control, but you left me no choice."

Something is screaming inside me. Oh, God. He can't really mean that he's killed him. He can't. *Please.*

My eyes are trying to look around again, for help, for sanity, for escape, but the librarian places a finger under my chin and forces my head up, makes me meet his eyes.

"That nice man is dead now, because of you. Think about that the next time you are tempted to interfere."

Hot tears are squeezing out of the corners of my eyes. "You're lying," I whisper.

"Am I?"

He's not. Somehow, without a doubt, I know that he's not. Oh, God. I close my eyes, letting the scalding tears force their way out however they can. He takes his hands from me, and I slide down to the floor. I don't look up, but I can picture him there, standing over me.

"Don't be late to class, now," he says in a completely different voice. And then I hear him jog lightly down the steps and away. I don't get up. I don't go to math. I sit there weeping helpless tears for Signor De Luca. And for Annie, and for myself.

Chapter | 08

As soon as I can pull myself together enough, I text Ryan: 911 SOUTH STAIRWAY. I don't know how long it takes him to come; time has gone away for me. Everything has gone away for me. Suddenly Ryan is just there, kneeling in front of me and asking me what happened.

"He killed him." I look up at Ryan, meet his eyes, desperate for him to convince me that this isn't true, to tell me he just saw De Luca in the hallway, that the librarian was lying. "He threw me against the wall and he said that De Luca was dead and that it's my fault."

Ryan sinks the rest of the way to the floor. "Oh, God."

"It can't be true. It can't be."

"Do you think he was lying?"

Yes. Yes. Yes. He had to be. It can't be true. "No."

After a moment, Ryan says, "We should find out. For sure."

He's probably right. Even though I'm already sure.

We go to Signor De Luca's classroom. There's a sub sitting at his desk. I've had her before; she's nice, kind of young and doesn't care if you do homework or read or whatever as long as you're quiet. But right now I hate her for being there, hate her for robbing me of my last shred of secret hope that Mr. Gabriel was lying after all.

The bell rings for the end of the period as we're standing there. Students stream out around us. The sub is packing up her stuff.

"Is Signor De Luca out today?" I ask her, trying to make it sound like a regular question, like nothing, like his life doesn't depend upon the answer. "I thought I saw him earlier."

"He had to leave early," she says. "Some emergency, I think." She looks up then and seems to realize that maybe she wasn't supposed to share that. "Or—I don't really know, actually. I just know that he had to leave early. I'm sure he'll be back tomorrow."

She smiles at us nervously and heads out, leaving us in the empty room.

We cut the rest of the day. Ryan drives us over to Signor De Luca's house. We ring the bell, knock on the door. We go into the yard and sit on the back porch until dark. There's a cat flap in the back door, and eventually the gray cat slips out through it and twines around our legs, meowing. Her soft, hopeful, hungry presence twists my heart in agony. Knowing that De Luca is never coming home to give her dinner, knowing that she will never know what happened to him, why he suddenly abandoned her, is suddenly more than I can bear. I scoop her up and sob into her fur for as long as she lets me.

Ryan sits silently beside me, his own tears leaking out from under his tightly closed eyes.

The next morning I go to Italian, still trying to hope that Signor De Luca will be there, scowling and pissed that we didn't come to see him at the end of the school day like we'd arranged. But of course, that's not what happens. Another sub stands in the front of the room. He informs us that "Mr. De Luca" has had to leave school due to a family emergency, and he is not expected back for the remainder of the year. This guy — Mr. Hubbard — will be covering until a long-term replacement can be found. I want to smack him. He doesn't even make us call him *signore*.

Annie is not here. I am half relieved, half sorry. But both halves wish I could see her face right now, see what her reaction would be to this news. Does she know what really happened? Did she know beforehand? Could she have stopped it? Did she try?

Did she *want* to stop it?

Did she help to kill him?

Ryan looks as defeated and miserable as I feel. But seconds after our shared hopeless glance, my text alert flashes silently at me from under my notebook. NO GIVING UP. CAN'T GIVE UP, OK? NO MATTER WHAT.

I want to type a lot of things back to him. But I can't seem to put the words together, and anyway, I know he already gets it. He's there, too. And it doesn't matter, because he's right. We can't give up. So I just say: OK.

He reads it, nods, puts his phone away. We pretend to pay

attention to Mr. Hubbard, who is trying to figure out how to continue Signor De Luca's lesson plans when he does not himself actually speak Italian. Inside, I am trying to make myself not give up. To imagine that there is something else we can try, to remind myself that the librarian killing De Luca only makes it that much more obvious that we have to figure out some way to stop him. Because *he is fucking killing people.*

You can't just let that stuff go.

It's just also perfectly clear that we can't try to get anyone else to help us. And the idea of the two of us alone against Mr. Gabriel is — I don't even know what it is. There aren't words for what it is. Well, okay, *ridiculous* is one possible word, and also *crazy,* and *terrifying,* and maybe *insanely stupid,* although that's two words, of course.

We trudge onward through the day, trying to not draw attention to ourselves, to not give Mr. Gabriel the slightest reason to suspect that we are up to anything else. It is not hard to appear hopeless and done. I skip lunch, because I don't think I can handle trying to seem normal to Leticia and Diane. When they see that something is wrong, they will not let it go until they make me tell them. Which obviously I can't.

I hole up backstage in the auditorium instead, in theory to distract myself with figuring out Sweeney's chair, but even the show doesn't seem important now. I just sit in a corner on the sawdust-sprinkled floor, waiting for the bell to ring, so time can move forward, so the day can eventually end. My thoughts are endless circling prophecies of doom. There's no way we can fight him. There's nothing we can do. It's ridiculous to try. I know we still *have to* try, that we can't just roll over and give up. But.

I glance up to check the clock and see Annie standing there.

"Hey," she says.

"Hey," I say back, autopilot. I'm afraid to move, to blink, to do anything that might reveal her to be some apparition of my own imagination. But she doesn't vanish. She's really here.

After a second she takes a step closer. "I hate fighting with you," she says quietly.

My breath catches. "Me too," I whisper.

She looks at me for a second, looks away, looks back. Takes a breath. "I know you don't like what's going on with Mr. Gabriel," she says finally. "I just wish I could make you understand."

I think very carefully about what to say here. "I want to understand. I'm just—just worried about you. About—what's going on. You get that, right?"

She nods. "I know. But that's only because you don't understand. I know how it must seem to you. But for me, it's—" She shakes her head, as if even she can't quite grasp what it is for her. "I finally know what it's like to be in love, Cyn. If you could only know how he makes me feel—so alive, and real, and . . . and *essential,* all these things I never was before. . . ."

"Annie—"

"I know you think I'm being crazy. That it's not really love, or whatever—"

I want to bite my tongue, but I can't. "It's *not* really love.

145

Can't you see what he is? Do you know what he's done? What he's doing?"

I wait for her to explode, but she doesn't. She looks at me, and she seems really there and lucid and of sound mind and all the rest. "You think I don't know that he's not just a man?" For a moment her face is as open as I've seen it in days . . . and, I think, a little scared. But only for a moment. "I know he's more than that. Better than that. And — and I'm better. He's making me better. Isn't that what love does? Lifts you up, makes you more than you were?"

"He's not —" But she's not listening. Not hearing. Can't. Won't. Her eyes are going sparkly and twinkly and a little loony. So much for lucid and present and sound.

"I'm going to be special like he is, Cyn. Special enough that we can be together forever. He told me. I just need to . . . There are things that need to happen, things he needs to do, that he needs me to do, and then he's going to take me away from all of this. From everything. So I can be with him always."

I curl my fingers into fists against the floor, my nails digging into my palms, forcing myself to sit there, feigning calm, and not get up and grab her and try to shake some sense into her. "Annie. Are you really here? I mean, are you really in there, hearing yourself? It's not love if he's making you do things. And he's not *special*. He's psychotic. A monster. Literally. A. Mon. Ster. He's *killing people*. He killed Principal Morse and Signor De Luca! And he plans to kill pretty much everybody! Do you understand? This is the guy you want to run away with?"

Her eye twitches, and I see in her face again, clear as day, that she does know, and that she won't let herself acknowledge it. She shakes her head again, as if it's just so sad that I'm so blind to the truth. "You just don't get it. You can't. You can't know how he makes me feel. It's like how you say Ryan makes you feel, only times about a million. And he wants *me*, Cyn. We want each other, and I'm going to go with him. That's all I want, forever and ever."

She blinks, and then she looks at me again, hard and straight and determined. Like she's fighting that part of her that won't see, but not nearly hard enough. "I know he's not a regular person. I know he's not . . . not human. I know he's going to take me somewhere that's not . . . here. That there will have to be some sacrifices." Her face goes a little wistful. "Do you remember when we used to be all obsessed with the Greek gods and goddesses in junior high? I feel like Persephone. He's stealing me away to the underworld, except I'm glad to go."

"He's not Hades, Annie. He's not some Disney version of the lord of the underworld, all misunderstood and maligned yet secretly good-hearted and just in need of someone to love. He's a *demon*. He *kills* people. He *likes* killing people. He sucks out their souls and kills them, and he's going to do that to the whole entire school. How can you just shrug that part off? Don't you care? Don't you care that he's going to kill all your friends? Including, I might add, me?"

She keeps her eyes on mine. "That's not true. I know you believe that, but it's not true. He may be a demon, if you want to use that word, but he's not evil. He's not a killer. He's not a monster. He's just different from us."

"Sure. He's different from us in the same way that serial

killers are different from kindergarten teachers. The way that rabid bears are different from gerbils. He is a monster, Annie. I think you know that he is."

She sighs, looks down. "I know you're trying to make me mad, but it's not going to work. It's not your fault that you don't understand. If you could hear the way he talks to me, the things he says . . ." Her sad resignation vanishes suddenly and she smiles dreamily at a spot somewhere above my head. "He writes me love poems, Cyn. He e-mails them to me at night so I can read them and feel close to him when we have to be apart. They're so beautiful. No one who was truly evil could write the things he does." After another moment in which I continue to stare at her in silent horrified and somewhat nauseated disbelief (*love poems?*), she meets my eyes again, but there's no connection there. "I just want you to know that I forgive you, Cyn. Whatever happens, okay? You're still my best friend."

She's killing me. She's *right there,* and I should be able to reach her, to make her see what's happening.

"What about your family?" I ask, grasping at straws now. "You're just going to leave them? You're just going to leave everything and everyone who cares about you?"

"Yes!" She says this with such unexpected vehemence that I actually jerk backward against the wall. "Who am I here, Cyn? Nice little Annie, who gets good grades and takes care of all the little kids who show up at her house and smiles at everyone and does what she's told and doesn't make any trouble but who never actually has a life of her own. Where's *my* adventure, Cyn? Where's my secret crush, my rule-breaking, my fiery passion, my hope for a future that holds some sort of *something*, that doesn't just lead back to the same life I've always had, where nothing ever changes and I'm never allowed to . . ." She breaks off, nearly in tears, then starts again. "Am I supposed to become my mother, with a house full of kids and a boring husband and endless loads of laundry and cooking and PTA meetings forever? Or am I supposed to go to college and grad school and get some all-consuming job that sucks my life away before it's even started? I have a chance for . . . for *everything*. To be alive in a way I will never get to be here. To be loved and wanted for who I really am, inside, the person no one ever sees behind the nice good girl I've had to be all the time, *always* . . ."

I'm so taken aback by this outpouring of secret pain that I can't even speak at first. "Annie," I manage finally, "you can be whoever you want to be. You don't need Mr. Gabriel for that."

She shakes her head again, dropping her eyes. "What if what I want is to leave here forever, to get to live the kind of fairy-tale adventure I'd never otherwise have a chance to have? I *love* him, and he loves me, and I don't care if that means I have to leave."

And you don't care if he kills everyone you care about, I think but don't say. It's pointless; she won't hear that part. I can't reach her. I can't talk her out of what she's feeling, or thinks she's feeling, or whatever. The only thing I can do is find a way to destroy the librarian. And hope that Annie will come back to herself when he's gone.

"I love you, Cyn," she says. "But I don't think I can be around you when I know you can't support me in this. I just — I just wanted to let you know that I wasn't mad anymore.

But please stay away from me from now on, okay? I won't be coming to classes anymore, so that will help. Mr. Gabriel has arranged for me to do independent study in the library for the rest of the semester. And very soon, of course, it won't matter anyway."

Because you'll be gone and we'll all be dead.

"Because I'll be gone. And I hope you can find a way to be happy for me, Cyn. In the end."

"Annie—"

"Good-bye, Cyn." She looks me once more in the eyes, and then she walks away.

I could run after her. But what would be the point? I'd just ruin her nice exit, and it wouldn't change anything.

The only way to change anything is to kill Mr. Gabriel.

So that is what I will do.

Somehow.

After school, Ryan and I head to his place to do a little Internet research.

I lean my head against the car window, staring blindly at the blur of passing roadway. I am still replaying my conversation with Annie in my head, trying to figure out what else I could have said or done to get through to her.

"You okay over there?" Ryan asks, glancing at me from the driver's seat.

"No," I say.

"Still thinking about Annie?" I'd filled him in earlier about seeing her.

"Yeah." I sit up, sighing. "I can't stand seeing her so . . . smitten. With him. I mean, I know it's not real, he's cast some kind of spell on her, but . . . still."

He's quiet for a moment, then says, "Well, that's why we're doing this, right? Trying to stop him? We'll figure something out, and before you know it he'll be gone and she'll be back to her old self."

"Right," I say back, trying to be heartened. And I am, at least a little. "No giving up."

"Right on." He turns the corner onto his street.

We head right upstairs to his bedroom. Ryan grabs his laptop from the desk and then flops stomach-first onto the bed. He flips the computer open in front of him.

He has left plenty of room beside him. It seems very clear that I am supposed to lie there.

Next to him.

On his bed.

"So what are we looking for exactly?" he asks, fingers poised above the keyboard.

"Um . . ." I drop my bag on the floor and sit sideways on the bed, kicking off my shoes. *LIE DOWN LIE DOWN LIE DOWN!* My brain is shrieking at me. *BEFORE HE MOVES BEFORE HE DECIDES TO SIT UP LIE DOWN LIE DOWN NOW!*

I lower myself down next to him.

"We could just start searching demons and stuff," I say, trying to focus, "but I already tried some of that, and there's so much crap and nonsense out there . . . I was thinking maybe we should look for a good *source* of information, instead of looking for the information itself, you know? Like an occult bookstore or something. There must be something like that around here somewhere."

Ryan starts typing. I try to catch a glimpse of what comes up in the auto-complete window of the search engine, but he's too fast. Thwarted, my brain shifts its attention back to the fact that his left hip is gently pressing against my right. I can feel all of my nerve endings straining toward him. *More,* they are chanting in creepy unison. *More more more.*

Quiet, I think at them. *Now is not the time.*

They fall silent, sulking. But they continue to strain. I feel them trying to force me to lean into him. My brain, unhelpfully, supplies a full-blown predictive scenario of what might happen if I do lean into him, and he leans back, and then we look at each other and all at once he thrusts the laptop off the bed and grabs me with those strong, rugged hands and pulls me close and closer until his mouth is soft-yet-firm on mine and the rest of him is not-at-all-soft against the rest of me . . .

Is it wrong to be feeling this warm and tingly and suffused with *want* when all these terrible, serious things are happening?

Yes. Pull it together, Cyn, goddammit.

I pull it together.

My nerve endings weep quietly, but I ignore them.

"Huh," Ryan says. "Well, it doesn't look like there's anything right here in town, but there's one on the other side of the lake. 'Books of Darkness: Your One-Stop Shop for Magic, Mystery, Hidden Secrets of the Universe.'" He glances over and smiles crookedly at me. "They also have Dungeons & Dragons tournaments and gaming supplies."

I grin back at him. "Sounds like just the place we need. You up for heading over there now?"

"The sooner the better, right?"

"All righty, then," I say, resisting the urge to shout to drown out my wailing nerve endings, who realize I am about to break what little physical contact they have been able to enjoy. "Let's go."

I stifle a sad sigh of my own as our hips break contact. But we have work to do.

Thirty minutes later Ryan executes a flawless parallel park down the block from the address we got from the website. We exit the car and walk along the sidewalk. Laundromat, minimart, nail salon, pet shop, Books of Darkness.

The front windows are painted entirely black. The door is black, too, with a red doorknob and splotches that I think are supposed to be blobs of blood dripping down beneath it. I am not entirely certain that this is a place I want to enter.

Ryan, however, doesn't hesitate. He grips the bloodred doorknob and turns it and pulls the door open. A black curtain hangs before us, and Ryan pushes through to the inner space beyond. With one last backward glance at the still-sunlit street, I follow him in. We have to try, I guess. Plus, all of my nerve endings are still straining after him with all their might, so it's not really very hard to step up behind him and emerge on the other side of the black curtain.

I stop in stunned surprise. Ryan is frozen next to me, similarly taken aback.

Warm recessed lighting illuminates a long wooden coffee bar and a café area serving cookies and smoothies and little organic sandwiches. A college-age girl with magenta hair and multiple piercings looks up from behind the counter and smiles brightly. Across from the bar, there's a large seating area with chairs and tables and a sign that says, D&D TOURNAMENTS RIGHT HERE, EVERY THURS. NITE! On the far side of the room, stairs heading down are visible through an archway. Above the archway, hand-painted lettering announces, THIS WAY TO THE BOOKS!

"Hey, welcome," says the barista. "Can I help you guys with something?"

"Uh, yeah," Ryan says after a moment. He gives me a little nudge.

Apparently it's my job to do the explaining. I don't really mind, especially since the counter girl is kind of cute and I'd rather he didn't speak to her directly anyway.

"We're looking for some books. For research. About—"

The girl holds up her hands to stop me. "Books are Aaron's department," she says apologetically. "I only know the coffee and snacks and the D&D stuff. Go on down and find him, and he'll get you what you need. If he's not at the desk, he's wandering around the shelves. Or, you know, in the bathroom."

"Oh. Um, okay. Thanks."

Ryan and I exchange puzzled looks as we start down the stairs.

The book room is less colorful than the café, but it's still not at all what you'd expect from the blacked-out windows at the entrance. The lighting is still really good. Rows of shelves are packed tightly with books, labeled with little signs that say things like WICCA AND SPELL BOOKS, MAGIC HISTORY, and CONTEMPORARY SCIENCE FICTION. There's a desk in the back corner, cluttered with piles of paperbacks and legal pads and a few big, thick referency-looking books. There's also a laptop hooked up to a large flat-screen monitor. The walls are a creamy off-white punctuated with pieces of artwork that appear to have been supplied by some local artist, with little cards by each one listing the title and the asking price. It seems to be a series on angels, from what I can tell at a glance. Pretty, and a little sad, somehow. Before I can examine them further, Ryan calls out beside me, "Uh, hello? Aaron?"

"One sec!" a voice responds from somewhere among the shelves. In the promised second, a guy appears from around a corner. He's maybe forty-something, with short, spiky brownish hair that I would say he appears to spend a little too much time on for someone his age. He is wearing a They Might Be Giants T-shirt. He sets down a stack of books on a side table and comes over to shake our hands.

"Aaron Litske, proprietor. What can I do for you?"

"We, uh, need some books," I say.

He grins at me. "That part I guessed. Any particular topics?"

I glance at Ryan and he nods encouragingly.

"Demons, I guess. And maybe their powers and how to stop them." I add nervously, "It's for school. You know, a project."

He doesn't seem to care about this last part. As soon as I say demons he takes off toward one of the rows of shelves.

"Demon possession, demon summoning, or demon in assumed human form?" he calls back over his shoulder.

Ryan and I look at each other again. "I guess the third one," I say, and Ryan concurs.

Aaron reappears with another stack of books, which he takes back to his desk. He sits and indicates a pair of folding chairs against the wall. "Why don't you tell me as much as you know, and we'll try to go from there?"

We sit and I try to think of how to begin. After a moment, I ask, "Is there a kind of demon who can look human, but then sometimes he's, uh, clearly not human?"

"Animal form? Or still mostly humanoid but with wings and fangs and such?"

"Wings and fangs," Ryan says.

"Hmm. Okay." Aaron starts typing. "What else? Powers? Behavior patterns?"

"He kind of turns people into zombies," I say. "Not real zombies. I mean, they're not dead, just sort of dazed and wandering around aimlessly and stuff. Temporarily. Mostly. We think he's sucking out bits of their souls."

"Or life force or whatever," Ryan adds. "He touches them and then they get all slow and weird and low-energy."

"Sometimes he kills people," I put in quietly. I don't want to think about Signor De Luca right now. "At least one looked like a ritual sacrifice kind of thing. There was a lot of blood."

Aaron nods, typing away. "Uh-huh, okay. Human aspect, siphons life force, requires at least occasional human sacrifice, probably in order to maintain his human manifestation. Is his ability to revert to demon form limited?"

"I'm not sure what you mean," I say.

"Can he do it anywhere, anytime? Or only sometimes, or only in certain places?"

"I think—I think only sometimes. I'm not sure about places. There was a symbol on the floor, though. When we saw him with the wings and fangs. The rest of the time he's a librarian."

We seem to have given up all pretense of school-project research. But I don't think Aaron really cares why we're asking. He's all business.

"Oh, good," Aaron says. "Always a good sign."

"That he's a librarian?" Ryan asks, sounding confused.

"That there was a containment circle—that symbol you saw on the floor. Usually that means the demon can only assume partial demon form by accessing his home dimension. If there was a drawing on the floor, he probably created a portal that existed only within the symbol. Meaning he couldn't just step out and be a demon all over the place."

We were right. That's why he hadn't chased us that day. But—

"But how does he get back out, then? I mean, when he wants to be human again? If he can't leave the symbol . . . ?"

"Human accomplice, most likely," Aaron says. "Someone he can trust to draw the right diagram and then to let him out again when he's finished."

"Someone—someone he's got under his influence?" He totally lied to me, that jerk. Annie must have still been there. Unless he arranged to have her come back later, I guess.

"Probably," Aaron agrees. "Or someone who just gets off

on helping demons, maybe in exchange for money or power. Demons can promise all kinds of things, of course. They don't always deliver, but by then it's usually too late anyway."

"Too late?"

Aaron nods, still typing and clicking away at the computer. "Demons aren't particularly trustworthy. Or loyal. Once they've got what they want, they often just kill their accomplices, unless there's still more they're going to need from them in the future."

Oh, Annie.

It's okay, my brain reminds me. *He's not going to kill her. He's going to make her his demon bride and take her away forever.*

Right. Thanks. *So* much better.

Ryan and I share another glance.

"So, how can we stop one of these demons?" I ask. "We can stop him, right? I mean, it's possible?"

"Well, let's see." Aaron starts scrolling through whatever information his typing and searching has retrieved. I try not to bounce impatiently in my seat.

"Okeydokey," Aaron says finally, looking up at us. "I think what you've got is a middle-grade demon; serious but not one of the big evil superstars or anything. It should be possible to destroy him. That's what you want, right? To kill him?"

"Yes." We say it together.

"Okay." Aaron resumes his clicking and typing. "Give me just a second here . . ."

We sit, striving for patience and calm. After a moment Ryan asks, "Will all the spaced-out people come back to themselves? I mean, once he's dead? Will they come back to normal?"

That's a good question. De Luca had thought so, but . . . he was wrong about at least some things, obviously.

Aaron holds up a finger in a *just a moment* gesture without looking up. From somewhere under the desk we hear the soft whirring sound of a printer coming out of sleep mode. Aaron clicks and types for another few seconds, studies the screen again, then grabs one of the books from his stack and flips through the pages.

"Okay. So the dazed thing is a side effect of having your life force siphoned away."

"Is it their souls?" I ask. "Is that what he's taking?"

"Eh." Aaron makes a seesaw gesture with his hand. "I don't know if I'd say *souls*, exactly. Maybe, but I think 'life force' is better." He perks up. "You kids play video games? You know how some of them have that life-indicator thing for each player? A red bar or something, showing how much life you've got left, or how many hit points, or whatever it's called in that particular game. And you can lose some of it and then gain more later and be okay, but if it ever gets down to zero, you're toast. That's more like what this is like, I think."

"So as long as he's only taken a little bit from each person, they can be okay after a while?" asks Ryan.

"Yes, I think so. I mean, hey, no guarantees, this is all just theoretical, right?" He laughs a little, and we laugh a little, too — ha-ha, of course, we're not actually *serious* here. "Anyway," he goes on, "I think anyone who's just lost a bit of life force to him should be fine eventually. But if he's got anyone directly connected to him, that's a different story."

I lean forward. "What do you mean, *connected*?"

"Some demons like to make themselves little, uh, helpers. Kind of like deputies with very limited demonic powers. People to help do their bidding, since sometimes the demons themselves are limited as to what they can do while they're pretending to be human."

"So would one of these deputies, for example, maybe be able to help him take people's life forces?"

Aaron thinks for a second. "Could be. Don't really know what all the variations are, but that certainly sounds possible. Anyway, anyone he's turned into a deputy will need to be severed from his control before he's destroyed, or they'll be destroyed right along with him."

"Oh," I say, sitting back in dismay. Ryan gives me a sympathetic look. "How — how do we break that connection?"

"I'd say you're looking at a three-step process. Step one is to bind the demon so that you can do the rest of it without him getting away. Or, you know, killing you. For this, you will need . . ."

He lays a book open before us on the table.

". . . this diagram," he continues. "You've got to either draw it first and then summon him into it, or draw it around him while he's standing still."

Ryan and I look at each other, then back at Aaron.

"How are we supposed to do that?" Ryan asks. "He's not an idiot. He's not just going to stand there."

"What about the first part?" I ask. "Summoning him into it?"

"Either of you ever do magic before?"

"Uh, no."

"No."

"Then I wouldn't recommend the summoning option. Way too much could go wrong." He pauses for a moment, thinking. "Here, I know."

Aaron scoots back in his chair and pulls open a drawer in the bottom right side of the desk. After a few seconds of rummaging around, he sits back with a pleased expression. "Try this," he says, holding out what looks for all the world like a small strobe light.

"A strobe light?" Ryan says dubiously.

"Little-known demon weakness. Catch 'em by surprise with one of these, and they freeze just like a deer in the headlights. You've really got to sneak up on him, though. If he sees it coming, it will never work."

Ryan takes the strobe light, still looking highly doubtful. I don't blame him.

"Step two," Aaron goes on, "is to sever the connection with whomever he's deputized. You'll need that person to be there for this, too. Now, there are two ways this could happen. You could convince him to release the person voluntarily, but that's probably unlikely. The other way involves a little magic ritual."

"Didn't you just tell us not to try doing magic?" Ryan asks. He's clearly starting to get irritated.

"This isn't as dangerous as the summoning spell. Or nearly

as complicated. You'll just need to mix together a few things, and then it's simply a matter of performing the symbolic ritual." He jots down a quick list on a piece of paper and hands it over to me. "I've got the hard-to-find ones here in the shop. The rest you should be able to find at any grocery store."

"And step three?" I ask warily.

"Step three is where you get to kill him. Well, that or banish him back to his own dimension. It depends how powerful he is. But it should get him out of your hair, either way. For that part, you just need to trace the diagram with something flammable — lighter fluid works nicely — and set it on fire. The combination of the flames and the containment circle will either drive him off this plane, or destroy him."

He stands up. "Just be sure to get all other flammable things out of the way, of course. And bring a fire extinguisher. You don't want to burn down the whole building."

We stand up, too. Aaron grabs the papers from the printer, which include instructions for drawing the diagram he showed us, along with a coupon for 20% off our first purchase in the store, and then slips into the back room to get some of the more unusual items on the ritual list. He comes back bearing an assortment of little plastic bags containing various substances. "Erica can ring these up for you upstairs."

"Thanks," I say, shaking his hand firmly. Ryan does the same, and then I can't help asking, "Hey, so, why do you make the front of your store look all scary and uninviting? It's really nice in here. You probably scare a lot of people off with the black windows and bloody doorknob."

Aaron smiles. "That's pretty much the point. We serve a

select clientele here. Just folks who already know about us, or find out through friends . . . or who come here because of some particular need, like you two. We don't want every college kid in town hanging out in here with their laptops and cell phones, ruining it for the rest of us."

"Oh," I say. "I guess I can understand that."

"Try to keep it under your hat, okay?" Aaron calls after us as we head upstairs.

No worries there. I'm certainly not going to go blabbing to anyone about our demon-research errand. I doubt Ryan will, either.

The magenta-haired girl rings us up at the counter and puts everything except the strobe light in a recycled Whole Foods paper bag for us. I take the bag and Ryan tucks the light under his arm, and we go back through the black curtain and into the outside world.

"So," Ryan says as we walk toward the car. "That was interesting."

"Yeah. You think he really believes in all this stuff?"

"I think he really does." Ryan hesitates, then adds, "I sure hope so, anyway. If he's just messing with us, we're likely to have a really unpleasant experience back at the library."

"Yikes. Good point."

Ryan unlocks the passenger door for me, then goes around to the driver's side and we both get in. The sun's going down, and the lighting is getting decidedly romantic to my eye. Okay, naked fluorescent bulbs are romantic to my eye when they're shining down on Ryan Halsey, but still. This is *objectively* romantic, I think.

"So what else is on that list?" he asks.

I take out the paper Aaron gave me. All the more esoteric items that he's already given us have little check marks beside them. The remaining items are all pretty standard. "Salt, baking powder, garlic, rosemary, white glue, and um . . ." I look up at him. "Paprika."

"Heh. Not what I would have guessed, but I suppose that's why we consulted the experts."

"I suppose so."

We sit there looking at each other for a moment in the darkening car, and *oh my God* I want there to be kissing, but I guess now is really not the time. *It could be the time,* my nerve endings whisper slyly at me. *Just lean forward and kiss him. DO IT! DO IT NOW!*

I can't.

I want to. I really, really want to. But I can't. What if he doesn't want to kiss me? What if he *pulls away*? I'd never recover. And we have work to do.

I busy myself folding the list, and Ryan clears his throat and starts the car, and off we go.

Maybe later, I promise myself silently. Maybe right before we actually go through with this crazy plan. Because then we might be just about to die, and so I might not have quite so much to lose.

Chapter | 09

It is Sunday night. I've got a Tupperware container filled with the mixture of ingredients from Aaron's list and a box of chalk (assorted colors) for drawing the diagram. Ryan has a steak knife for the severing ritual and the lighter fluid for the end part. The strobe light is in his backpack, along with extra batteries, matches, a lighter (in case something happens to the matches), a crowbar, a mini fire extinguisher, and a box of chewy chocolate chip granola bars, in case of sudden low blood sugar.

Annie is tied up and gagged in the backseat, wriggling furiously and trying to yell through the scarf we stuffed in her mouth.

I turn around to look at her again. "I'm so sorry, Annie. Please, just try to relax, okay? I swear, you will understand and forgive me eventually."

Her eyes narrow to angry slits and I hastily turn back around.

It had been pretty easy to kidnap her, really. She hadn't told her parents she didn't want to see me, and so I just walked inside her house without ringing the bell, like I have ever since we were little, and her mom, who was knee-deep in laundry and half watching TV, waved me around to the back of the house where Annie's room is. Annie was sitting at her computer with headphones on, and I was able to jump her almost before she even realized I was in the room. With the usual thumping, running, and screaming sounds of too many little kids in the basement/rec room downstairs and the turned-up volume of the television in the living room at the front of the house, there was no danger of anyone hearing the struggle. I let Ryan in through the window, and while he finished tying her up, I e-mailed a quick vague-but-worried note to Mr. Gabriel in what I hoped was a good imitation of Annie's style, saying she needed to talk to him and that if he saw this, he should meet her in the library at midnight. It took all my self-control to resist looking for some of those "love poems" she'd mentioned while I was in her e-mail, but I knew I couldn't risk the distracting and time-consuming throwing up they would probably induce. I left a note on the bed in a decent approximation of Annie's handwriting, saying that she was going over to my place to help me study for a test. After that, we bundled her quickly out the window and into Ryan's car. The whole thing took less than ten minutes.

Of course, then we had to hang out in the car with Annie

tied up in the back for several hours, waiting for midnight. That part was harder.

"Ready to do this?" Ryan asks.

"Not really. But I guess it's now or never, isn't it?" I look over at him in the dim glow from the distant streetlight. We're parked on the street closest to the back entrance of the school. The e-mail we sent Mr. Gabriel asked him to leave the door propped open for us, but Ryan's got the crowbar just in case.

We get out of the car and close the doors on Annie's renewed struggling. It seemed best to leave her here until after we get Mr. Gabriel immobilized. If something goes wrong and we don't make it back . . . well, then Annie will have bigger problems to worry about than being tied up in the backseat of a car, anyway.

We stand there a moment more, both apparently equally reluctant to put the next part of this insane plan into motion. Because this next part is where everything either works and we win, or it all goes horribly, horribly wrong.

"This is really crazy, you know that?" I ask Ryan.

"Yeah." He clears his throat. "Hey, I just — you know, in case we're about to die —"

Oh my God. He's going to kiss me. He's going to kiss me in case we're about to die. Which doesn't even necessarily mean that he really has *liked* me liked me all this time, since maybe he just wants to kiss *someone* before he dies and I'm the most convenient candidate — *Shut up*, I tell myself. *Shut up and accept that he really does like you and he wants to kiss you! He's going to kiss you! Right here and now!*

"Yes?" I prompt, a little breathlessly.

He pauses, looking back at me very seriously. And then: "It's been a pleasure working with you, Cynthia Rothschild." He sticks out his hand.

I stare down at it.

He wants to *shake hands* in case we're about to die?

I look back up at him, confused. But only for a second. Then I reach out and take his hand. Because, hey, you can't leave someone hanging like that. And besides, if that's the best I'm going to get right now, I'll take it.

It doesn't have to be, my brain points out in a very sane and level voice. This is unusual for my brain, so I pay extra close attention. *This is your moment — the moment you were waiting for. You could pull him toward you right now, grip that hand for all you're worth and pull him close and plant your mouth right there on his. Because you might be about to die, you know. You really might. So you really should kiss him. It could be your one and only chance.*

Yes, I think. My brain is offering very wise counsel here. I'm going to do it. I'm going to kiss him. I'm going to kiss him right now.

But I don't.

I return his firm, professional grip and let my nerve endings bask in the warm touch of his skin against mine for several long seconds. *Remember that,* I tell them. *That might be the last good thing that happens to us in this lifetime.*

I take a breath. I nod. He nods back. He releases my hand. I reluctantly allow this. My fingers curl in against my palm in remembered ecstasy.

And then we dart across the street and creep over to the service entrance behind the Dumpsters.

The door is propped open like we'd asked, and I start to breathe a sigh of relief, grateful that at least we won't have to try forcing it open. And then it starts to swing farther inward on its own, and from the darkness behind it a voice says, "Annie? Is everything—"

Oh, no! Oh crap! Oh crap!

Ryan wrenches his backpack from his shoulder and thrusts his arm inside, bringing out the strobe light just as the door opens enough to reveal Mr. Gabriel standing a few feet beyond the entrance. Ryan flicks the light on just as the librarian's eyes begin to narrow in understanding.

And then he freezes, midglare, staring at the flashing light.

"Now what?" Ryan whispers. "We can't do it here!"

"I don't think we're going to get a second chance!" I whisper back. Aaron never actually said how long the strobe light will keep Mr. Gabriel frozen. "Stay there, and I'll draw the diagram around him right where he is. I think he's far enough inside that we'll be able to close the door once I'm done. It will be fine."

God, I hope I'm right.

I push the door carefully open the rest of the way until it catches, safely back against the wall. Then I fumble for the chalk and kneel down beside Mr. Gabriel's frozen form. My skin is crawling from being this close to him, but I try to ignore it and focus on making sure to draw a continuous line with no breaks in it at any point. It takes me longer than I expected. I keep shifting along the floor, checking the line, checking the printout from Aaron, trying to draw while my hand is shaking crazily.

"Good?" Ryan says from behind the flashing light when I finally sit back.

"I think so. Yes. Okay."

He turns off the strobe light.

I'm blind in the sudden darkness, and I freeze, afraid to move and accidentally break the circle. I hear Ryan's breathing from somewhere to my left, and closer, a stealthy shifting sound that makes me want to scream.

"Oh, nicely done," Mr. Gabriel says from the darkness beside me.

I stay perfectly still, willing my eyes to adjust *right now,* so I can see if Mr. G. is safely contained or not. It's still too dark. The waiting is killing me.

"Did it work?" Ryan asks. Apparently the waiting is killing him, too.

"Oh, it worked," Mr. Gabriel says in an amused voice.

"How do we know?" Ryan asks, a little defiantly. "You could be lying."

"If it hadn't worked," I tell him, "we'd probably be dead by now."

"Oh. Good point."

Mr. Gabriel chuckles, and says nothing.

Slowly, shapes start to become clear around me. There's just a little light coming in from the streetlights, and other than a few residual ghost images, I seem to have recovered from the strobe's glare and then sudden extinction. As soon as I can see the edges of the symbol clearly enough, I ease carefully out of my crouch and back away. Mr. Gabriel is standing at what I think might be parade rest in the middle of the chalk symbol. I expected him to be angry, but he seems to be taking it all in stride. It occurs to me that he could be faking.

"Do you think he could be faking?" I ask.

Ryan squints at the librarian. "I don't know."

"Only one way to find out," Mr. Gabriel says, and throws himself forward.

I shriek and leap backward, but he slams to a stop at the chalk line. He could be faking that, too, but I am pretty sure I saw his hand press up against some invisible obstacle right before he stopped moving. Pretty sure. But we need to keep going, because we can't go back, and so we need to assume that he's really contained in there.

Ryan finds a light switch, and of course only a fraction of the lights are working, and at least one is flickering annoyingly, but the familiar fluorescent glow of substandard school lighting makes me feel a little better. We're in a kind of vestibule that connects to the loading dock and the service elevator. Metal shelves hold cleaning supplies against one wall, and there's an old desk that I guess belongs to the janitor or maybe the security guy who mans the service entrance during the day.

"Okay," I say. "Step two."

"Ooh, what's step two?" Mr. Gabriel asks. He's standing very still about an inch inside the edge of the symbol. His voice is still amused, but his eyes don't seem to be laughing, exactly. He has them fixed on me in a very unpleasant way.

"Shut up," Ryan tells him. To me he says, "Are you sure you're okay staying here with him while I go get Annie?"

"No need for that," says a new voice.

We all turn to look.

For one long, uncomfortable beat, no one says anything.

Then, with considerable effort, I find my voice.

"*Aaron?*" I ask incredulously.

Aaron, *Books of Darkness* Aaron, is standing just beyond the doorway. With Annie. She's still gagged and her arms are still bound with the rope, but he's untied her legs. He's holding a knife to her throat. His knife is a lot bigger and scarier looking than Ryan's steak knife. Which is still in the backpack anyway.

"What are you *doing* here?" I say.

He doesn't look at me. But Annie does. She looks at me, and then at Ryan, and then at the librarian, and then back to me, and her eyes are even slittier and angrier than they were before. She starts trying to yell things through the scarf that I'm really glad I can't understand, but then Aaron says, "Shut up," and presses the knife more firmly against her skin and she shuts up. Her eyes continue to radiate hatred, though.

"I don't believe we've met," Mr. Gabriel says, holding out his hand as far as the chalk will let him. "I'm John Gabriel. And you are?"

"Aaron Litske," Aaron says, not moving. Of course, he knows about the significance of the chalk. He's not going to reach over and break the circle. But what the hell is he doing here at all?

"Is there something I can do for you, Mr. Litske?" Mr.

Gabriel asks calmly, undeterred by Aaron's failure to fall for the handshake trick.

"I'm here to make a deal," Aaron replies just as calmly. "I'll release you—"

"No!" Ryan and I both shout.

"*Shut up!*" Aaron shouts back, and in that second he doesn't look anything like calm. He looks—I don't know what to call it. Excited, terrified, nervous, happy, and a little sick, all combined into one huge scary overpowering emotional state that lies somewhere far, far away from the land of normal, sane, comprehensible human feelings. The knife makes a visible dent against Annie's throat, and I can't move for fear of him hurting her. And then he swallows and seems to regain control, and his face gets smooth and calm and regular-looking again.

"Take me with you," he says to Mr. Gabriel. "To the demon world. I'll release you and give you this girl and all I ask is that you take me with you when you go. I need to go with you."

Mr. Gabriel looks interested. "Really? That's a new one, I have to say. Usually people ask for cash or eternal youth or a lifetime of free cable. Are you sure? That's your price?"

"Oh, yes." And I think we can all hear the naked desperate *want* in those two short syllables.

Okay, I acknowledge to just myself, all nice and silent inside my own head. *Aaron is not a kooky yet good-hearted bookstore guy who happens to believe in demons. Aaron is a frickin' loony bird.* Awesome.

Because really, this situation was not messed up *nearly* enough already.

Mr. Gabriel appears to think this is an acceptable offer. He smiles warmly at Aaron in the uneven illumination. Aaron relaxes visibly. And that is when Annie lurches forward, ignoring the line of blood that appears on her neck as she pushes past the knife, and throws herself into Mr. Gabriel's arms.

Breaking, of course, the containment line as she does so.

Before Aaron can even fully register what has happened, Mr. Gabriel has closed the space between them. He's still cradling Annie with one arm as he backhands Aaron across the face with the other, hard enough to knock him senseless. At least, I think he's only knocked senseless. He's definitely crumpled and motionless against the wall. I cannot spend too much time pondering his life status, because the demon librarian is clearly one hundred percent free and very, very pissed off.

I expect him to kill us now, but instead he turns to look at Annie. "He hurt you," he says.

She shakes her head, denying, and the librarian gently pulls the scarf from her mouth and unties her arms and hands. Then he leans down and runs his tongue along the line of blood, licking her skin clean. Annie closes her eyes in what appears to be ecstasy. I close mine in what is nausea.

I open them again when I sense that Mr. Gabriel has returned his attention to me.

He stands facing me, one arm curled casually around Annie's shoulders. She's leaning against him, eyes still closed. Smiling.

Mr. Gabriel is not smiling. He shakes his head and makes a sad face.

"I'm very disappointed in you, Cynthia. I thought I had gotten through to you. I thought I made it clear that further interference would bring serious consequences."

"Are you going to kill me now?" I ask. I'm proud of myself for getting the question out without my voice breaking. (I know. Like *that* matters. But still.)

The librarian rolls his eyes. "Not you," he says. My eyes flick to Ryan before I can help it. Mr. Gabriel looks exasperated. "Not him, either. Come on, now. I'm not throwing the whole show under the bus just because you can't follow instructions. But I am going to kill someone. You betcha. Any suggestions?"

I don't say anything. I can't even muster up a good glare. We were so close! And now the situation is worse than ever. He knows we haven't given up. And he's going to kill someone just to punish me. I remind myself that he's planning to kill a whole lot of people, that not trying to stop him would be way worse, because then pretty much everyone in the school would end up dying. *But you weren't supposed to try and fail,* my disheartened brain points out. *You're not being punished for trying. You're being punished for screwing it up.*

I know this is unfair. How could we possibly have predicted Aaron's completely random and bizarre intrusion? What the hell was that? But it doesn't matter. I still feel responsible.

I look at him standing there, his arm still draped around my best friend. She looks so happy. It breaks my heart to look at her. I keep my eyes fixed on the demon librarian instead.

"Why Annie? Why can't you just leave her alone?"

He turns to look at her, and his gaze softens, just like he

really is in love with her. She opens her eyes and looks back at him adoringly.

"I knew as soon as I met Annie that she was the one," he says. "All her good qualities just shine right out from within her. But more than anything else, I couldn't resist her innocence. She's pure. Unsullied."

I find myself feeling a little confused. "But—she can't be the only—I mean, for example, I certainly don't want you to pick *me*, but I'm not, uh, sullied either. . . ." Not that it's any of *his* business, but I would hate for Ryan to think . . . I mean, not that it's currently any of his business, really, either, what my sexual history is, but since I don't actually *have* a sexual history, it doesn't seem fair for him to get entirely the wrong idea or anything.

Mr. Gabriel laughs like this is the funniest thing he's ever heard.

"I don't mean virginal, although that's a nice bonus, of course. I mean that her heart is unsullied. She's never been in love, never had her heart broken. She's been waiting for me."

Annie doesn't contradict this. I don't think she's even fully present right now. She's just standing there transfixed, staring up at him, soaking in the sight and sound of him. Mr. Gabriel might not have sucked out her life force, but he's turned her into a zombie all the same. Just a different kind.

But I'm going to get you back, Annie. Even if you hate me forever.

Mr. Gabriel is still talking. "I'm going to show her what real love is all about. Fire, and passion, and pain and devotion beyond anything you can ever imagine." He looks away from her with obvious effort, turning his gaze first on Ryan and then on me, his face hardening with contempt. "Human love is ridiculous. Stupid and empty and fleeting. Humans don't know what love is. And teenagers!" He laughs again, even harder than before. "Teenagers are the worst! You think you're in love with this one here, but you don't even know him. You can't see who he is, can't read his soul, can't feel what's inside him. You think he looks hot in his gym shorts, and that must mean you love him. That's not love you're feeling in your loins there, my dear."

I'm not sure how my face hasn't burst into flames from the fires of mortification this little speech has set there. It takes me a second to make my voice work. "That's not — I mean, I don't —" I can't even attempt to think of what a suitable response would be here. I can feel Ryan's eyes on me, but I can't bear the thought of meeting them with my own just now.

Mr. Gabriel's all revved up at this point, though, and so a suitable response isn't actually called for, apparently.

"Annie is coming home with me, to be my queen. Well," he allows, "my queen as soon as I win the fight for the demon throne, which, among other considerations, requires me to have a human consort ready." He rolls his eyes again, waving his hand dismissively in the air. "It's a thing."

He turns back to Annie, and I see that he's a little transfixed himself, staring back at her. He takes her hands and kisses them gently, first one and then the other. "I will take such pleasure in showing her what real love means. Slowly, for thousands and thousands of years. You'll all be long gone, but Annie and I will just be beginning. And I will take that sweet, trusting, innocent heart of hers and slowly twist it into something else, something knowing and damaged and evil and corrupt."

He looks up suddenly and flashes one of his dazzling smiles. "Like me!"

Now I can meet Ryan's eyes, because, seriously, the demon's confessional lecture here is way worse than anything he can expose about my loins. Ryan looks as horrified and nauseous as I feel. This is more than just evil, soul-sucking, people-killing, demon-villain type stuff. This is sick, messed-up, serial-killer, borderline-pedophile, criminal insanity of the most disgusting and appalling kind. And it's all being channeled right at Annie, who can't really be hearing this and giving it the ol' thumbs-up. I'm even more sure now that she's not really here in this moment with us. She's firmly inside her own head, lost in romantic daydreams starring the version of herself she wants to be and the version of Mr. Gabriel that she's convinced herself is real. I know from daydreams, and I know exactly how many light-years away they can be from reality sometimes.

"You know she doesn't really want that, right?" I ask as if he could somehow not know this. "She's not in love with you. She's in love with some made-up idea of you that doesn't come anything close to what you really are."

"She wants it," he says, and reaches out to caress her face while he does. "She may not understand yet, but she will. And she will have plenty of time to come around. So much time. With me. You do want that sweetheart, don't you?"

Annie leans blissfully into his touch, like his hand is made of silk or velvet or some of those really high-thread-count sheets.

I can't stand it.

"Get *away* from her!" I scream at him, lurching forward, grabbing her arm, trying to pull her away, to make her stop *looking* at him like that. She swats at me, suddenly aware of my presence again and clearly not happy about it, and Ryan is shouting something and I'm not listening to either of them because I'm suddenly remembering that I have this super-roach thing going on, right? And so I don't *have* to stand it. I don't have to let him stand there and touch her and tell us all about how he's going to mess her up until every last remnant of who she is is gone. I can stand up to him, instead.

Mr. Gabriel grabs my upper arm hard enough to make me gasp. Everyone else is still shouting, but they're muted in the background and I can hear him very clearly over everything. "You may be resistant to my considerable charms," he is saying, "but I can certainly still hurt you."

With abrupt and violent speed he strikes out, and the pain is astounding as I go flying backward and crash into the wall. For a second there's just blur and blackness, but as I slide down toward the floor I realize I actually see stars. Huh. I always thought that was just something people said.

"Cyn? Oh, God, Cyn, are you okay?" Ryan's voice, from somewhere nearby. In fact, he seems to be right next to me. That's good. I like when he's next to me.

I blink about a hundred times, trying to restart my brain

and make the room come back into focus. It does, finally, and I see that Ryan is sort of propping me up with his body, which is very nice. But I also see that Mr. Gabriel is standing there looking down at us with his arm around Annie again, which is not very nice at all.

The librarian is all business now. "This is the last time I'm going to tell you. If you do anything else to annoy me, if you try to tell anyone, if you try to explain to one more person what is happening, raise even the tiniest bit of suspicion, I will kill both of your families, all of your teachers, all of your friends, and a few other random people for good measure." He smiles just a little, apparently at the thought of all that killing. He thinks a moment and then adds, "And also some puppies. And babies." The smile disappears. "Are we clear? For reals this time?"

He doesn't wait for an answer. He makes a gesture and he and Annie vanish. In the last split second before she's gone, Annie gives me the finger.

And then it's just me and Ryan in the dirty service vestibule. Shocked and hurting and horrified and alone.

Chapter | 10

Well, not *quite* alone.

There is a muffled groan from across the room, and suddenly we both remember Aaron.

"Huh," Ryan says. "I thought he was dead."

"He's going to wish he was dead," I say. Then I say: "Ow." Because everything hurts.

"Can you sit up?"

"I think so."

Everything still hurts, but sitting doesn't seem to make it any worse. Ryan shifts over to sit beside me.

Aaron groans again. We look over at his crumpled form.

"What do you think we should do about him?" Ryan asks.

"Kill him?" I say hopefully. Okay, I am kidding. Or at least half kidding.

"He did seriously screw things up," Ryan agrees. "But . . ."

I sigh. "I know. We're not going to kill him. I might hurt him a little, though."

"I won't stop you."

More groans. Aaron's body shifts scratchily against the floor.

"I guess we should get that knife," I say. I can see it. It's lying on the floor a few feet from where Aaron is groaning and shifting.

"I've got the steak knife, too," Ryan reminds me.

"Good. Then we can each have one." I know I should get up, but it's so nice to just sit here. Sit here and not move and feel Ryan's comforting presence directly beside me, even if he didn't actually want to kiss me before he died.

"What are you thinking?" he asks.

"I am thinking that our good friend Aaron owes us a little something. And I can't think of anyone more likely to have some suggestions for what the hell we are supposed to do now."

"We can't trust him," Ryan says.

"I know. That's why the knives."

"Hmm."

"Do you have a better idea?"

He sighs. "No."

"And no giving up, right? Still?"

The slightest pause, and then: "Right."

"Okay." I take a deep breath and then start the slow process of getting painfully to my feet. Ryan hovers nearby, apparently ready to catch me if I can't handle the whole standing thing. I think I'm okay, though. A little dazed, but all my parts seem to be working.

I step carefully forward and then pick up Aaron's knife from the floor. I think it's a hunting knife. It's huge, with a long, polished hilt. Ryan finds his backpack and digs through it until he finds the steak knife, which we'd wrapped in a towel. He takes it out and looks at it, then looks at Aaron's knife.

"Trade?" he asks hopefully.

"Ha. No way."

He nods and steps around to the other side of Aaron. We stand there looking down at him for a moment.

Then I kick him in the ribs.

He groans louder, but still seems mostly unconscious. I pull my foot back to kick him again, but Ryan puts out a hand to stop me. "Cyn. We don't want to have to take him to the hospital or something." He crouches down beside Aaron, who is facedown, and ungently rolls him over.

Aaron groans again and moves one arm to shield his eyes.

"Hey," I say. "Hey, asshole. Wake up."

His groans are becoming more word-like, but I'm still not hearing actual words. I am also not feeling an abundance of patience. I kneel across from Ryan and take my giant knife and place the tip against Aaron's throat. He stops groaning. He shifts his arm down very slowly and opens his eyes.

"Welcome back," I say, smiling pleasantly. "Did you have a nice nap?"

Aaron looks back and forth between Ryan and me. "Dammit," he says softly.

"Yeah," I agree. "That didn't go so well, huh? You didn't get what you wanted *and* you made two people very, very angry with you. Two people who kind of need a good reason why they shouldn't stab you to death with their big knives right about now."

"I'm sorry," Aaron says hoarsely. "I thought it was my only chance."

"Nope," I say. "*This* is your only chance. Right now. We need a new plan for getting rid of the demon and getting my friend out from under his influence, since our last plan got kind of messed up when you *totally screwed us*. Tell us what else we can try, and we will let you live."

"If it works," Ryan puts in.

"Good point. If it *works*, we will let you live." I give him a little tap with the knife. "Start talking."

"I'm sorry," he says again. "I don't think there is anything else you can try."

I tap him again, a little harder. He flinches.

"Wrong answer," I say. "Try again."

"Please," he says. "I swear. I know it's my fault, but he'll be ready for you now. I don't think you'll get another chance."

"Dude," Ryan says, leaning in. "I seriously would *not* piss her off any more than you already have. She really wants to kill you."

I nod solemnly. "I really do."

"But —" Aaron is beginning to look a little panicky.

Ryan puts a hand on his shoulder. "Just take a minute and think, okay? We'll wait. You know a whole lot about demons.

And you seem like a pretty smart guy. I'm sure you can come up with something."

We fall silent. Aaron closes his eyes, either to help him focus or just to avoid looking at me watching him. I'm sure I don't look very friendly.

Ryan and I look at each other from our positions on either side of Aaron. We don't smile or speak, but I think we can both feel the other person's *thereness* in what is a very good, solid, reassuring kind of way. I know I can, anyway. Feel it. It makes me acknowledge once again how very, very glad I am that he is here with me in all of this. And I don't care what Mr. Gabriel thinks. I *am* in love with Ryan, and not because of my loins. My loins are in love with him, too, sure, but that's beside the point. Maybe before it was just a lusty teenage crush, because of his beautifulness and his good vocabulary and his knee-buckling ability to render silliness and surliness and need and want and pain and loss and joyful insanity as Sweeney onstage. And that sweet twisty smile he gives to girls who tackle him in the hallway.

But it's more than that now. He's brave and good and he's making himself face this terrible, unbelievable thing that's happening, and he's trying to help me save Annie and the school and everything else. He's smart and quick and resourceful and plays an excellent good cop to my bad cop, and he still remembers his Boy Scout knot-tying skills, which is both adorable and highly useful (as evidenced when he helped me overpower and then tie up Annie in a not-too-uncomfortable-while-still-entirely-stable way).

And yeah, I know it's almost certainly unrequited; the pre-death handshake pretty much made that clear. And I can't bear to think too much about Ryan hearing those things that Mr. Gabriel said about how I feel. But none of that changes anything. I'm in love with him anyway, dammit.

"Okay," Aaron says suddenly. He opens his eyes. "Okay. I think — I think I might have an idea."

"Let's hear it," Ryan says. I demonstrate encouragement by not pressing any harder on the knife.

"Well, at this point you can't hope to just sneak up on him again. I mean, that's pretty obvious."

"That's not an idea," I say. "That's an unhelpful observation."

"What I mean is," he continues speedily, "I think the only option is to get some help. You can't try cornering him again on your own."

"We tried getting help," I say blackly. "The librarian killed him." It is getting harder to not press on the knife.

Aaron swallows and hurries on. "I don't mean another human being. I mean help from another demon."

Ryan and I look at each other again. I can't tell what he's thinking. I can't even tell what I'm thinking. This sounds simultaneously like a very good and a very terrible idea.

Aaron sees that he at least has our attention. "I really think that's your only chance. And it's a *good* chance. He's strong, but he's not invincible. Not to another demon."

I sit back on my butt, letting the knife break contact with Aaron's neck, but still holding it prominently in my hand. I don't think he's going to bolt, and my knees were starting to ache from kneeling. I regard Aaron silently. He looks shifty and nervous, but I don't know if that means that he's trying to trick us (*again*), or just that he's afraid I might still be thinking about stabbing him to death.

"Why would another demon want to help us?" Ryan asks.

"Because they're not all best friends down there, you know," Aaron says. He grimaces. "Can I sit up? Please? I promise I won't try anything." When we don't object, he pushes himself awkwardly to a sitting position. "Ow," he says. "Anyway. Demons are generally not cooperative entities. They fight one another constantly. They form alliances sometimes, but ultimately it's every demon for itself. And right now there's even more rivalry than usual, because the demon king is dead, and all the demons who hope to replace him are getting ready to take their shot."

We're both staring at him. "How do you *know* this stuff?" Ryan asks finally.

He shrugs. "You saw my store. This is what I do. I've been studying and communicating with demons longer than you've been alive."

"You'd think you'd do a better job of not messing up demon containment circles, then," I mutter.

Aaron shoots me a resentful glance. "I know demons. I forgot about teenage girls. I never thought she'd run to him like that. I didn't really get how far gone she was."

I feel myself go very still. "What does that mean? How 'far gone' is she?"

"Oh. Not — I didn't mean —"

I look him right in the eye. "Do not lie to me, Aaron.

Seriously. If I find out you are lying to me I will stab you without any hesitation. What do you mean?"

He shrugs again. "I just mean that she's really buying it. It's not too late to get her free — I swear — but she's not even trying to fight it, as far as I could tell. And, hey, I only saw her for a few minutes. I might not have the whole picture."

"But?"

"But from what I saw, she's not super interested in seeing what's really happening. She wants to believe in whatever lies he's told her."

I can't really argue with him on this one. That's how it seems to me, too. I wish I'd known some of that stuff about how trapped she felt, how not-seen. I had no idea.

"So you think another demon would be willing to help us?" Ryan says, getting us back on track.

"I — think so. You can never really tell what demons will do. But if he's making a play for the throne, which I bet he is if he's here, draining people —"

"He is," I say. "He said something about that. How Annie was going to be his queen, et cetera, et cetera."

"All right, then," Aaron says. "So he's automatically got a bunch of enemies who also want to be the next demon ruler. There's a really good chance one of them would be willing to make a deal with you if it meant taking him down."

"A deal," Ryan says. He looks unhappy. "Like, a deal with the devil, basically, is what you're saying."

"Demons," I say. "Not devils."

"Ehh," Aaron says, "there's a lot of overlap there, sure. But demons don't break their deals. They can't."

Ryan is shaking his head. "But you said, before — you said that they turn on their helpers once they get what they want."

"Oh, sure. But that's because the helpers generally don't make deals — they get seduced, either through magic or just regular human greed. They volunteer. They trust the demons to treat them well in return for their services. You can't trust a demon to do anything they don't have to do. But if you make a deal, they have to do what they agreed to. You just have to be very, very careful that you understand the deal when you make it. They honor the letter, not the spirit. They will gleefully slip through the tiniest loophole if you let them."

Ryan looks even more unhappy. "You're not really selling it," he says.

"You don't really have much choice," Aaron says frankly.

"He's right," I say.

Ryan throws up his hands. "But — weren't you listening to what Mr. Gabriel just *said*? How he's going to kill all our friends and babies and puppies if we tell anyone?"

I blow this off. "I'm sure he meant other *people*. Telling demons about demons can't really count."

"Cyn."

"Yes, okay, that's not a very strong argument. But Aaron's right — we don't have a choice. We can't do this on our own. Not now. And we can't do nothing."

Ryan doesn't say anything for a minute. I suspect he is trying very hard to think of another alternative. I let him. Because, hey, if there is another alternative, that would be fantastic. I would be all over it.

But eventually he just sighs and looks back at me, defeated.

I turn to Aaron. "All right. How do we contact another demon?" He opens his mouth and I point a warning finger at him. "Remember: Lying? Stabbing."

He nods, barely seeming to hear me. His face has taken on an odd and somewhat disturbing animation.

"I can do that for you," he says.

We both roll our eyes.

"Seriously?" Ryan asks.

"Because you've been so awesome thus far with all the helping?" I add.

Aaron actually looks wounded. "I *said* I was sorry. I had—reasons. But I won't try to screw you again, I promise. This could be my way to help make amends."

Ryan sighs again. "We still can't trust him," he says to me.

"I know. So we'll be careful. But who else do you know that can contact demons?"

"There's that Wiccan girl in my gym class."

"Funny. But I don't think Wiccans deal with demons. Also, I'm pretty sure she would fall into the category that would inspire Mr. Gabriel to start killing our families if we tried to enlist her services."

"Probably."

We turn back to Aaron, who is watching us expectantly. "Okay?" he asks.

"Yeah, okay," Ryan says. "Contact away."

Aaron looks appalled. "I can't do it *here*," he says. "I need my stuff. I have to *prepare*. It's not like I'm just going to pick up the phone and dial up the demon world. We have to go to my apartment."

Ryan holds up his hands in defeat before I can say anything. "I know, I know. We don't have a choice." He sighs again. "Let's go, then."

We take Ryan's car. Aaron makes tentative noises about driving his own car home, but we ignore him. I make him take shotgun; I don't like the idea of him sitting behind us.

"How did you even know where to find us?" Ryan asks as he starts the car.

Aaron looks slightly embarrassed. "I followed you."

"Since *Friday*?"

He shrugs. "You were obviously in a hurry to take care of your demon. I knew if I followed you long enough you'd eventually get down to it."

I'm very creeped out to realize that he's been watching us this whole time. I know, compared to everything else, a little spying seems pretty insignificant, but still. Ew.

Aaron's apartment turns out to be right above the store. There's a normalish living room lined with bookshelves and an amazing kitchen with lots of pots hanging from the ceiling and expensive-looking shiny metal appliances and a *ton* of plants — neat little potted herbs and other green leafy things growing on the windowsills and on top of the cabinets and wherever else space allows. Through another door I can see what appears to be his bedroom, also sporting bookshelves and with stacks of books on the floor beside the bed.

He offers us beverages and snacks, which we decline, and then leads us into another room in the back of the apartment.

This room is obviously where the demon stuff happens.

The windows are tightly covered with blackout shades,

and the walls, floor, and ceiling are all painted black. There's a low table against one wall holding an assortment of candles and containers and more stacks of books. When he turns on the light — which is red — a huge glowing diagram appears in the center of the floor.

"You don't bring a lot of ladies home, do you?" Ryan asks.

"Not anymore," Aaron says, rather mysteriously, and without any hint of bitterness or irony.

He moves around the room, selecting items from the table with a sure hand, lighting candles and setting them at certain points along the lines of the diagram. I expect him to consult some books or something, but he seems to know exactly what he's doing. All of his movements have the practiced air of ritual about them. Even the last few minutes that he spends in front of a small mirror near the doorway, checking his teeth and messing around with the arrangement of his hair.

"All right," he says finally, in a breathless, anticipatory kind of voice that reminds me uncomfortably of Annie. "Here we go."

He closes the door and points to the far wall. "Have a seat over there, and don't say anything until I say it's okay. Okay?"

"Okay." We say it together, with the same obvious reluctance. But what else can we do? We have to trust him to do this part. We walk over to where he indicated and sit on the floor, our backs against the wall.

Aaron sits cross-legged at the edge of the diagram. He takes a few deep, long breaths, and then makes a slow series of gestures in the air before him. He starts speaking in a low, measured voice, words that I can't quite catch and that don't seem to be anything resembling English.

At first it's just Aaron, gesturing and speaking, and then all at once there is suddenly and undeniably another presence in the room. It's like the air gets heavier and darker — a feeling of fullness in the space where before there was just empty air. Aaron picks up a knife I hadn't seen him lay beside him, and without pausing his flow of words he slices a neat line along the inside of one forearm.

I gasp, but Aaron doesn't show any sign of having felt the pain of that cut. He leans forward and holds his arm inside the boundaries of the diagram, letting his blood drip down onto the floor.

The fullness grows . . . fuller.

Aaron doesn't move. He keeps his eyes fixed on the inside of the circle, avidly watching his blood begin to make a small, sickening puddle.

And then there is a demon standing there.

She's in half-human form, like Mr. Gabriel was that time we walked in on him. She looks like a gorgeous fortyish woman with serious curves, but there are long, sinuous horns twining up on either side of her head and what looks like a pair of giant fins stretching out behind her. Her hands aren't quite human hands; the fingers taper into long hooklike claws. The claws are painted red.

"Hello, mistress," Aaron breathes, gazing longingly at her like she's the only woman who ever existed in the whole world.

And then I get it. Oh, man.

He's in *love* with her.

"Oh, hell," Ryan mutters beside me. Clearly, he's just come to the same realization.

The demon's (demoness's?) head whips toward us, then back to Aaron. She does not look happy.

"What is this?" she asks suspiciously. Her teeth are pointy. "I thought we agreed you were not to contact me again."

"*You* agreed," Aaron says. "I obeyed. As always."

She raises an eyebrow. "You call this obedience?"

He hasn't taken his eyes off her once. "I have a very good reason for summoning you, my mistress."

"Uh-huh. This should be good."

"I have an offering."

That doesn't sound good. Beside me, Ryan's face is grim. He looks exactly like someone who is trying very hard not to say *See? See? I told you!*

"There is nothing you have that I want, worm."

"I have information about one of your rivals and an offer to help you diminish him."

This stops her for a moment. Then she shakes her head. "Aaron. Why don't you ever learn? You insist on continuing to bother me with your nonsense, and you use these ridiculous porous circles that allow me to *hurt* you. . . ." On the word *hurt,* she gestures and Aaron jerks upward, gasping, as though being lifted by an invisible hook. She looks at him a moment, then makes a small circling motion with one long finger-claw. He screams, blood suddenly seeping through the front of his T-shirt.

But he still never takes his eyes from her, and his gaze is as adoring as ever.

Aaron is a more than little messed up.

The demoness considers him for another few seconds, then shakes her head again, this time in what looks like resignation. "All right," she says. "What is this about? Quickly, before I grow even more tired of you."

"These two are trying to bring down a demon who has inhabited their school and taken one of their friends to be his consort," Aaron says quickly and calmly, for all the world as though he isn't dangling from nothing and bleeding from at least two places.

"So?"

"They seek assistance, and will bargain."

She flicks a contemptuous glance at us, then looks back at Aaron. "Seriously? You want me to help a couple of teenagers save their high school?"

"The demon calls himself John Gabriel."

"Ah."

"And the girl has some kind of resistance."

I stare at him. "Hey! How do you know about that?"

"Your demon librarian said something about it. Before he threw you across the room."

Ryan's eyes get very narrow. "I thought you were out cold that whole time."

Aaron attempts a shrug, which doesn't quite work given his awkward physical situation, but the general message comes across. "I went in and out of consciousness a few times."

I feel stupidly embarrassed that he knows about my roach-iness. "Yeah, well, you saw how much good it did me. He can still kick my ass, apparently. He just can't mesmerize me or suck my soul out like he can with everyone else."

Suddenly I have the demoness's full attention. I immediately wish I didn't.

"Rrrrrreallllly," she purrs. She turns away from Aaron and he drops to the floor like a bag of rocks.

I scramble to my feet, because I don't like how it feels to be looking up at her. Ryan stands up beside me. The demon-ess stands at the edge of the circle, gazing at me intently. I wonder suddenly if she can hurt me the way she was able to hurt Aaron. Fucking Aaron. Who the hell intentionally creates a demon containment field that allows the demon to reach through it and make holes in your guts?

"Come closer," she says.

"Uh, *no*," I say. "Sorry."

She widens her eyes slightly and repeats the command more forcefully. "Come. Closer."

Beside me, Ryan takes a step forward.

"Hey!" I say, grabbing his hand and pulling him back. I glare at her. "Quit it!"

"Interesting," she murmurs. "You really are resistant. Not your little friend, though. Just you."

"So?"

Ryan abruptly jerks upward into the air with a yelp, taking his hand with him. I twist to stare up at him. He stares back, clearly on the edge of (understandably) completely freaking the hell out.

"So *come closer*," the demoness explains, "or I will rip his intestines out through his eye sockets."

Fucking *Aaron*.

"Okay! Okay. I'm coming, see?" I take a slow step toward her, then another, glancing back and forth between her and Ryan. "Just put him down, all right? Gently! Please."

She waits until I reach the circle's edge, then releases him. He drops a little less hard than Aaron did. Maybe that's what passes for gentle for a demon. At least his guts appear to still be intact.

From the floor, Ryan gives me a little wave that seems to be meant to indicate that he's okay.

"Now," the demoness says, "let me get a look at you."

Then she closes her eyes and holds up her hands, or whatever they are, palms out. I feel a weird tingly sensation. Not good-tingly, like the kind Ryan inspires in my loins and various other places; this feeling makes me imagine thousands of tiny stinger-bearing insects hovering about a millimeter away from the entire surface area of my skin.

The demoness inhales deeply, and then exhales in a long, slow, shuddery breath that I can't feel against my face even though she's only a few inches away. She opens her eyes, and her gaze is focused and sharp and alight with interest.

"Oh, yes," she says, baring her pointy teeth in a terrifying smile. "Did your demon tell you what we call creatures like you?"

"Yeah, yeah, I'm a giant super cockroach. Ha-ha, so funny. Hi*lar*ious."

Her smile stretches even wider.

"So. I believe we can be of assistance to each other. You want to drive out this demon, yes?"

"I want to get rid of him forever and save my friend," I say carefully, mindful of Aaron's warning about deal making.

She nods. "I can help you. In return, you must allow me to borrow your resistance."

Uhhhh. "How will that work, exactly?" I ask.

"Your John Gabriel is preparing to fight for the demon throne. I . . . have just decided to do the same. When the fight begins, you will let me draw upon your resistance, which will give me the advantage I need to defeat my rivals."

"But how are you going to 'draw upon' it exactly? Will I get it back?"

"Think of it like . . . sharing an umbrella with me in a storm. You will have a little less of it for yourself, but only while you're holding it so that I can benefit from its protection along with you."

That doesn't sound so bad.

"How would you help me save my friend?"

She thinks for a moment. "I will give you two powerful items to use at the time of the battle. One will sever the demon's hold on your friend. The other will be a kind of shield to help protect you. It will deflect the demon's power back at him, but only once."

Aaaand now I am not following this at all.

"But—his power doesn't work on me. If I'm only, uh, sharing the umbrella, why wouldn't I still have enough—?"

She shakes her head. "It's . . . a small umbrella. And it will be raining very hard."

"Cyn," I hear Ryan say from behind me. "This isn't sounding like such a good idea."

I make shushing motions at him with my hand without turning around. Of course it's not a good idea. None of this is a good idea. There's just no better choice available.

Anyway, I'm still trying to understand. "But he won't even be here — he'll be wherever you are, fighting, won't he?"

"You will need to be present, in our realm, at the time of the battle."

"Cyn, no!" Ryan shouts, at the same time that Aaron cries, "*What?* You'll take *her* but not me?"

The demoness's face tightens in annoyance. She flicks her claws and I whip around to see Ryan and Aaron both slump over.

"What did you just do?" I say in a carefully controlled voice.

"They're fine," she says. "I just needed them to shut up and let the ladies finish their chat."

"Okay," I say, although it's totally not okay. I am suddenly aware that I am now, for all practical purposes, alone with her in Aaron's creepy demon room. "So get on with it."

"At the time of the battle, I will bring you here. Your demon will be bringing your friend along with him, too. He'll have to. You will use the items I give you to sever their connection and protect yourself from his power while I am borrowing your resistance. Then, once I destroy the others and win the battle, I will send you back to your own world."

"Me and Annie."

"Yes."

"Alive and unharmed."

"Not killed or harmed by me. I cannot make any promises for anyone else."

"And if you don't win?"

"I will win."

"Okay, but if you *don't*?"

"Then we both lose. And your friend, too."

"You're not giving me much in the way of guarantees, here, lady."

She smiles coldly at me. "There are never any guarantees. For any of us. I will keep my bargain, assuming I am alive and able to do so. If I'm dead, you will likely be, too. Or will wish you were. Your friend will be lost. If I win, you will get what you are asking for. Make your choice."

I suddenly remember something else. "Can you stop Mr. Gabriel from killing everyone else in the school? He's planning to do that at the end, before the fight."

"I can try to force his hand sooner than he's expecting. That's the best I can do. I can't stop him from draining your schoolmates between now and then. I can't stop him from killing in general. But I might be able to stop him from getting his last deep drink at the end." She tilts her head, considering. "That's extra, though."

I squint my eyes at her. "Extra?"

"Not part of the original bargain. It raises the price."

"To what?"

"You must return to the demon realm twice more, at times of my choosing, to assist me."

"No."

"That is not negotiable."

There is no way I'm going to agree to that. I'm sure once will be bad enough.

"Fine. Forget it. I'll find some other way to stop him from killing everyone. We'll stick with the original deal."

"No."

"What do you mean, *no*?"

"The original deal is off the table. New deal or no deal. Take it or leave it."

"You can't do that!"

She smiles her disturbing pointy smile and says nothing.

I feel very strongly that I should not agree to this new addition. But I need her help. *Annie* needs her help. The whole damn(ed) school needs her help.

"Once. Once more, at a time of your choosing."

"Twice."

"What if I'm busy?"

Silence.

"What if I'm not able to come?"

"You will be."

"What if I say yes but then I just don't come when you try to make me come back?" I realize I should probably not be saying everything that pops into my head right now, but I'm genuinely curious about this point.

"You will not be able to refuse. It will be part of the deal."

"Like, I'll be magically compelled to obey?"

"Something like that."

I shake my head. "Oh, no. You spell it out. Clearly and completely. I want to know exactly what I am agreeing to before I agree to anything. Spell out all the terms, right now."

She sighs, but does it anyway. "You agree to be transported to the demon realm for the coming battle for the throne and to lend me the power of your resistance to aid me in my fight for demon rule. This will be a temporary lending of power, and I will release it back to you upon my victory or my death, whichever comes first. You further agree to return twice more, at times of my choosing, to lend me your resistance again. In return for all of this, I will give you the tools you will need to free your friend from her demon master and to protect you from one direct assault of his power, provide you and your friend safe passage back from the demon realm following the battle, and do my best to prevent your demon librarian from killing everyone in the school before he departs."

I try to channel my favorite fictional lawyers from TV — kicking ass and taking names, etc. "You will also do your best to see that Annie and I survive to be returned to our own world. And when you do your best to prevent Mr. Gabriel from killing everyone, your top priority will be making sure that Ryan Halsey survives." I indicate his attractive yet unconscious form behind me. I feel a little guilty as I say that part, since I know Ryan would probably not agree to being put first over everyone else that needs saving. But I don't care. If I have to go to the goddamn demon world, not once but three times, I'm going to get whatever I can out of it. And if that means I can make sure he survives this thing, I'm going to do it.

I hurry on with the rest. "Also, when you summon me

those two more times in the future, the specific terms of the assistance I will be giving you will be negotiated at that time, my approval not to be unreasonably withheld or delayed. And you can't whisk me away on the day of my future wedding, while I'm giving birth or about to give birth or have just given birth to a child, while I'm operating a motor vehicle or heavy machinery, or while I'm having sex. Or if I'm in the bathroom. And you have to do it in such a way that won't be suspicious to any normal people who happen to be around who don't know about demons and stuff. And you have to return me safely, alive and unharmed, if you can, both times. And then after the second time you have to leave me alone forever."

"Agreed."

I'm startled by the swiftness of her reply, and quickly try to review everything that's been said to make sure I'm not overlooking anything important. I can't think of anything, and I don't know what else to do other than agree. I don't want to. I really, really don't want to. But getting her help seems like the best chance — probably the only chance — of getting me and Ryan and Annie and as many other people as possible out of this alive.

"Agreed."

I feel another tingly sensation, this one a little painful, like all those insects stabbed me just for a second with their many tiny stingers. Then it's gone.

The demoness makes another gesture and I hear groans behind me.

"Worm," she says, addressing Aaron. He snaps to as much attention as he can, half lying on the floor.

She looks at him a moment more, then favors him with a small smile.

"You have done well. With your friend's assistance, I will now be in a position to move forward with my plans for the demon throne. I will therefore be in need of a human consort from which to create my future mate. You will be ready when I call you."

Aaron can barely speak from what appears to be overwhelming joy. "Y-yes, my mistress," he manages in a hoarse whisper.

She blinks and disappears.

"Cyn?" Ryan asks softly. "What happened?"

"I'll explain on the way home," I say. "Right now I just want to get out of here." I go over to help him up. "You okay?"

"Yeah," he says, but he lets me help him. "I'll live."

Yes, you will, I think but don't say. And I realize that while I'm prepared to tell him the other terms of the deal, I'm not going to say anything about the going back twice more, or about making his life the demoness's top priority.

There's really no reason he needs to know.

Chapter | 11

When I get home, it is all I can do to drag myself up the stairs. My parents are asleep, of course; there's a note on my door telling me that there are (surprise!) takeout leftovers in the fridge if I haven't eaten yet. I suppose it's a good thing that my parents don't seem at all concerned when I stay out all hours on a school night. Or at least a convenient thing. I crumple up the note and toss it on the floor. I can feel myself moving very slowly as I go into my room and drop my bag. I don't think very much about anything as I get changed and wash my face and brush my teeth.

And then I go back to my room and close the door and sink slowly down onto the edge of my bed and start to freak out.

I'm going to hell.

I am literally going to hell. Because where else do demons live when they're at home? It's either hell or something like it, right? Some other place that's not here that is filled with demons. A place where they steal young, innocent human people and take them away forever and turn them into something they are not. And I'm going to *go there*. On purpose.

In the moment, earlier, when everything was happening, I didn't really have that much time to be scared. But now, apparently, the time for being scared has arrived. Because I am absolutely terrified.

I don't want to do this. Oh, God. I'm sorry, Annie, but I don't want to do this.

Too late, my brain reminds me.

I snatch at that idea. Is it? Is it really too late? She didn't say that this first visit to the demon world was set in stone, exactly. Just the second two, once she had fulfilled her part of the bargain. I mean, what if I just didn't go? Didn't let her borrow my resistance? Then she would just be free of her part of the deal, right? Well, and also she would be pissed, and would probably kill us all. But I *could* not go. Maybe.

I should have gotten more clarity on that point.

I make myself back away from this line of thought. It doesn't matter. I'm not going to back out. I have to do this. For Annie, and Ryan, and everyone else, too.

I lie back on my bed, willing myself to breathe. Deep breaths, in and out. *It's okay,* I tell myself. *It's okay. It's going to be okay.*

Probably not, if you really think about it, my brain says.

Shut up! I shout at my brain. (I really hate my brain sometimes.) *It will be okay. It has to be okay.*

I get under the covers and close my eyes and try to make myself go to sleep. I'm so tired that it should be easy, but behind my eyelids I can see the burning red flames of my hazy imagined idea of the demon world. I wonder if it will hurt, going there. If it will be hot, if I will be on fire, if everything will be on fire. I didn't ask her if it will hurt. I didn't ask her what it will be like.

Because it doesn't matter. I have to go. I have to save Annie.

I'm not sure if that's my brain talking or some other part of me, but it makes me realize that under the fear, I am really, really mad. *Why? Why does it have to be me? I just want to build the set for the show and be secretly in love with Ryan and not have to fight demons or save people or deal with any of this!*

But it doesn't matter what I want, and I know it.

And it does have to be me. Because there's no one else who can give the demoness what she wants and make her help us.

I lie there, and try to breathe, and try not to think. I lie there and will myself to fall into oblivion, to get what few hours I can of not being here and present and awake and scared.

Eventually, I do fall asleep. I know this because at some point the nightmares begin. Nightmares involving Mr. Gabriel and Annie sucking out Ryan's soul together while I watch and he screams and Aaron and the demoness laugh and laugh and laugh. Nightmares of formless demon shapes reaching for me from every direction, trying to rip me apart into a stringy mess of blood and bones and tatters of dull gray brain tissue. Nightmares of pain and fear and hopeless struggle and knowing that I cannot win, and that all of it will be for nothing in the end. And permeating everything, the glowing red pulsing fires of hell, waiting to consume us all.

I gasp awake, sitting up in bed.

I know what to do for Sweeney's chair.

The next day at school, they announce that we have a new principal.

They have preempted our usual first-period classes for a special assembly and herded us all into the auditorium. I sit with Diane and Leticia, who have saved me a seat. Annie is nowhere to be seen. Ryan is toward the back with his usual crew.

I am barely functioning. I think I got about an hour of tormented sleep before I woke up with the chair idea, and then I was at my desk until I had to leave for school, making notes and sketches and plans. I was tired then, and I am even more tired now. My five-second cold shower only revived me temporarily, and my continued efforts at remaining conscious are not going very well so far. Diane keeps poking me awake.

Assistant Principal Jensen finally walks up to the podium and waits for us to quiet down. He thanks us all for our attention and our strength and courage in getting through what has been and continues to be such a difficult time, and he thanks Assistant Principal Levine for serving as acting principal for the past few days, and then he introduces us to Principal Morse's replacement.

The new guy vaults up onto the stage to say hello. His name is Kingston. He looks like an off-duty army general but without the crew cut. Tall and maybe somewhere in his late forties or early fifties and super fit looking and kind of handsome in an older-man kind of way. He grips the podium with both hands and gives a short little speech with just the right blend of *sorry we have to meet under these circumstances* and *we are going to get through this together* and *this is clearly the best student body ever* and *hey, isn't it exciting to be young and in high school?*

I don't like him. But that's probably just because of what happened to lead to him being here. Not his fault.

But I still don't like him.

For no real reason I turn around to look at Ryan and he's looking back at me across the auditorium. He doesn't like the new guy, either, I can tell.

We go through the motions of the day. Everything feels even less real than usual to me, thanks to my lack of sleep. I show up in classrooms and force my eyes to stay open and my head to stay upright. English, AP Physics, lunch, math, health, history. I can barely remember which class I'm in when. I write things down; I pretend to pay attention; I think about Annie and Ryan and Aaron and his demoness ladyfriend and above all Mr. Gabriel and what he will do if he finds out we are trying again to stop him. I try to seem cowed and beaten and exhausted, none of which is super hard right now. In the back of my mind, I gently cradle my plans for the Sweeney chair that I am going to start working on at rehearsal today. I exchange texts with Ryan between classes to confirm that we are both still alive.

When the bell finally rings at the end of history, I am relieved beyond all sense. I can sleep in study hall and then I can go to rehearsal and see Ryan and think about the play and the chair and not about demons or best friends who have gone crazy or anything else besides murderous barbers and pie shop proprietors and dead people being cooked into meat pies. Fun things. Just for a little while.

I turn the corner, heading toward study hall. Leticia and Diane had better *let* me sleep, or I will have to hurt them. I am thinking of possible ways I will need to reason with them when I suddenly realize that someone is standing in front of me.

I stop walking just in time to avoid a collision. Looking up, I see that the someone is our new principal.

"Well, hello!" he says in just the kind of booming voice you would imagine.

I try to muster up some kind of energy for a reply, but before I can even try to say hello back, he grabs my hand to give me an enthusiastic handshake.

The electric-shock feeling hits me as soon as his fingers close around mine.

Suddenly, I am very awake.

"Oh, *crap*," I say, staring up at him. His eyes, just for a second, flash with twiny black flames.

Principal Kingston raises his eyebrows at me. He does not release my hand.

"Well," he says. "That explains a few things."

He starts to say something else, then stiffens, glancing behind me. I feel a crawly tingly awfulness at the base of my spine, and sure as anything I know that what Principal Kingston is looking at is Mr. Gabriel.

There is a moment of silence.

I try to pull my hand free from Principal Kingston's grasp, but he won't let go. I twist around to look over my shoulder at Mr. Gabriel.

He smiles.

"I see you've met my friend Cynthia," he says. "She's a pain in the ass. Super-roach, you know." Except he doesn't say *super-roach*, he says that incomprehensible nonword with the pointy jagged syllables that hurt my ears, but I know what he means.

I'm still trying to pull my hand free from Principal Kingston's.

"I believe this territory is clearly marked," Mr. Gabriel goes on, talking over me to the other man. "Seriously, George, not cool."

"Your wards were weak," Kingston says, shrugging. "Looks like you're spreading yourself a little thin, John. Not focusing your energy in the best places, perhaps."

Mr. Gabriel looks at me then, and for a second his pleasant facade slips into a glare of pure fury. I realize in that moment that taking out Signor De Luca and being trapped, even temporarily, by our containment circle must have cost the librarian more than he'd let on.

"I've got it under control," he says, returning his gaze to the new principal. "Get lost."

"Well, *that's* not going to happen," Principal Kingston says. "I like it here. Have you seen my office? It's huge!"

I take my other hand and try to pry Principal Kingston's fingers loose. He doesn't even glance at me.

"So . . . how do you want to do this?" Mr. Gabriel's voice is closer and I pull a little more frantically at the principal's hand.

"Well, I'll be honest, John. I was thinking of just taking you out, taking this place over, setting up shop here until the battle."

"Trying."

Principal Kingston rolls his eyes a little. "Sure, right. Trying. But look, John. Maybe it doesn't have to be that way. Neither of us really needs to waste energy on that kind of thing, right?"

I take my foot and place it squarely against the principal's thigh for leverage as I continue my efforts to free my hand.

Mr. Gabriel sounds surprised. "Alliance?"

"Why not? Truce, at least. Maybe pool our resources. Then we can divvy up the school however makes the most sense, focus on getting ready for the big event."

There's a moment while the librarian apparently thinks this over. "Well, I'll admit, George, I would prefer not to deal with more distractions right now. I've got a lot on my plate."

"So, deal?"

"With terms."

"Of course," Principal Kingston agrees.

"I've selected a consort. She's off-limits, obviously."

"Obviously."

"And they're doing *Sweeney Todd* for the fall musical."

"Oh, yeah?" Principal Kingston is visibly arrested by this news. "Well, so the cast and crew is off-limits then, too, right? When's the show go up?"

"End of next week, actually. Perfect timing. I can get you the performance times."

"I adore *Sweeney Todd*. Have you seen any of the rehearsals? Do they have a good cast?"

"Excellent cast. Sweeney is amazing."

Principal Kingston shakes his head in happy disbelief. "I'm so excited."

I have stopped trying to extricate myself. I'm just standing there at this point, listening and staring back and forth between them.

Thinking of Ryan seems to remind Mr. Gabriel of my presence. He looks at me again, his smile fading.

I turn to Principal Kingston. "Okay, so, I'll just be going," I say.

Now they're both looking at me.

"Let me go," I tell Kingston very seriously.

His hand grips mine a little tighter.

"I'll scream," I say. And then I realize I shouldn't *tell* them; I should just start screaming. I inhale, but before I can make a sound, Principal Kingston yanks me forward and turns me around and wraps an arm around me, his hand clamping firmly over my mouth.

"What should we do with this one?" he asks Mr. Gabriel. "Together, we might be able to . . ."

Mr. Gabriel looks thoughtful. He takes a step forward.

"I'm tech director!" I shout into Kingston's hand, or try to. It comes out sounding pretty much like *MM MMm MMmm MMM!*

They both seem to understand me, however. Mr. Gabriel

makes a pained face. "The set's mostly done," he says. "She's probably replaceable."

I glare at him, ready to scream very unpleasant things at him through Principal Kingston's fingers, but then suddenly there are voices approaching. Kingston flings me away, and he and Mr. Gabriel turn as one toward the other end of the hall. They are all benign, friendly smiles and nonthreatening body language. The voices materialize into Mrs. Foster and Miss Daniels while I slam into the far wall, trying to catch my breath.

"Good afternoon, ladies!" Kingston booms. The ladies titter, even Mrs. Foster, who has to be about eighty years old.

I don't wait to see what happens next. I run.

I spend the rest of eighth period in the auditorium. Mr. Henry is there, but he just gives me a little salute and goes back to grading papers. He teaches freshman English when he is not teaching drama and directing awesome musicals.

I sit in my usual seat.

Our new principal is a demon.

And now he's, like, partnering up with Mr. Gabriel.

So instead of one demon, we have two.

I just want to make sure I'm getting it all straight in my head.

Shit.

I pretty much just sit there running those same few sentences through my head for the next half hour or so. Eventually the bell rings, and Mr. Henry puts his papers away and takes out his *Sweeney* notes. I watch kids start trickling into the auditorium.

Ryan arrives and sees at once that something new has happened.

"What now?" he asks, dropping into the seat beside me.

"Principal Kingston is a demon."

"Shit."

"Yeah. He's teaming up with Mr. Gabriel. They're going to share the school, I think. Until it's time for them to try to kill each other."

"Shit."

"Yeah."

"What are we going to do?"

"I don't know."

We sit there for a few minutes, not talking.

Finally, Ryan pokes me in the side. "Want to help me run lines?"

I shrug. "Okay."

We run his lines until Mr. Henry starts rehearsal proper. Today they're running all the chorus scenes. They begin with "God, That's Good!" in which all the townspeople are loving the meat pies, having no idea about the central secret ingredient. It's also the number in which Sweeney's fancy chair first makes its appearance. As much as I would love to, I don't have time to sit and watch. I grab my notebook and head backstage.

It is chair time, my friends.

I collect my tech minions and bring them out into the hall so we won't have to whisper.

"Okay, you guys," I say. I spread my notebook pages out on the floor before them. "This is what we're going to do."

There is minimal chatter. I have trained them well. A few intelligent questions and they are off and running.

I love my minions.

The new design is actually pretty simple. No crazy twisting, no backward flip down the trapdoor, no disembodied meat hooks that swoop down from above and impale the victims. (In my defense, I only *very* briefly entertained that last idea. It would have been cool, though.)

It's all about atmosphere this time.

Once Ryan has slashed his customer's throat, he'll pull a lever to open the trapdoor, which will reveal the pulsing red light of the fires — of the oven, and also a metaphoric representation of the fires of hell — below. Then the chair itself will tilt forward, letting the still-dying victim see exactly what is waiting there for him before he plunges down, terrified and bewildered, into heat and flame and death.

The stage lights will dim simultaneously each time this happens, and Sweeney (who is often singing and looking out at the audience while he murders people in the chair) will be partially bathed in a hellish red glow himself.

The flames, of course, will just be red and orange and yellow gels over lights, and there will be cushiony soft things for the victims to land on. And they'll be going front-first, so it will be even easier for them to land safely and correctly once they're out of view of the audience. It's going to work, and it's going to be awesome.

Mr. Henry wanders out with a cup of coffee; the cast must be taking a break.

"That the new chair plan?" he asks, nodding toward my papers.

"Yup." I gather them swiftly together and stick them back in my notebook.

"Not going to show me?"

"Nope. You'll have to wait and see."

He gives me a long, considering look as he takes a sip. "Is it going to work?"

"Yup."

He raises an eyebrow. "Is it going to be awesome?"

I grin. "Yup."

He nods. "All right, then. I trust you. Can't wait to see it." He starts to turn, then turns back and points at me. "Demo by Friday, yeah?"

"You got it, Mr. H."

He nods again and gives me a flourishy carry-on wave and wanders back into the auditorium.

I carry on.

The next morning, both Mrs. Foster and Miss Daniels are absent.

I push past more and more blank-eyed students in the hallway, making my way slowly to the library. It's ridiculously stupid of me, but I can't seem to stop myself.

Mr. Gabriel is in there alone, sitting at the circulation desk.

I walk up to the desk. "Did you kill them?"

He holds up one finger in a *just a moment* gesture, then finishes typing something at the computer before finally looking up. "I'm sorry, Cynthia. What were you saying?"

"Did you kill them?" I ask again.

"Kill whom?"

I try to give him a withering glance, but I don't really have it in me. Mostly I'm just feeling numb.

"Are you guys just going to keep killing people? Like, daily?"

He scoots over on his tall wheely chair until he's sitting opposite me.

"Not *daily*, no. Maybe every other day. We do have to kill people occasionally to maintain the gateway and stuff." He says this like he's explaining some library policy to me, like why the borrowing period is only two weeks (one week on audiovisual materials). "Besides, I told you someone extra was going to die because of your little extracurricular activity over the weekend. Did you like those two nice teachers? I do hope so. They died screaming, you know. Screaming and begging for mercy. It was fun."

"I really, really hate you," I say.

He smiles. "Oh, Cynthia. I can't wait until I win the throne and can really start in on cultivating Annie for her new life as my queen. I think, if I haven't already killed you, which is still kind of a toss-up, FYI, I'm going to see to it that we come visit you sometime. So you can see what I've done to her. You know, once it's really started."

"You've already started, you asshole."

He laughs, actually throwing back his head to guffaw with abandon. I wait until he regains enough control to speak.

"Oh, my dear girl. I haven't started at all. You wait. You'll see. I think I might have to leave you alive just to have the pleasure of showing you what real starting will look like."

I pick up my bag and wander back out into the hall. They are easy to spot all the time now — the students who just drift along, there but not-there, drained of some essential ingredient in their personalities. Here and there I see other kids who seem aware enough to look around them in confusion, wondering what the hell is wrong with everyone else. Some of the affected ones will come back to themselves later, or tomorrow, or the next day. They'll be relatively fine, like Leticia, or like Signor De Luca was, until he was dead. The ones who spend the most time around Mr. Gabriel, though, and now Principal Kingston, too . . . they probably won't really come back. They'll just keep getting worse, little by little, until there's nothing left of them at all.

I walk past Mrs. Foster's room, where another sub is writing some notes on the board.

I stop and lean against the wall.

This isn't going to work.

The deal we worked out, that *I* worked out — that deal with the demoness only comes into play when the actual fight for the throne takes place. Which seems to be at least a week and three-quarters away, because Gabriel and Kingston both seem pretty hell-bent on seeing *Sweeney Todd*.

Which means more and more people are going to get pieces of their souls sucked out.

And more and more people are going to die.

We can't just sit by and let that happen.

I can't.

We have to try something else.

Chapter | 12

In Italian, I tell Ryan about Mrs. Foster and Miss Daniels. This is feasible because Mr. Hubbard is a complete joke, and there are no consequences for talking or changing seats or anything else. Every once in a while he'll look up from whatever he's doing up there at Signor De Luca's desk and say, "I hope all that talking is being done in *Italian*," then stare around the room with what I suspect he believes is a very meaningful expression. Then he'll ignore us for a while again and pretend he thinks we're working on whatever lame textbook exercises he gave us to do.

"We have to do something," I say when I have brought Ryan up to date.

"We *are* doing something," he says. "Or you are, at least." He is somewhat frosty on this last point. We haven't really talked about my demoness deal since the night it happened. Clearly, he still does not think it is a wonderful idea.

"That's too far away. At least until after the show, and they're going to keep killing people until then!"

He looks around, I guess to make sure no one heard me. I suppose that is not really the sort of thing you should shout out in the middle of class. But no one is paying any attention.

"So what do you suggest?" he says finally.

"We could make Aaron contact the demoness again. We could ask her for advice."

"No way," he says. "Are you crazy? We can't trust either of them. It's too dangerous."

"It's too dangerous not to!"

"Cyn —"

"Ryan —"

It goes on like this all period.

It continues throughout the day, via text and one semi-heated whispered conversation in the hallway after seventh period. He is making me crazy, and not in the usual good-crazy way. This is bad crazy. This is angry crazy. I don't understand how he can be so stubborn. Also, it's confusing to feel both kinds of crazy at the same time. I still want to tear his clothes off, but now I also want to punch him until he sees reason. (And no, FYI: I'm not advocating violence as way to solve your differences. Just because I *want* to punch him doesn't mean I *would*. [Just as I am not, alas, tearing his clothes off just because I want to.] But he sure has been making the idea tempting today. [The punching idea. The tearing-off-his-clothes idea is always tempting.])

When the bell rings, and Ryan appears to be inclined to

make his way to his eighth-period class, I grab his arm. "We're not done here."

He looks at me, then sighs and nods. "Okay. Come with me."

I follow him down the stairs and past the gym and through what I guess might be the gym teachers' (currently unoccupied) office and then into a large closet that appears to be the final resting place of a lot of old sports equipment no one has had the heart to throw away. Ryan closes the door behind us. We sit among the torn hockey nets and deflated basketballs. We're each leaning against opposite walls, but the room is narrow enough that our legs come to about the same place in the middle. They're not quite touching, but they could be.

There's only a little dim light coming in through the door's tiny window. For a moment we just sit there, and I can't help it, for a few seconds I forget about all the terrible demon crap and even that I'm angry and just feel excited to be hiding with my hopeless crush in a dark, dirty closet, cutting class and sitting in close proximity. I can feel my calves straining to close the few inches that separate them from Ryan's. My nerve endings are so greedy. *He's right there,* I tell them silently. *Can't you just be happy that he's right there?* They cannot. They want more, and I can't really blame them. They want to touch him. They want to mingle in codependent bliss with his nerve endings. They send suggestive messages about what can happen in dark rooms when a boy and a girl are alone together and at least one of them has the wherewithal to make a move. I try to block out these very appealing images. Now is not the time.

If not now, when? they whisper back at me. My left leg twitches, trying to edge closer.

Stop it, I tell them more firmly. No one is making a move. No one is just going to "go for it" here in the old-sports-equipment graveyard; no one is going to lean in and kiss anyone; and no, absolutely not, no one is going to very slowly just casually begin to take off their clothes NO THEY ARE NOT STOP BEGGING STOP IT!

I clear my throat awkwardly. I have no idea what Ryan has been thinking about while I have been struggling against my baser impulses. I have no idea what he thinks about ever. I know he doesn't think about the kinds of things I think about, or else there would totally have been kissing that night when we were about to try to kill Mr. Gabriel. It is known among teenage girls (although not always acted upon, often to our eventual sorrow) that the best course is to judge boys by their actions, not their words. It's so easy to imagine what you want to imagine, to pretend that the things they say mean what you want them to mean. But when they have a chance to kiss you before they think they are about to die, and they do not so kiss you, it is a pretty clear sign that they are not secretly in love with you.

Of course, he knows now that *I* am secretly in love with *him.* Unless he thinks Mr. Gabriel just made that up. I try to believe that is possible. Ryan hasn't ever mentioned it or asked me about it or anything. And, as must go without saying, I have certainly not brought it up myself.

So what *is* his deal? I suppose he really could just want

to be my friend. Not "be my friend" in the sense of just not wanting to be my boyfriend, but actually *be my friend* — get to know me better, hang out with me, talk about stuff, whatever. But he's got so many friends already. I can't imagine he really needs another.

"So?" he says finally. "Got any other ideas that I can shoot down?"

I smile despite myself. "I've really only got the one," I say apologetically. I proceed cautiously. "I know you hate this plan, but I really think Aaron is our best chance."

"It's not a plan."

I don't say anything to this.

"Are you sure they're going to keep killing people?" he asks after a minute. "It wasn't just — just to punish us for the other night?"

My smile drops away. "It may have been partly about that. But Mr. Gabriel said they need to kill people to 'maintain the gateway,' which I guess is how they get here from . . . from wherever they were before. He seemed pretty clear that there will be more killing."

Ryan shakes his head, more in frustration, I think, than denial. "Why hasn't anyone noticed? At least three teachers have gone missing in the last week, and everyone knows that Principal Morse is *dead* —"

"They still think that was a heart attack, remember. Mr. Gabriel must have done something demony to make them overlook any blood he might have been . . . missing." I hurry on, not wanting to think too much about that. "And that sub said De Luca had some kind of family emergency . . . There's probably some very plausible and rational story circulating about Mrs. Foster and Miss Daniels, too."

"It just seems so unbelievable that everything — school, life, the show — everything just keeps going while teachers are dying and people are getting their souls sucked out. . . ."

Yeah. He is not wrong about that. And it's not actually that people haven't noticed at *all*. I've watched other kids stare around at the slow-moving students in the hallway, seen them try to snap their strangely unresponsive friends out of the inexplicable daze they seem to have fallen into, heard teachers whispering and wondering what the hell is going on with everyone lately. People can tell that something is wrong. They are not, on the whole, stupid. But maybe they also sense that what is wrong is not something that they can deal with or even truly believe, and so they let themselves get . . . distracted.

The show is actually one of the things distracting people. Which would be awesome — okay, it's still a little bit awesome — but it is also troubling. Because I feel more than a little guilty being part of something that's interfering with people realizing what's happening. But I also feel more than a little proud of being part of something that everyone is talking about.

Much of it is Ryan's doing, of course. He blows me away every time he gets up on that stage. And yes, okay, Ryan knocks me off my feet a little just by standing around and breathing. But he is *amazing* as Sweeney. It's not just me; everyone can see it. Mr. Henry is practically beside himself. And word is getting around. There is buzz among the populace. Everyone connected to the show is telling their friends, and even the teachers have been getting the word. Advance ticket sales are off the charts, which doesn't usually happen, I can tell you.

The other thing distracting people is Principal Kingston.

He's been here just over a day, but somehow it feels like he's been here much longer. He is a constant presence. His booming voice welcomed us this morning on the PA system just like he'd been doing it for years, and his energetic form is already somehow a familiar sight in the hallways. He pops into classrooms to see what's going on; he attended last night's volleyball game and a Model Congress session. Impossibly quickly, he is becoming beloved by both students and teachers. Perhaps on some unconscious level they take in his virile good humor and can-do attitude and obvious physical strength and leadership qualities and they think he's going to be able to save us from whatever is happening.

Which would be funny, if it weren't so horrible.

"That's why we have to do something," I say again, bringing us back around, full circle.

Ryan looks at me in the semidarkness. I still have no idea what he is thinking. Why are boys you like always so hard to read?

"You're right," he says finally. "We do have to do something. But not that. Not Aaron again. Not summoning more demons."

I suddenly remember how the demoness had him dangling there in Aaron's apartment, threatening to rip him apart. I, at least, have my roachy goodness to protect me in some ways. He's entirely vulnerable. I don't know why this didn't occur to me until now. I'm such an idiot. No wonder he hates this plan.

Hesitantly, I try: "But if Aaron made a different kind of containment circle, one that wouldn't let her hurt us —"

"We couldn't trust him to do what we asked. You know that, Cyn."

I do know that. "Yeah," I say reluctantly. "But . . ."

"Just — let's take a little more time to try and think of something else. Okay? You're right, we can't just sit back and let people die when we're the only ones who know what's really going on. Of course not. But there's got to be something else we can try. Give me at least another day."

"All right."

But I am lying.

It's not all right. And I am not going to give him another day. I appear to have decided, just in this moment, that I am going to go to see Aaron on my own, and not tell Ryan. Because I know what needs to be done, and I don't need his permission, and I don't need to force him into a position where he does something he's terrified to do in order to try to prove that he's not terrified. Which is surely what would happen if I keep pushing on this. Or if I told him I was going to go alone.

But I *will* go alone. I will take care of it and that will be that. Depending on how it goes, I might tell him later. Or not.

He smiles at me in the dimness, and I feel guilty but also certain that I am making the right call.

I smile back. Argument over. Yay.

"So," he says, raising an eyebrow. "What should we do for the rest of the period?" He is looking straight at me.

My throat closes up and I need a few seconds to remind myself that he *does not like me that way*, and so clearly he didn't mean that to sound the way it sounded. My nerve endings all jumped instantly to attention at his words, of course (they like to believe what they want to believe, even though I know better, and they have all *kinds* of ideas for what we should do for the rest of the period), and I know I will just have to try to patiently talk them down. But their influence is hard to ignore; I feel my smile go twisty before I can get myself under control.

"What?" Ryan asks, his own smile growing twisty in response. Which (a) doesn't help, because *oh my God* his twisty smile is ridiculously sexy, and (b) doesn't mean anything, since it's clearly just some automatic mirroring thing, not actually a sign that he knows what I am thinking and is thinking the same.

Unless he does know what I am thinking. Unless he did believe what Mr. Gabriel said, and he knows that I like him and is enjoying how easy it is to make me blush. Can he tell that I'm blushing? It's probably too dark in here for that. Definitely. Definitely too dark.

"What?" I say back. "Nothing. What do you mean? I don't know. What time is it?"

I bite the inside of my lip to stop myself from adding any other inane comments to this already impressive array. He shakes his head, eyes crinkling, and I don't know what that means either. It's so easy to imagine exactly what we could do in here for the remaining time before the bell rings. Alone, undisturbed, in the semidarkness, enjoying a moment of respite from the horrible evil danger we know is waiting out there in the rest of the world. I wish so much that I had the guts to just close the space between us and kiss him.

You can! You can! my pounding heart insists. Or maybe that's my loins talking. It's hard to tell them apart at times like this. They're all tangled up together.

You and Ryan could be all tangled up together.

SHUT UP. My whole body is a traitorous mass of unrealistic impulses and faulty decision-making skills. Obviously, there is no way I can try to kiss him. If he wanted to kiss me, there would have been kissing by now. If I made a move, it would be an awkward and terrible disaster. Catastrophic. And we have to work together on this whole demon thing. Not to mention get through the rest of the show. And if I went to kiss him and he didn't want to, I would never be able to look him in the eyes again, ever.

But what if he does want to kiss me? What if he did mean to sound suggestive? What if that was his way of making an actual suggestion?

But it wasn't. I'm sure that it wasn't.

Was it?

I look back at him, and I'm sure I must look as confused as I feel. He holds my gaze for another few seconds before getting up to his feet.

"Auditorium until rehearsal?" (We have rehearsal every day now, since the show is getting so close.) He reaches down to help me up.

I take his hand, which makes everything a million times worse, but in the best of all possible ways.

"Sure."

Right before he lets go, he gives my hand a little squeeze.

I have no idea what that means either.

But I liked it anyway.

We say hi to Mr. Henry and then I tell Ryan I'm going to go work on the chair. Which is partly true. I go backstage to survey the progress being made so far and to plan out what needs to happen next. But once I hear Mr. Iverson start the vocal warm-ups, I leave things in the hands of my capable minions and slip out through the backstage door.

Then I pay a visit to Books of Darkness.

I take the bus, which is slow and annoying, but it gives me time to think. And to recover from all that time alone in the semidark with Ryan.

Aaron is not overjoyed to see me. He can tell at once that I want something. And I think it makes him nervous that Ryan isn't with me. Like he can tell that I want something of which Ryan does not approve.

"What?" he says ungraciously.

I tell him what. There is some arguing. But I win. I have to win, in the end. Because if I don't hold up my end of the deal, he doesn't get to go to the demon world to live forever in demony bliss with his scary ladylove. And so he has an interest in keeping me happy and marching onward unflinchingly toward that final battle.

He summons the demoness for me. She does not seem very surprised.

"Hello, worm. Hello, roach."

I roll my eyes. "Ha-ha, once again, so funny. Seriously, that never gets old."

"What do you want?" she says, and it sounds as though she is really curious and not just annoyed. Maybe she is hoping I will want to make another deal.

"There's another demon at school. He's pretending to be the new principal."

The demoness nods. "Yes, word has been getting around about that sweet setup your librarian has going on. It's not surprising that other demons are starting to push their way through."

"But—how can they? I mean, if it was that easy, why aren't they all over the place, all the time?"

"Oh, it's not that easy. Not usually. But your demon has already created a gateway into the school, you see. And until recently, he had it strongly warded, to prevent followers. But the wards were weakened, and now he can't keep everyone else out. They're starting to find their way in."

And I realize, again, that it's my fault. I made Mr. Gabriel divert his attention or his energy or whatever, by trying to stop him, and that made his wards get weak, and that let the other demons start to get through.

Demons.

Plural.

"Wait. You mean—you mean *more* demons are coming?"

She smiles. "Oh, I'm certain of it."

"How many are we talking about?"

She shrugs. "Hard to say. But there's a limit, since all the demons will need fresh kills to help maintain their power once they get through, and if enough people die, some of your kind are going to take notice, and that could become — inconvenient."

I blink at her. "Well — what can we do? How can we stop them?"

Now she laughs, pointy teeth flashing. "You cannot stop them, my dear. If they can push their way through, they're going to. There's nothing you can do about that." She seems to notice my distress. "But don't worry. Most of them are minor demons. As long as none of them are real contenders for the throne, our deal will still be good, and you will still get to bring down your librarian demon and save your little friend."

This is not at all the conversation I'd hoped we'd be having. I know she said before that she couldn't stop Mr. Gabriel from killing in general, but I thought — I don't know — she'd have some tips or something, at least for stopping Mr. Gabriel and Principal Kingston from killing people left and right, day after day. I am realizing that I have perhaps been a bit naive.

"But — but you're saying that in the meantime, more and more demons will be showing up and sucking out people's souls and killing people?" Why does she not see that this is a problem? "We can't just sit around and let that happen!"

"Not really much you can do about it, I'm afraid. Just try to keep your head down until after the show on opening night. That's when things will be . . . happening."

This is how Alice in Wonderland must have felt. I mean, yes, Alice seemed to take events pretty well, all things considered, but still. Every conversation she had in that book made less sense than the one before, and eventually all connection to reality was basically stripped away to nothing. These conversations I have been having with demons make me feel that way.

"Opening night? You mean, of *Sweeney*?" That can't really be what she means, but I don't know how else to interpret it. "How do you even know about that?"

"Oh, everyone knows about that. That's half the draw, I think, honestly. All demons love *Sweeney Todd,* you know. And it sounds like your boyfriend is really amazing. I can't wait to see it."

I am trying very hard to come up with something to say when the demoness winks out and is gone.

I spin around to look at Aaron.

"Sorry," he says. "I can't hold her here. She was done talking, I guess. They're not big on good-byes and stuff." He doesn't seem put out by this, however. If you can still want to be with someone who sticks her finger-claw remotely into your guts and makes you bleed, I guess you don't really sweat the little things like good-byes.

The show is still a week and a half away. That's a lot more time for killing and soul-sucking and additional demons. There has to be something we can do in the meantime. There has to be.

I look at Aaron.

He is gazing lovingly at the circle where his demoness had been. Or her likeness or projection or whatever.

I already know he is not someone I can trust. I try, half-heartedly, to convince myself that maybe I can. I mean, he wants me to survive and carry out my part of the bargain and all that, right? He's not going to mess with that.

But he might. He might make some other deal, or he might just get overexcited and screw things up again. I can't risk it. Which is really too bad, because he is the only person I know who knows anything at all about demons.

And then I stop, and stand there, frowning.

I have just been struck with a really unpleasant idea.

I take a cab back to school and even get in some actual work before rehearsal ends. Ryan does not seem to have noticed I was gone. He gives me a ride home, and on the way we talk about how great the show is going to be and pointedly avoid all other topics.

The next day at school, before homeroom, as has become usual since Annie stopped speaking to me, I sit with Diane in the hallway that everyone calls the band wing, which is next to the auditorium. Diane, as a clarinet player, has a legitimate reason to hang out in the band wing, but no one really needs a legitimate reason to be there. It's just one of those places people go. Mostly the theater crowd and the band crowd, but occasional other random people, too.

We sit on the floor, our backs to a row of lockers. We're just sitting, not talking, which is something I can do with Diane that I can't do with many other people. She does a good companionable silence. We're both kind of lost in our own thoughts, staring into space. We both notice the shoes that have stopped in front of us at about the same time.

"Excuse me," a polite voice says. "Can you tell me where the office is? I seem to have gotten turned around."

We look up. A middle-aged woman smiles hesitantly down at us. A new sub, I'm guessing. Diane points left.

The sub turns to follow the direction of Diane's finger, squints, then turns back. "Um, thanks."

She leaves.

I watch her walk to the end of the hallway and ask someone else, who also points left. The woman wanders off. Just before she disappears from view, two more unfamiliar adults walk by, a man and a woman this time, from the opposite direction.

As they pass the junction with the band wing, they turn their heads. Slowly and simultaneously.

They are looking at me.

Invisible fingers seem to crawl up my back. I shudder involuntarily.

"You okay?" Diane asks.

"Uh, yeah. Just a chill or something." I smile reassuringly at her before looking back down the hall.

The strangers keep their eyes on me until they cross out of my line of sight.

I count three more unfamiliar faces in the next ten minutes.

Then there's a familiar one.

"Hey," Ryan says. This is new. I don't usually see him in the band wing in the morning. Usually he's off hanging out with his friends (his other friends?) in the cafeteria or the school yard or wherever they like to go.

"Hey," I say back, squinting up at him. "What's up?"

Diane suddenly remembers something she needs to do somewhere else. Before she goes she makes kissy faces at me behind Ryan's back until I successfully glare her away.

Ryan slides down next to me, taking Diane's place against the locker. For one crazy second I think maybe he's going to say something about us, about how he doesn't just want to be friends, about how he really wanted to kiss me in the sports closet yesterday but didn't quite have the nerve.

"What's up with all the subs?" he asks.

I close my eyes. *Stupid, Cyn. He does not like you that way.*

"I think they're demons," I say.

"Seriously?"

"Yeah. Not all of them, maybe. I think there was one we saw earlier who was just a regular human woman. But some of them are definitely not, you know, normal. I mean even for subs."

"Huh," Ryan says. "That doesn't seem good."

"Nope."

Silence. Then: "Why are your eyes closed?"

"I don't know." *So I don't have to see how close you are and still so incredibly far away.* I open them. He's looking at me oddly. "What?"

"You're a strange one sometimes, you know that?" He's sort of half smiling as he says this, I guess to communicate the fact that he doesn't mean it to sound entirely like an insult. But it's clearly not entirely a compliment either.

"Um. Thanks?"

Before he can say whatever he might have said next, a pair

of burly unfamiliar security guards wanders down the hall toward us. They both turn to stare at me as they go by. Their faces are long and blank; their eyes look dead and empty. Ryan and I stare up at them silently until they finally have to look away or start walking backward. And then one of them actually does start walking backward, so he can keep looking at me, until the other one notices and gives him a smack on the shoulder and makes him turn back around.

"Okay, those guys were hardly even trying to pass for human," Ryan says. "That's just sloppy workmanship."

There are ten more minutes until homeroom. I want to close my eyes again. I don't want to see how many more demons there are at school today.

I keep my eyes open anyway, though.

We sit there on the floor, watching too many students with listless expressions, watching not enough others looking concerned and suspicious. I sit, and I enjoy the fact that Ryan is sitting next to me (he is also capable of a good companionable silence, it seems), and I try not to think too much about what I have decided to do later this morning.

After Italian, during which I try to act just like someone who does not have a troubling and secret plan up her sleeve, I ditch second period and force myself to go to the library. I stand outside for several minutes before I can successfully make myself go in.

Mr. Gabriel is seated with a laptop at one of the tables, working on a PowerPoint presentation about the Dewey decimal system.

"Really?" I can't help it; it just slips out.

He clicks Save and turns to face me, ignoring my question. "Can I help you with something, Cynthia?" he asks.

Okay. Okay, go.

"Yes," I make myself say. Then I make myself sit down at the table across from him.

He looks at me, eyebrows raised expectantly.

Deep breath. Then: "I might be willing to make a deal, after all."

His eyebrows climb even farther up toward his hairline.

"But not the one you offered that day at rehearsal. Something else."

He tilts his head slightly toward the library doors, and I hear the lock slide into place.

"I'm listening," he says.

"So, okay. I could not help but notice that you are no longer the only demon invader in the school," I begin. "I mean, obviously Principal Kingston is another one, but I know there are more. I saw several of them this morning. And I get the sense that they might not be the last."

Mr. Gabriel says nothing. He just watches me, waiting.

"And I heard what Principal Kingston said, about the wards or whatever, and how they got weak because you were, uh, distracted. With other things."

"Indeed." His eyes are getting that look like they want to start twining and flaming at me.

"So, I get that that's maybe a little bit my fault. That you got distracted," I go on quickly. "And while I still, you know, hate you and everything, I am not exactly excited about

239

having all these extra demons here, sucking out souls and stuff. And so I'm wondering if there's anything that I can do, to help you strengthen the ward-things again and stop more demons from showing up. I know that this roach thing I've got going on gives me some resistance . . . I thought, maybe, I could help you somehow, using it."

Mr. Gabriel leans back in his chair, still looking at me.

I wait.

"What are you up to?" he asks finally. "I know you're not just giving up on trying to stop me. You *can't* stop me, but I know you won't really accept that. I can't figure out your angle here."

"There is no angle. I mean, yes, you're right, I haven't given up on trying to save Annie," I say. "But I haven't yet figured out how to do that, and in the meantime, I can't just sit here and let more people die and get their souls siphoned away until there's nothing left. Not if there's a chance that I could help stop it. Having you here is bad enough; having you and a whole bunch of other demons sucks even worse."

He squints at me, then shakes his head. "I don't get you, Cynthia. I offered you a free pass, for you and your hopeless love interest, and you turned it down."

"Because for that deal I had to give up on Annie. And I won't give up on Annie. This time I'm the one making the offer, and so I get to set the terms." I pause, then add, "And my love interest is *not* hopeless. There's been significant progress!" That's not exactly true, of course, but Mr. Gabriel doesn't need to know that.

"Kudos," he says. "What are your terms, then?"

"I help you close your gates or whatever to stop more demons from coming through. In return . . . can you stop the demons who are already here from killing and draining everyone?"

He's still squinting at me. "You realize I'm still planning to kill and drain pretty much everyone myself at the end, right?"

"I know you're planning to try. I told you, I haven't given up on trying to find a way to stop you. This gives me more time. And if nothing else it gives everyone a stay of execution, right?"

"Hmm."

I can see he doesn't think this is a good enough deal for me. I can't let him get suspicious. "And you promise that no matter what, you won't hurt Ryan. You won't hurt him or kill him or suck out any of his soul or let Principal Kingston or any other demons hurt him either. Not just until the show, but forever."

I should have thought of asking for that before, anyway. My deal with the demoness only really obligates her to *try* not to let him die. Not quite as much of a guarantee as I would like.

"Ah," he says. "Now, that makes more sense."

"I want to save everyone," I say. "But if I can't — then I at least want to save him."

This is absolutely true. And I think Mr. Gabriel can hear it in my voice.

He stops squinting and leans forward, hands clasped on the table, all business. "The only way to reinforce my wards at this point is through a significant ritual sacrifice," he says. "I thought about arranging some mass poisoning in the

cafeteria or something, but the consequences of killing a suf-
ficient number of people would be too much for me to easily damp out. Police would come, the school might be closed
down . . . I can't risk it. Not now.

"If you are indeed willing to help me, however, there is
another possibility. I could kill the other demons who have
come through instead. That would actually be a far more powerful sacrifice, and of course no one would miss them."

Now it is my turn to be squinty. "Why haven't you done
that already, then?"

"I can't do it myself. I need to kill them all at once for the
sacrifice to work, which would require luring them to some
single location, and there's no way I could do that without raising suspicion. But you . . . there is a way that you could help me
get them all in one place. It's actually something that you are
uniquely qualified to do."

He goes on to explain that all I would need to do is "tag"
them for him. Which turns out to basically just mean touching
them after dipping my hands in some special substance that
Mr. Gabriel will provide. That's it. The tagging will allow Mr.
Gabriel to draw them all to one place, probably without them
even realizing they're being drawn, and then he and Principal
Kingston will kill them and fix the wards.

"But — Kingston — ?"

"I can't hurt Kingston until the actual battle, because of
our truce. Which means he'll have to be in on this plan. And
it will work better with the two of us anyway. And that part
isn't your problem. All you need to do is tag the others. I don't
think it will be very difficult for you. They've all heard there's a

super-roach here, and they will be interested in you, which will let you get close. But your resistance means they won't be able to charm or glamour you or otherwise get inside your head or turn you from your objective, even if they have minor protection spells going. And they'll never suspect you're working with me. If I tried to compel anyone else to do this, they'd be able to detect my influence. But you'll be clean, acting of your own free will, and they will never know what's coming."

I have to admit that I am not exactly excited about helping to kill a whole bunch of demons. I don't think I could be excited about killing anyone, demons or not, present company excluded. But if I don't, more human people are going to die. So, easy decision. Save Ryan, save at least some of the other students and teachers in the school, and cut down on the amount of life-energy sucking that will be going on between now and the show.

Yeah, it's not perfect, I know. But I think it's the best I can do.

I extend my hand toward the librarian, and we shake on it.

"Deal," I say.

"Deal."

Chapter | 13

I am pretty much ready to start right in here, get with the tagging, let's do this thing, etc. But of course there are preparations and Mr. Gabriel needs to confab with Principal Kingston and so I am sent off to class with instructions to come back later.

So now it is later, and back I come. I ignore my twinges of guilt at keeping all of this a secret from Ryan. It would be wrong to tell him. Selfish. He would only be mad, and it's too late for him to try to talk me out of it anyway. I just need to get through this on my own. And it's not even that big a thing. It's not like I have to kill the demons myself. All I have to do is touch them. Easy peasy.

Principal Kingston is sitting at one of the long tables, flipping through a copy of *Sports Illustrated*. He looks up as the doors close behind me.

"Our little roach girl! Come in, come in. Mr. Gabriel's finishing up in the back. Have a seat!" He indicates the chair across from him.

I sit and look at him warily.

"I have to say, I was surprised when Mr. Gabriel told me about your offer," he says, leaning forward over his magazine. "But I think it's fantastic that you're able to see the big picture here. Thinking outside the box and all that. And even if your reasons are a little misguided, I am happy to be doing business with you. People so rarely consider alliances with their enemies to reach the greater goal these days. It's a shame, really." He shakes his head, apparently at the shame of it all. "So! How are your classes going?"

I am saved from ridiculous small talk with the demon principal by the demon librarian's emergence from the office behind the circulation desk. He's carrying a large blue ceramic bowl with both hands, which he places on the table in front of me.

"All right," he says. "Ready to begin?"

"How is this going to work, exactly?" I ask. All kinds of misgivings are starting to flutter around deep in my belly region. I ignore them as best I can.

"All you need to do is place your fingers in this liquid. It will make you able to tag the other demons with just a touch, and I'll be able to draw them to where we want them. You let me know when you've got them all, and then Principal Kingston and I will take it from there."

I look at the liquid dubiously. It looks like dish soap.

"What is it?"

"Palmolive. The base substance doesn't really matter, although thicker liquids tend to hold the magic a little better."

"And this stuff smells a lot better than, say, tar or congealed gravy," Kingston adds.

They are both looking at me expectantly.

I push back my sleeves and take my rings off, then gingerly lower my fingers into the bowl. It is so almost exactly like soaking your cuticles pre-manicure that I am half expecting Principal Kingston to whip out a nail file. Instead he glances at Mr. Gabriel and then reaches out and clamps his hands over mine, holding them in place.

"Hey! What—"

"This next part might hurt a little," Mr. Gabriel says from behind me. "But it's important that you don't take your fingers out until I'm finished. Principal Kingston is just helping to make sure that happens."

My misgivings have exploded forth from the little corner I had stuffed them into and are flinging themselves around inside me like mad, damaged birds. I had instantly tried to jerk my hands away when Kingston grabbed them, but it's like being encased in concrete. They didn't move a millimeter.

"This wasn't part of the deal." I direct my words over my shoulder to Mr. Gabriel.

"We never discussed the details. You should have asked more questions. And anyway, it won't be *that* bad. It only hurts for a few seconds. Now be quiet and let's get this over with."

I don't really have much choice. I sit and glare at the principal, who smiles pleasantly back at me.

Mr. Gabriel starts saying some of those jagged-edged words and suddenly my fingers feel like they have burst into flames. The world goes red and after a second I realize I am screaming. The Palmolive has clearly become acid or liquid fire or something equally horrible and Mr. Gabriel's voice gets louder and Principal Kingston is nodding at me encouragingly across the table. I throw myself backward, or try to, but Kingston's hands still have mine fast and all I succeed in doing is twisting my arms painfully and nearly falling out of my chair.

"Stop it! Please, stop it, oh, my God my *hands*—" My initial shocked screams have mutated into crying, pleading whimpers. The pain is beyond anything I've ever experienced. I can barely process that I'm actually feeling this. It doesn't seem possible.

Mr. Gabriel growls a few final syllables and there's kind of a silent *whoosh* and it feels like something is being sucked in through my fingertips and then the fire goes out and there's just a throbbing memory of awfulness. Principal Kingston releases me and I yank my hands back, terrified of what I will see, expecting the flesh to have melted clean away to bone, or worse. But there's nothing. I hold them up, twisting them around. There's no evidence of what they have just suffered through. They don't even have a soapy residue.

"Oh, you're fine," Mr. Gabriel says dismissively. "Teenagers are such babies."

"You *asshole*," I say, standing up to, I don't know, maybe punch him in the face or something, but he steps neatly back and just points to the chair.

"Sit down so we can go over what you need to do. A deal's a deal, Cynthia."

I stand there a moment longer, my poor hands curled into furious fists at my side. Then I sit back down. Because he's right, and I still have a job to do. And the quicker we get on with things, the quicker I can get the hell out of here.

They think there are about twenty other demons in the school at this point. They know about the security guards, and most of the rest are probably subs. All I have to do is touch them, skin to skin. Hands are probably easiest, but I am welcome to use my imagination. Once I get them all, to the best of my knowledge, I am to let either Gabriel or Kingston know. And then I'm done.

There's one more thing.

"You need to be able to tell who the demons are, of course," Mr. Gabriel says, which sounds reasonable, except there is something about the way he says it that makes my nerve endings shudder, and not in that good Ryan kind of way. Also, I am still extra-hating him for the acid-dish-soap thing.

He takes a step toward me. I get up out of the chair so I can back away more easily.

"Okay," I say. "How will I do that?"

"You need to let me touch your eyes."

I back away some more. "No way."

"It won't hurt."

"That is not the point. There's got to be another option."

Mr. G. shakes his head. "There's not. Don't be difficult." He comes toward me again, and I run around to the other side of the table.

Principal Kingston gets casually up out of his chair and grabs my arms, yanking them up behind my back.

"Ow! What are you, his hired thug? Get off me!"

"Now, Cynthia. Don't make such a fuss. Mr. Gabriel is just making it possible for you to carry out your side of the bargain. An unfulfilled bargain satisfies no one." He makes it sound like something you'd have embroidered on a pillow. He pulls my arms up another painful couple of inches. "Stop whining and do what needs doing, young lady. I don't want to have to send you to detention, but I will if you make me."

Mr. Gabriel has by this point circled around the table. He reaches out and takes hold of my face with one hand, his fingers resting just under my jawbone and his thumb pressing into the skin below my eye.

"Now, just hold still," he says softly, and the thumb and forefinger of his other hand come slowly at my face, in pretty much the way they would if he were about to gouge my eyes out. I clamp my eyes tightly shut. I expect him to try to force them open, but he just makes an exasperated sound, and his fingertips come to rest on my eyelids instead. There is a flare of power that makes me gasp, but it's not quite pain I'm feeling, and so I guess he's not exactly a liar. About this part. After a second they both release me.

I open my eyes.

Mr. Gabriel and Principal Kingston stand a few feet away, watching me. I stare despite myself. They both have a kind of red glowing halo above their heads.

"All the demons are going to have that?" I ask.

"Yes."

"How long will it last?"

Mr. Gabriel shrugs. "Not sure. Long enough, anyway. Now, off you go."

No one needs to tell me twice. Off I go indeed.

My fingers are still throbbing quietly as I walk down the hall outside the library. They don't hurt anymore, exactly; it's more of a pulsing hyperawareness. I find it hard to believe that other people can't see it. I hope the demons will be as unsuspecting as they are supposed to be. I realize too late that I forgot to ask what happens if I touch a non-demon. That seems like important information, but there is no way I am going back in there now. They might decide I need some other dose of demon magic to better serve the bargain. I will just not touch any non-demons until this thing is over with.

I begin seeing the demons right away. I have to admit, the halo thing is pretty handy. Not all of them are as obviously inhuman as the security guards.

But, God, there sure are a lot of them. I think Gabriel and Kingston's estimate of twenty was a bit on the conservative side.

I approach the security guards first, because they seem kind of stupid and also because they are standing conveniently nearby. Security guards in our school don't generally wander around in pairs, but I guess these two only did minimal research.

They stare again as soon as they notice me. I decide to use that as my opening.

"What?" I say, marching over to them. "Why do you keep staring at me?"

"We know what you are," one of them says in a scratchy voice. "Roach." Only he really says that horrible demon word for it, of course.

"I don't know what you're talking about," I lie. I flip my hair angrily. "Who's your boss? I'm going to tell him you're acting inappropriately toward the female students."

I turn as if to go, and the guard on the left grabs my wrist. *Gotcha.* I start, naturally, trying to pry his fingers loose. There is a slight feedback vibration, different from the static-electricity feeling I have come to expect — kind of like typing on a virtual keyboard with the vibrate feature turned on. I take this to mean the tagging has been successfully accomplished. The demon does not seem to notice.

The second demon puts his hand out, clearly intending to push the other one back warningly (he seems to be the brains of the operation, such as they are), but I deliberately misinterpret his movement and slap his hand away. "Don't you start, too!" I snap.

The first one lets go, finally, and I take a step back. "If you bother me again, I really am going to tell," I say. I turn to leave, and this time they don't try to stop me.

Two down, a whole lot more to go.

After a few awkward oops-my-hand-slipped-so-that-it-accidentally-touched-your-hand maneuvers and other nonideal approaches, I finally settle on appointing myself the student government welcome ambassador for the new substitute teachers. There's no way they can really know there's no such thing, and it allows me to march right up and shake their hands while explaining my nonexistent role as their student liaison.

There end up being thirty-two all together. I think. I'm making my third full circuit of the school, blowing off yet another class, and I don't encounter any more glowing red halos that I haven't already tagged. If there are secret demons hiding out in secret rooms somewhere, I don't know how to seek them out. And the day is almost over, and I want to be finished.

I head back to the library. Mr. Gabriel is showing his Dewey decimal PowerPoint presentation to a group of students, but he looks up when I poke my head in.

"All finished with that special project, Cynthia?"

"Yes, Mr. Gabriel. Just wanted to let you know."

He thanks me and I retreat, relieved to be done. It's a study hall day, and so I can just go and sit and try not to think too much until rehearsal. I reflect a little anxiously that if we do end up surviving this mess, I'm going to have some serious work ahead of me to catch up in all my classes. But whatever; that's still way, way better than dying. And not my immediate problem anyway. I have had a weird, hard day; I deserve forty-five minutes of peace and quiet.

I look up and see that Ryan is leaning against the wall ahead of me.

For the first time in pretty much ever, I am not one hundred percent happy to see him.

"Hey, you okay?" he asks. "You haven't been texting. I

wanted to make sure Mr. Gabriel didn't kill you or something."
He smiles, even though it's not actually funny.

I smile back anyway, because even now I can't help but smile back. But I don't want to talk about what I've been doing all day, and I don't want to lie, and I'm not sure how I can avoid both of those things at the same time.

"Yeah, sorry. I'm fine. Just distracted, I guess."

His too-perceptive eyes take me in for a few seconds. "You sure?"

Dammit. "Yeah. You know, it's just — just everything. Sometimes I succeed more than others in not thinking bad thoughts. I'll be okay." I give him another smile, a little twisty despite myself. "Better already, in fact."

I can't quite believe I just said that.

He smiles again too, a little wider than before. Acknowledging my accidental flirting? Liking it? Embarrassed on my behalf and trying to cover for it? As usual, I cannot read him at all. But I can feel myself grinning stupidly back at him. Even with everything else going on, his smile still makes me have trouble standing. And thinking. And breathing.

After one more awkward moment in which I simultaneously want him to look away and to never, never look away ever, he says he'd better get to class. Before he leaves, he takes my hand and squeezes.

"It'll be okay," he says. "We'll think of something. No giving up, right?"

"Right."

I don't know where this recurring hand-squeezing thing is coming from, but I am not going to complain.

He gives me one of those chin-first nods and walks away.

It's not until he's gone that I remember how I wasn't going to touch any non-demons.

Crap.

I don't know what to do. I can't run after him. I mean, I *could*, but then what? I really, really don't want to tell him about my side deal with the librarian. And probably the tagging doesn't even work on people at all. Wouldn't Mr. Gabriel have mentioned that, if it did?

Probably not, actually.

The bell rings, and I make myself go inside. It will be fine. I'm sure it will be fine.

I take out a book and stare at it, not reading.

And then, after a few minutes, my fingers suddenly feel — odd. *More* odd. The throbbing intensifies, and I find myself staring at the wall. Through the wall. Toward — what? I want to get up. I want to get up and go out and walk down that hall.

It's the librarian, I realize stupidly. He's drawing the tagged demons to the place where he and Kingston are going to kill them. I can feel the pull of whatever he's doing. It's not quite compelling me to go. I can feel it, and it makes me want to move toward that place, but I can resist it. It's like when you know there's ice cream in the freezer and you really want it and you have to sit there reminding yourself about how you really, *really* want to fit into those pants you bought that are a little too tight and so should not eat the ice cream and you know this and so you can resist, but it's hard and unpleasant. But you can still do it. Usually.

But what if I'm able to resist not because I'm human, but

because of my roach thing? What if Ryan is also feeling the draw and can't resist?

He won't even know that he should. He'll just feel like he wants to go there. It might not even occur to him to question why he wants to go.

I get up as slowly and casually as I can and take the bathroom pass from the front of the room. The teacher covering study hall doesn't even look up from her papers. I walk slowly over to the door and open it and step through and close it behind me.

And then I run.

I let my pulsing fingers lead me down one hall and then another. I realize I was sort of assuming the destination would be the library, but instead I'm being drawn up another floor, to one of the science labs. I pass a couple of demons who are walking along, chatting, not really noticing where they're headed. "Hey, no running in the halls!" one of them calls after me.

I keep running, obviously.

The throbbing in my fingers is getting even stronger. I can tell now that the place I'm being drawn to is the last lab at the far end of the hall. Partly this is because of the intensity of the throbbing, but it is also because Ryan is standing outside, his hand on the doorknob.

I manage a burst of extra speed and throw myself at him, tackling him to the ground almost in the way I used to fantasize about, except for the throbbing fingers and the close proximity of many demons masquerading as substitute teachers and other high-school staff. Also, I never thought about how much it would hurt when my knees and elbows slammed into the floor like that.

"Cyn! What—"

"Shh!" I roll off of him and let him get to a sitting position. But when he tries to stand, I yank him back down.

"Hey!"

"Hey, yourself. I don't know where you think you're going, but you need to just forget it."

"But—" His forehead wrinkles up in confusion. "I have to, uh—"

"No, you don't. There's, um, something else going on here. Something not for you."

He still looks confused. Understandably. And kind of annoyed.

"What's going on, Cyn?"

I take a few final seconds to search frantically around in my brain for any ideas about how to not have to tell him. The two chatting demons open the door and go inside and close it behind them again. They pay no attention to us.

My brain fails completely to help me out. Stupid brain.

I take a deep breath and force myself to look Ryan in the eyes. "So, okay. Remember how we were talking about what we could do to stop all the extra demons from killing extra people and draining extra students and stuff?"

"I remember how I thought your idea was too dangerous," Ryan says, dangerously.

"Yeah, well, I didn't agree with you."

"You went to Aaron? Without me?"

"Well, yes. But actually, he was completely unhelpful. As

was what's-her-name. Oh! Except that she said the final-battle thing is probably going to happen on opening night. After the show, of course."

Ryan closes his eyes for a second and shakes his head, as if to clear away some of this nonsense I am tossing at him. "So, then what did you do?"

Yeah. This is the part I really didn't want to get into.

"I made a deal with Mr. Gabriel."

"You what?!"

"I know. I know! It seemed like a good idea at the time. And it *was* a good idea! I mean, it is, still, at this time, too. I think it's going to work out, and at least we'll only have two demons to deal with instead of more than thirty!"

He speaks slowly and quietly. "What was the deal, Cyn?"

I tell him the deal, leaving out the part about making Gabriel and Kingston promise never to hurt him but including how I must have accidentally tagged him when he squeezed my hand outside of study hall. "I'm sorry, I had meant not to touch you, not to touch anyone—"

"What, forever?"

"No! Just until after they were done with whatever they were going to do."

"And what are they going to do, exactly?"

"I don't know. Destroy the other demons and use the power released by the mass sacrificial killing to shore up the wards or whatever and stop other demons from coming through."

The whole time we've been talking, there's been a low rumble of voices coming from the other side of the wall. Just regular talking, like there was a science lab cocktail party going on, with friendly teacher chitchat and little groups of small-talkers and stuff, possibly drinking colorful alcoholic beverages out of glasses in the shapes of test tubes and beakers by the light of many artfully arranged Bunsen burners. I notice now that the sound of the voices has suddenly disappeared. Could it be over already? I guess I thought there'd be more, I don't know, *ritual* to the ritual sacrifice. Like when Mr. Gabriel went all demony in the library that time with the blood and the shapes on the floor and everything. This was so quick and quiet.

Then, the screaming starts.

Ryan and I look at each other, wide-eyed, our argument temporarily forgotten.

There is more screaming, lots of it, and someone—some*thing*, remember, they're demons, bad evil murderous treacherous demons—something throws itself against the door. I guess it's possible it's *been* thrown, but the hand-shaped silhouettes slapping desperately against the frosted glass of the window suggest self-throwing. There are other sounds, wet, horrible sounds, that I can't quite identify. I do not try too hard to address this.

"Cyn," Ryan says. "Are you sure they're all demons?"

"Yes!" Of course they are. Right? I mean, they have to be. I saw the halos.

Which I was able to do because of whatever Mr. Gabriel did to my eyes. What if it just made me see them randomly?

No. That's dumb. I can't start questioning that now. Gabriel and Kingston both had the halos, and so did the security guards, and I know they're all demons . . . and all the rest I tagged were new, strangers, and they had the *halos*, dammit, and they were, they have to be . . .

The screaming is still going on. There is now a streak of what I think is blood across the window. The hands and whomever they belonged to are gone.

In that moment I know I'm going to open that door. I need to see — something. Something to reassure me that they are, in fact, all demons. I have no idea what that would be.

I stand up and move slowly toward the door. I expect Ryan to try to stop me, but there must be a part of him still responding to the tagging, because he just comes silently along with me.

Slowly, I turn the knob and open the door a tiny crack.

Something huge and dark and screaming comes flying at the opening, and in the single frozen moment before I am able to slam it shut again I am satisfied that nothing in that room is human. The door shudders violently as the thing smashes against it, but somehow the door stays closed. Gabriel and Kingston must have done something to it, secured the room somehow, so no one — no *thing* — could get out.

Ryan and I back a few steps away, still staring at the shifting shadow shapes that can just be seen through the thick frosty glass.

"Yup. I'm sure. All demons."

"Okay." He's silent a moment, then adds, "But, you know, not okay. Not really, Cyn. Jesus. How could you just go and do that, without even talking to me?"

"I tried talking to you! You were too afraid to try anything!"

He glares at me, surprised and hurt, and I instantly regret those words.

"I'm sorry," I try. "That's not what I meant. I just meant that you didn't seem to like anything I came up with —"

"You only came up with the one stupid plan!"

"And I was afraid that if I told you about *this* stupid plan, you'd try to talk me out of this one, too. Probably because you'd be right, that it was stupid and too dangerous. But I couldn't just sit back and do nothing. If we do nothing, *everyone* is going to die." I take a breath, realizing that I'm angry at him again. "And besides, it worked! I saw a chance, and I took it, and it worked. So don't go criticizing me for having stupid plans. At least I tried *something!*"

He's quiet for a minute more, and I'm not sure what that means or what he's thinking, and we stand there looking at each other in the otherwise empty hallway, hearing only the muffled crashes and screams and other sounds from the sealed lab room. They are beginning to taper off.

"All right," he says finally, and I don't know whether that means *all right I understand* or *all right but I kind of hate you* or just *all right I'm done talking about this right now.* I don't ask. "You're done here now?" he continues.

"I think so." My fingers aren't throbbing anymore. And the deal was only that I had to do the tagging; I would never have even come here if it weren't for having accidentally involved Ryan. "Yes."

"So let's just get out of here, and we can talk more later."

That sounds like an excellent idea.

But we are still standing there when we hear the door swing open.

We spin around and I register two things. One: the noises have all stopped, and two: a woman has just stepped inside that room. I catch just the trailing edge of her skirt as she goes in. She leaves the door open behind her, and I can see bits and pieces of — things — scattered around the floor and the walls. And a little hanging from the ceiling, too.

"Well," a female voice says into the silence. "I guess it's a good thing I like to be fashionably late."

"Dammit, Cynthia," Mr. Gabriel's voice calls from inside. "You missed one."

Apparently he knows I'm out here. I step toward the door, Ryan right beside me. We lean in.

Gabriel and Kingston, looking human again, are standing at the far end of the room. I can't see the woman's face, because she's turned toward them and away from me, but I can see the red halo glowing over her head.

"I just got here," she says. "I must have missed your invitation. I just felt something interesting going on and thought I would come investigate."

"But we closed the gate," Kingston says. "The wards —"

"Yes," she says. "I think I got through right at the last possible second. Really, it appears my timing was stunningly perfect. As usual."

Mr. Gabriel and Principal Kingston both appear to be temporarily speechless. They just stand there glowering at her.

"Well," I say. "We'll just be going. You guys look like you've

261

got some catching up to do. And, uh, cleaning up." I am trying very hard not to look at anything other than the three demons who are still standing upright and alive.

The woman turns around, finally. I am not really all that surprised to see it is Aaron's demoness. She *had* mentioned that she'd wanted to see the show.

"Yes, run along," she says. "I'm sure we'll see you around." She winks at me.

We run along.

Chapter | 14

The bell rings as we make our way back down the hall. We stop by Ryan's eighth-period classroom, then study hall, to respectively retrieve our belongings. We are quiet the entire time. We are nearly to the auditorium when Ryan asks, "Did you know? That she was coming?"

"No," I say truthfully. "Although I can't say I'm surprised."

He nods sort of to himself, without looking at me.

"Ryan —" I touch his arm. He stops, but still doesn't look at me. "I'm sorry I didn't tell you what I was doing. Please don't be mad at me."

"I thought we were in this thing together, Cyn," he says.

"We are! We totally are! I just — I thought I was doing the right thing. I'm sorry."

Now he looks at me. "How could you think that going to Aaron *by yourself* and then going to Mr. Gabriel *by yourself* and making a *secret deal with him* was possibly the right thing?"

"Because you didn't want to come with me to Aaron's, and if I'd told you I was going alone, you would have come anyway, and I didn't want to make you do that! And yes, I was pretty sure you would hate the idea of making a deal with Mr. Gabriel, and so I didn't tell you that, either."

"Why didn't *you* hate the idea of making a deal with him? Have you forgotten what he is?"

"No! Of course not! I did hate it! But I could see that it would work. And it *did* work. You have to see that. At least now there are only two —"

"Three."

"Ah. Right. Okay, three. Still, better than thirty!"

Ryan sighs and presses the heels of his hands into his eyes for a minute.

"And — look, you couldn't help me with that part," I go on. "It was something only I could do, because of that super-roach thing."

"You still should have told me."

I'm not so sure about that, but I nod anyway. "I know. I'm sorry. I really am."

His hands find their way back down to his sides. He turns to face me directly. "No more secrets, Cyn. This nightmare is bad enough without feeling like I can't even count on you to tell me what's going on."

"Okay." Once again, I know that I am lying; there's no way I'm going to tell him about the two-more-times-to-the-demon-world addendum to the agreement with the demoness. Or that I made all the demons promise not to hurt him. But those are *old* secrets. I tell myself that I am only promising not to keep any *new* secrets. This doesn't sound very convincing, even inside my own head. But I can't worry about that now.

"Okay," he says.

We stand there for a moment, and then by mutual unspoken agreement we start walking toward the auditorium again. As we're heading down the aisle toward the stage, I say, "Hey, can you stay after rehearsal? I need your help testing out the chair."

He looks relieved, although whether it's because of the subject change or because he's just glad to hear I'm finally about done with the damn chair, I'm not sure. "New prototype?"

"No prototype. This is it. This must be it, because we are out of time. I have to show it to Mr. Henry before the week is out, and I'd rather make that tomorrow than Friday. And I want us to practice it a few times before I let him see it. I've got Claude staying, too." Claude is one of the chorus guys who gets his throat slit by Sweeney in the second act.

"Sure, of course." He gives me a tiny hint of a smile, which lightens my heart enormously. I wasn't sure if he was ever going to smile at me again. "Is it going to be awesome?"

"Yup," I say.

"Glad to hear it." His smile flashes to full power for just a second. "Can't wait to try it out."

Later, I tell Mr. Henry that we'll lock up after we're done and shoo him away. I don't want him to see it until it's perfect. And it will be. My minions have done excellent work.

And, if I do say so myself, my design was pretty excellent, too.

I ask Ryan and Claude to sit in the audience so we can show them how it's going to look. My team and I have already moved the chair to the upper level of the pie shop/barbershop set piece, and removed the sad folding chair that had been standing in for the real thing until now. Jessica, my trusty tech-crew volunteer, has already practiced going down the trapdoor dozens of times, but this is our first time with an audience. I signal to Tom and Liz in the lighting booth and the houselights go down. The stage is currently lit as it will be for the start of "Johanna (Quartet)," which is when several throat-slittings and body-dumpings happen in the show.

"The chair looks great!" Ryan calls out, and Claude nods beside him.

I wave this away. The chair in its dormant state is not the thing that is awesome.

I check that everyone we need is in position. "Okay," I say, projecting my voice toward Ryan and Claude. "For the purposes of this demonstration, I will be Sweeney"—I hold up the gleaming silver razor (blunt-edged, of course) that I have borrowed from the prop table—"and Jessica will be you, Claude."

Jessica gets into the chair.

"So—the song is going along, lots of lovely singing, la-la-la." I move around, shifting the basin, pretending to lather up Jessica's face, doing a general approximation of what Ryan will be doing during the song. "Then, when it's time for the killing—" I mime slitting Jessica's throat (she makes an extravagant *oh my God what happened I'm being killed* face) and then pull a hanging chain we've installed from a beam above the stage. On cue, Tom and Liz dim the ambient stage lights slightly just as the trapdoor swings down and open in the section of the platform in front of the chair. Pulsing red light glares up from the gaping hole. I release the lock on the chair with a foot pedal, and the whole contraption swings forward, dumping Jessica front-first down the trapdoor and into the pulsing fiery light. I know from watching an earlier test run that my own face is also bathed in the evil red glow, giving me an appropriately demonic visage, and I hold up the razor so the red fire can be reflected in its surface as well. It's a beautiful effect with the dim lights everywhere else: Sweeney (or me, in this case), standing above the hole in the floor, holding up the razor and reflecting the heat and fire spilling up from below. (In the show the razor will be dripping with fake blood, too, which will only make it better.)

"Nice!" Ryan shouts. He and Claude stand up and start clapping. Claude gives a long whistle as well.

I grin at them. Jessica pokes her head out from around the doorway on the lower level and waves merrily.

They jump up to the stage to check out the mechanics. There's a giant mattress piled with extra cushioning beneath the trapdoor, of course, and the lights are set back far enough that there's no danger of Claude or anyone else smacking into one on the way down. The trapdoor itself is large, so that the opening can be large, so that there won't be another incident of someone's head making unintentional contact with the edge of it after getting half caught in a slightly faulty hinged seat — a design flaw of the previous chair that was more closely modeled on the 1982 Broadway production and was not quite ready to be tested at the time that certain people, who have since been demoted to cleaning crew, decided to try it out.

Anyway. None of that matters now, because that chair was nothing. This chair is the best chair ever.

"It's the best chair ever!" Claude says enthusiastically. "Reset it, I want to try!"

Ryan catches my eye from where he's standing in the pie shop/cellar area section of the stage. He's smiling. "That's one fantastic chair," he says.

"Well, it's not just the chair, obviously," I say, tucking my hair behind my ears and bending down to reset the chair for Claude. "It's the whole setup." I glance at him again shyly, unable to help myself. "Did you like the lights?"

"The lights were amazing. It's like the fires of hell are blazing up from the oven below. It looks — really great. Nice job, Cyn."

He holds my gaze again, still smiling, until I can't take it and I have to look away. Luckily the red lights will hide any blushing that might be happening in my general facial region. Ryan climbs up to the barbershop level and I start showing him and Claude how it all works, and I come to a startling realization: I'm happy. Despite everything else going on outside this auditorium, right now, in this moment, I'm happy. The chair is awesome, the cast and crew are excited, Mr. Henry is going to love it, my partner in demon fighting seems to have forgiven me for my sins, and all of my old delicious tingly Ryan-related feelings are singing out from various places in my body as my cells awaken to his very near proximity. Also the stage lights are making everything feel kind of warm and nice and toasty. I give in to it. I can feel sad and scared again tomorrow. Tonight, I just let myself feel happy until it's time to go home.

The demoness — who calls herself Ms. Královna — turns out to be our new Italian teacher. She's actually pretty good. Worlds better than Mr. Hubbard, although, admittedly, Mr. Hubbard set the bar pretty low. She tells the class she is from Slovakia but that she speaks several languages, including Italian, English, Danish, and Mandarin. She wears low-cut shirts and tight dresses, and all the boys in the class and a few of the girls suddenly seem intensely interested in learning Italian as well as they can. Even I get a little shivery when she says *bravissima* in that sultry voice of hers. Even though I know full well what she is.

But, hey — out of all the demons I have met, she is my favorite by, like, infinity.

Other than a single startled yet not really super-surprised glance on Friday morning when we walk into class and see her, Ryan and I don't discuss the demoness's presence. We also still haven't talked about the whole going-to-the-demon-world thing. There's nothing to say, really. He was there; he knows I made a deal, although, thank God, not all the details. But he knows I have to go. I know I have to go. So talking about it seems pretty pointless. I'm certainly not going to bring it up, and I'm grateful that he hasn't either. We only have a little time left before the time (the next time) when we might die. I don't want to spend it fighting or being more sad and scared than I have to be.

We showed the chair to Mr. Henry and the rest of the cast Thursday at the beginning of rehearsal. It was even better than when we showed Ryan and Claude, because this time Ryan and Claude were in full character and we had the fake blood and everything and it was *perfect*. Mr. Henry got up and hugged me and told me he was proud of me, and I had to work really hard not to start leaking around the eyes. The rest of the evening we ran all the scenes and numbers that involved the chair, and I just sat there in the audience and watched and loved it and was happy. Again. This time I could feel some other things lurking around underneath the happy, but I ignored them. Or tried to. *One week,* my stupid brain reminded me. One week from tomorrow would be opening night. And then—I had no idea what then.

Shut up, I told my brain. *I have a week. Leave me alone.*

My brain backed off, but I was not fooled. All the bad terrified and sorrowful thoughts and feelings were still there. Waiting.

I spend the weekend missing Annie even more than usual. I guess because it's the last weekend before I either save her or die trying. I almost call her so many times. But instead I lie on the floor of my room with my headphones, like I used to do in junior high whenever I was sad, and listen to all my favorite musicals over and over and over. I know there is probably something else I should be doing. Running intervals, maybe, or learning karate, or brushing up on my knife fighting, or maybe just praying a lot. I mean, there are *demons* infesting our school and people are still getting pieces of their souls sucked out every day and Principal Morse is dead and Signor De Luca is dead and Mrs. Foster and Miss Daniels are dead and probably more people are going to die before the end, although hopefully not too many if we can succeed in doing all the things we are hoping to do when the time comes. And I know that. Of course I do.

But that is part of the magic of musical theater, dammit. That it can be awesome when everything else is awful, that it can make you feel better when life kicks you in the face and then stomps on your head while you're lying there on the ground whimpering and then makes out with your boyfriend while making you watch, when there seems to be no hope and you have trouble seeing the possibility of happiness or a future or anything else. Musical theater can save you, even if only for two or three hours at a time. Sondheim especially can save you, although, of course, he's not the only one, and person-ally I think *Sweeney Todd* can save you almost more than any-thing else, except maybe *Les Misérables* (Schönberg / Boublil) or, possibly, *The Secret Garden* (Norman / Simon). Oh, or *Chess* (Tim Rice and those guys from ABBA). Or *Into the Woods* (see? Sondheim again). But I don't know — right now I am thinking that *Sweeney* has them all beat.

And so, yeah, demons, and death and scary terrible terri-fying things waiting around every corner, sure, and, for some of us, impossible journeys to some hellish underworld on the agenda very, very soon. Whatever. The awfulness isn't going anywhere. It will be there waiting for us all next week. And so for now, I am listening to my favorite songs and dreaming impossible dreams and ignoring the reality of the swiftly approaching future as much as I possibly can.

Tech week for the show begins on Monday, which means full run-throughs every night with reworkings of whatever needs it afterward and frequent stops to work out lighting issues or sound cues or any other tech-related thing that might need to be smoothed out. (Except the chair. The chair works perfectly every single time. It is the best chair ever.) Rehearsals go late and then later, and all of us are exhausted and it's getting kind of hard to tell who's walking around like a zombie because they've had part of their life force sucked out and who's just sleep deprived because of the show. It's just as well, because it means it takes all my brainpower just to make it through the day, and so I don't have a whole lot left for being terrified at the slow but steady horror-show countdown going on in the back of my head.

I'd been using *Sweeney* as a frequent excuse to avoid Diane and Leticia, because I'm so bad at keeping things from them and they are so good at seeing when something is up. But this week I have lunch with them every day. Because, I guess, I know that these lunches together might be the last. At least for me. I'm trying to have faith that no matter what, the demoness will fulfill her part of the bargain to stop Mr. Gabriel and Principal Kingston from killing everyone before they head home. So Diane and Leticia will go on having lunch together for the rest of the year, and next year, and for as long as they want to thereafter. Maybe forever. Even if I don't save Annie and make it back alive.

But I want to get *my* last lunches in, just in case they really are my last. Tech week insanity is a well-known phenomenon among the friends of the theater crowd, and so they will not question any odd behavior on my part now. So I can relax a little about that, at least. We studiously do not talk about Annie. She has pretty much disappeared from regular life at this point, but somehow everyone seems to be overlooking this fact, or else some demony hocus-pocus has made L&D not quite able to notice the fact that our friend is all but gone.

So we talk about Leticia's crazy food preferences and Diane's out-of-control shoe fetish and collectively dissect the words and actions of a certain Ryan Halsey (the parts I'm able to tell them, anyway) to try to determine why he seems to like me but not like me and sort out some kind of meaning from all the various mixed signals.

"He gives you a ride home every night," Diane says for the third or fourth time now. "Every night. A boy does not do that if he doesn't like you. You're not even remotely on his way home!"

Leticia is less certain. "I guess he really could just want to be friends. I mean, you're awesome, Cyn — who wouldn't want to be friends with you? I would give you a ride home every night without necessarily wanting to kiss you."

This is oddly distressing. "You wouldn't want to kiss me?"

"I said not *necessarily*."

"I'm sure she would love to kiss you," Diane says sooth-ingly. "We all would. That is not the point." She pauses, then adds, "Are you sure he likes girls? Maybe you're just not his type."

"I'm not sure of anything," I admit. And I'm not. I feel like Ryan and I have grown crazily close in the last couple of weeks, and yet in some ways I still don't know him at all. We spend all this time together, but we don't talk about anything other than demons and *Sweeney Todd*. Granted, those two topics do sort of eclipse pretty much everything else at the moment, but still.

Diane begins to list all the couples she knows who started out thinking each of them had no interest in the other, with detailed descriptions of how they finally ended up getting together to no one's surprise but their own, and Leticia inserts her trademark acerbic and hysterical commentary, and I'm sitting across the table laughing so hard I want to cry, because if I don't get to come back, I'm going to miss this so much.

Today, Thursday (which, just to place you in time here, is the day before opening night, T minus one and counting), Ms. Královna stops me in the hall.

She ushers me into Signor De Luca's room and closes the door behind me. I can still see the red halo over her head. I am starting to think that whatever Mr. Gabriel did to my eyes is not ever going to wear off. I haven't yet decided whether I am happy or upset about this.

"I have two things to give you," she says. "The items you will need to bring with you to the demon world."

She goes to the desk and opens a drawer. Then she lays two things on the desktop.

One of them is definitely a protractor. You know, those

half-moon-shaped things with the space in the middle and the little lines that you use to measure angles. It's made of metal and the surface is rather scratched up.

The other one appears to be a biology textbook.

"Hmm," I say. I look at her, trying to see if she is kidding. If we were in one of Annie's drawings right now, I would be a wavy-haired stick figure with skeptical eyes and little question marks floating around my head.

"This one will sever the link between your friend and the librarian," she says, indicating the protractor. "The other will protect you, just once, from his direct attack. You must not attempt to use them for these purposes until you are fully in our world."

She doesn't seem like she's kidding.

I look at the items again, then back at her.

"You realize that's a protractor and a biology textbook, right?"

She gives me an impatient look. "That's what they are in this world. They will be what you need them to be when you cross over."

Cross over. I still can't really believe that's going to happen.

I pick up the protractor and the book. "So, how's that all going to work, anyway?" I ask, very obviously trying (and failing) for casually. "The whole 'crossing over' thing?"

"You will know when it happens," she says, and she is smiling in a very non-comforting way.

"I don't want to know when it happens. Well, I mean obviously I don't want to *not* know when it happens, but I want to *also* know now, ahead of time, what it will be like."

"There is no way to explain what it will be like. I don't really know what it is like for humans to cross. I know what it's like for demons to come here, and it's not very pleasant. I imagine it won't be very pleasant for you, either."

"That's it? Really? You can't tell me anything else?" I am suddenly kind of pissed off. "I thought we were working together on this thing. I help you, you get to be queen of the demons, I get to save my friend, et cetera? Why won't you tell me everything you can to help me? If I end up screwing things up and dying, you're not going to have your roach-umbrella, you know. It's in your best interest to help me. So help me, dammit!"

She rolls her eyes.

"I cannot help you in this way. Why do humans always think they want to know everything?" She takes a step toward me, then another, her tight pants making whispery fabric sounds as her shapely thighs brush past each other. "You want me to tell you it will be terrible? Terrifying? It will. You will be dragged across a boundary you were never meant to cross, you will be thrust into a place in which you do not belong, where you will be meat and prey to everything around you, and you will need to keep your head and function and do what you came there to do despite this. There is no way to prepare. You will either be strong enough or you won't. You will succeed or you won't. You will survive or you won't. There is nothing I can tell you that will make one bit of difference."

She is standing right in front of me now. I can smell her spicy-sweet perfume, and if I look down, I know I'll get a full view of her impressive cleavage in her very low-cut shirt. Her eyes are bright and intense, and I realize she cannot wait for this whole thing to go down. She can't wait to go home and fight to the death.

Demons are fucking crazy.

"Fine," I say. "Sorry I had questions about this impossible, horrible thing I'm about to do. I'll just take my lame-ass magical items and go."

I clasp the book and protractor to my far-less-impressive cleavage, which I guess maybe isn't even technically cleavage at all since I'm not wearing low-cut anything, and head for the door. I'm sort of expecting her to say something else, some last parting words of wisdom or advice, some relenting, grudging admission that there is perhaps something she can tell me after all, and I even slow down toward the end to give her a chance to speak up, but she doesn't say anything. I open the door and walk out. The textbook is heavy. I am disappointed and annoyed.

When I get to class, I slide the textbook and protractor into my backpack, which is already stuffed with snacks and extra ponytail holders and vitamin C drops and other tech week survival gear. I suppose I'm going to have lug them around until tomorrow night.

My grumpy mood doesn't last, though. It can't. Because tonight is *Sweeney* dress rehearsal, and I can't wait. I can't wait to hear Ryan sing and watch him own the stage, can't wait to assume my stage-left-curtain perch, where I will sit with my headset and rule my technical kingdom and feel the magic of the show taking hold of everyone who experiences it. Tomorrow I will have to be freaked out about what is going to happen after the show, but tonight I just get to immerse myself in the whole spectacular glorious miracle that is musical theater. I am so pumped up about this, so ready to be happy and in the middle of it, that I am totally unprepared for the shock of catching a glimpse of Annie after seventh period, and it knocks the breath right out of me.

She's in the library, of course, sitting on a stool behind the circulation desk, scanning some books' bar codes with a little handheld scanner and putting them in neat, perfect, Annie-style stacks. This is the first time I've seen her in over a week. Since that night that everything went so wrong with the containment circle and Aaron and she disappeared with Mr. Gabriel. She hated me that night. It was clear on her face, how angry she was, how furious and appalled and disgusted, how much she hated me. I am riveted by the sight of her, like my eyes have been thirsty for her all this time, dying of thirst, and now they cannot stop drinking her in and would not turn away even if I had the heart to try to make them.

She looks happy. She is smiling her brightest Annie smile and she looks like she is exactly where she wants to be, without a care in the world, without anything dragging her even the tiniest bit down. I realize that I have stopped short in the middle of the hall, that irritated students are swerving around me on either side, but I don't care. I am still completely incapable of looking away.

I miss her so much. And if I don't stay strong and functional and manage to succeed and survive tomorrow night, I will lose her forever, for good. No backsies, not ever. And Mr.

Gabriel will turn her into something else, blacken her good, sweet heart and destroy everything about her that I love.

Aaand . . . speak of the devil.

He emerges from the back office, and while my whole body wants to convulse with fury and hate and hurt, Annie's face lights up to a place so beyond happy that I almost have to squint in order to keep looking. He puts his hand on her shoulder, and she looks up at him like he's her favorite movie star and God and Gandhi and Santa Claus all rolled into one. And while they are careful, even now, not to engage in inappropriate public school behavior, I can see the dark promise in his gaze as he looks down at her, and her own answering openness and willingness and *wanting,* and I have to fight myself to not throw up or scream or dissolve from the awfulness of everything right there in the middle of the hallway.

Mr. Gabriel's posture straightens slightly, and instantly I know that he knows I am there. He starts to look up, very slowly, to raise his eyes to the library doorway, to catch me standing there so he can smile his evil smile and bask in the delightful knowledge that he is killing me with what he is doing to my friend. I can't bear it. I turn and run, like a coward, before his eyes can meet my own. I know he'll know that I couldn't face him, but I refuse to accept the shame that wants to cling to my mind and heart. Let him think he's won; let him think I'm beaten; let him think that he has nothing to stand in his way as he makes his final play tomorrow night. When it counts, when it matters, I will face him. And I will win.

I repeat this in my head, over and over, as I run and then

walk and then stop and lean against the cold, smooth third-floor wall. *I will win. I will win. I will win.*

I *will* win.

And until then I will go back to focusing on what is good, and making the most of all the moments I have left before the final showdown has to start.

And that's what I do. It takes a little while to shake off the Annie and Mr. Gabriel sighting, but eventually I manage. I go to the auditorium and drop off my stuff and inspect my troops and check the prop table, and soon enough I am able to lose myself in the excitement of dress rehearsal, in Mr. Henry's adorable last-minute panics about things that are absolutely fine, in the costumes and the sets and in everyone running around getting last-minute items in place, in the anticipatory, barely reined-in promise as Mr. Iverson leads the cast in vocal warm-ups, and in Ryan's deliberate catching of my eye when Mr. Henry calls places for the run. I mouth, "Break a leg" at him and he smiles one of his devastating smiles and points at me as if to say, *You too,* and then he disappears behind the set.

And it's awesome, and I know I'm totally overusing that word but I don't care, and for as long as it lasts, the only demons I think about are the ones in Sweeney's and Mrs. Lovett's own minds and hearts, and that is fine by me.

That night when Ryan drives me home, he parks in front of my house instead of just stopping to let me out. I no longer expect that he is ever going to kiss me (even though this would be a *perfect* setting and opportunity, just FYI), so I indulge in no imagined scenarios of him leaning across the armrest and planting his lips on mine. Nope. Not one.

"What's up?" I ask, when he doesn't explain why (if not to kiss me) he has parked the car.

He is silent for another few seconds, not looking at me. I wait. He's clearly working up to something.

"Are you sure you want to go through with it?" he asks suddenly.

"What?" I don't know what I was expecting him to say, but it was definitely not that.

He turns to face me. A streetlight throws a narrow column of light across his cheek. "The last time we saw Annie, she seemed pretty determined to go with Mr. Gabriel. Maybe . . ."

"Maybe . . . ?" I echo back at him. I am a little afraid to find out how he might be planning to finish that thought.

He takes a breath, and I can see him preparing for me to not like what he's about to say. "Maybe sometimes people want things that other people can't understand, but that doesn't necessarily mean that they're completely wrong to want them. Maybe Annie has reasons that we don't know about. Maybe it's not our place to stop her from going after what she wants, even if it seems like what she wants is totally crazy."

"*You* are totally crazy," I tell him. "Are you listening to what you're saying? Annie was not herself that night. She hasn't been herself since that goddamn librarian materialized in our library and made eyes at her over the encyclopedias. You never really knew her before he showed up. I've known her practically my whole life. And the Annie I know would never want something like that. Never."

But even as I say this, I am thinking about the last real conversation Annie and I had. The things she said about everyone's expectations, and how alone and trapped and caged in she has felt. The things she's been feeling that I never even suspected. Maybe it's not true; maybe those are just things she's telling herself she's always been feeling so that she can justify what she thinks she wants and not see the truth of what Mr. Gabriel is really doing to her . . . but I don't think so. At least, not entirely. That felt real, those things she said. I never would have guessed it, any of it, but now I believe that she really has been feeling that way, at least some of the time. Maybe a lot of the time. Maybe the cheerful face she's always showing to the world is more of a mask than a window. And I was her best friend, and I never saw.

I try to really think about how she described her life. The future that seems unalterably laid before her, the good-girl persona she has worn for so long that she doesn't know how to be anything else. Or didn't, until now. Could this really be her one chance to let go, to stop being who everyone else wants her to be and instead to be the person she dreams herself, inside? To be wanted in that fierce and powerful way by someone, to reject the life she'd resigned herself to — to have that dark fairy tale that she has secretly longed for, that she had buried in despair of ever having anything close to what she wanted? Maybe there is a part of Annie, the real Annie, a big part even, who truly wants this.

I try to imagine accepting that. And I can't.

"No," I say out loud. "Even if she thinks she really wants this — even if she *does* really want it — that doesn't make it okay. Mr. Gabriel is a monster. He's told us straight out that he's planning to destroy her, to take away who she is and make her something else. That's not love, and that can't be okay. It just can't. Sometimes people are wrong. Sometimes they want bad things. Sometimes, if you care about them, you have to try to save them from themselves."

Ryan is quiet for a moment.

"If that's true," he says finally, "maybe I should be saving you. Maybe I should be stopping you from risking your life to save hers. Even if that's what you really want." He meets my eyes then, and he's more serious than I have ever seen him before. "I don't want you to die, Cyn. Annie wouldn't want you to die, either. Although, honestly, I'm a little tired of thinking about what Annie wants. Maybe it's time you let Annie take responsibility for herself and think about what's best for you for a change. Doesn't your life matter? Don't you have things to live for? Why does Annie's life get to be more important than your own?"

I'm staring at him, angry and shocked, and . . . confused. Because part of me is wondering if he's not at least a little bit right. Where does my responsibility truly lie? Even if I'm sure that I'm doing the right thing, do I have the right to stop Annie from doing what she thinks she wants? What she thinks is right?

If everyone thinks they are right, and they can't really all be right, then how do we decide who's wrong?

I shake my head. No. I can't go down that road. All I can do is what I think is best. And deep down, under the confusion and the fear and the wanting to still be alive for my own future, I can't really believe for one full second that letting my best friend be stolen away by a murderous evil demon is in any possible sense the right move here.

Ryan can tell what I'm thinking; it's clear in the hardening of his expression.

"Cyn—"

"Ryan, please. Just stop. I don't want to fight about this. I don't want to fight at all. I made my choice."

"What about my choice? What if my choice is to not let you just go off and get yourself killed?"

I close my eyes, trying to get my bearings. He is confusing me in more ways than one. Under any other circumstances, I would be really, really happy that he cares about me enough to be saying things like this. I would be thinking about what it might mean. But right now, the last thing I need is a reason to doubt what I'm doing.

"Ryan, I have to. I can't choose my happiness over Annie's life."

"What about your *life* over Annie's life? Could you choose that?"

I shake my head again. I'm crying a little, I realize, which makes sense, because even though I've been trying really hard not to think about it straight out like this, the whole thing sucks so bad, and it's totally not fair, and I wish—I wish so much that it weren't happening. "I'm the only one who can save her, Ryan. Do you really think I could live with myself if I just gave up on her? If you really care about me, you won't fight me on this. You'll do everything you can to help me, so that I can save Annie and survive and come back alive. Believe me, I don't want to die. But I have to save her first. I *have* to, Ryan. She's my best friend. I can't just let her go."

And suddenly I'm crying full force, dissolving in tears and racking sobs and wretchedness in exactly the way I have not allowed myself to do since this whole stupid-ass thing began.

Ryan reaches over and takes my hand. He doesn't say anything else, just holds my hand, which I grip tightly back, and lets me cry.

Finally, much later, when I seem to have cried myself out, he pulls back, just a little. He looks at me, which I'm sure can't be very pleasant given what a snively mascara-running mess I must be right now. He brushes his thumb gently under one of my eyes, then the other, wiping away the last of the tears.

"Okay," he says softly. "Okay. I won't try to stop you, and I'll do everything that I can to help."

"Thank you," I whisper, still sniffling.

Then he moves his hands to the sides of my head and holds it firmly, staring into my eyes.

"But you'd better damn well make it through this alive, Cyn. Do you hear me? Get in there and get Annie and get the hell back out. Promise?"

I nod as much as his grip on my head will allow.

"Say it. I need to hear you say it."

"I promise. I'll come back. I promise."

"Okay, then." He nods back. "It's a deal."

Chapter | 15

I awaken to the sound of my text alert.

I reach over and pull my phone groggily toward me from my bedside table. It is a text from Ryan. It says, IT'S THE DAY OF THE SHOW, Y'ALL.

The combination of him not only quoting *Waiting for Guffman* to me but also trusting that I will get and appreciate the reference is almost too much delightfulness for me to handle first thing in the morning.

But I manage.

I am not awake enough to manage much else, though, including coming up with a clever and appropriate response, so I just text him a smiley face in return.

For a few minutes I just lie there in bed feeling happy. *Again.* It *is* the day of the show, y'all, and Ryan thought of me as soon as he woke up and wanted to share his excitement with me in exactly the perfect way, and I am smiling at the ceiling like an idiot and it is all really, really good.

Then I think about what has to happen after the show, and all of the happy goes away.

No, no, no.

I don't want to feel like this yet. I still have time, dammit. I take a deep breath, and then I begin to talk myself through this. First, I am going to enjoy the day and the growing anticipation as the hours pass and the show gets closer and everyone looks forward to it together. The very fact that it might be my last day ever is going to make it all the more precious and important, and I am not going to waste said possible last day ever feeling sad and scared.

Not. Going. To. Happen.

I am going to live this day to the fullest in every cliché way imaginable. So yes, all-day anticipation, and yes, pregame excitement, and then the actual show will happen, and it will be amazing. And it will. Because no matter how much it rocks during rehearsal, no matter how awesome it is the night before, when it's for real—when the audience is there and reacting and you can feel them feeling the magic of everything and the funny parts are getting laughs and the sad parts are getting sadness and it is one hundred percent clear that they are right there, right with us, loving it—there is nothing on earth that is better than that.

The show is going to be incredible.

Especially every scene involving the chair.

And after . . .

After I will finally get to save Annie from the evil librarian and put an end to this nonsense once and for all.

And so I make sure my magic protractor and textbook are in my backpack and I get myself to school.

None of the teachers even try to have real class today. There are countless games of hangman and lots of "independent reading and discussion." The teachers, in fact, seem almost as excited as the students. Over the past several days, suspicious numbers of them seemed to be randomly working late, just happening to wander into the auditorium on their way to the parking lot, and then not leaving until rehearsal was over. And those who came and saw have clearly been talking to the rest, telling tales of wonder and excellence. The students, too, have heard the buzz, and additionally they are the friends and the boyfriends and girlfriends and siblings and secret and not-so-secret admirers of the cast and crew, and so they are probably still more excited than the teachers, who maybe want to support Mr. Henry and the students that they know in the show but mostly just want to *see* the show and possibly, as a bonus, feel superior to the teachers they know at other schools that have lame musicals that no one cares about at all.

The day goes by in a blur of nonclasses and texting Ryan and receiving encouraging words and good-luck hugs from Leticia and Diane (both Ryan related and show related). When the final bell rings at last, I take my minions out for an early preshow dinner to celebrate and fortify ourselves with ceremonial burgers and shakes and to pass the time until call, which is at 5:30 p.m. There is lots of nervous chatter and many self-congratulatory statements, but mostly we are just waiting for the clock.

And then, eventually, 5:30 p.m. arrives.

And so we all assemble back in the auditorium.

And now it's starting, for real.

The auditorium is the same auditorium it has always been, but it is also different — better, special, alive and suddenly seeming almost self-aware with its own power, thrumming with potential energy and promise. The orchestra chairs and stands are set up and waiting for their designated occupants. Mr. Henry is running around with happy frantic purpose. Busy silhouettes flit about in the lighting booth and backstage in the wings, and I am so excited and glad that I am here and still alive and a part of this.

Usually we all drop our stuff off in the band-wing classroom set aside for that purpose, but tonight I tuck my backpack quickly and quietly under the prop table. No one will touch it — everyone has learned exactly how serious I am about not touching things on the prop table that are not your own personal assigned props — and the aura of *don't you dare* that blankets the top of the table extends, I am certain, to the area underneath it as well. Maybe there will be plenty of time after the curtain calls for me to go and get my special demon-fighting loot from the other room, but maybe not. It seems best to keep it close at hand.

Preparation continues in various forms and speeds and styles until around 7:00 p.m. Then Mr. Henry calls us all together on the stage. Everyone is either in full costume and makeup or dressed in black for backstage ninja action.

"I am so proud of each and every one of you," Mr. Henry says, looking from one face to another, around the circle we have automatically and unconsciously arranged ourselves into. "I always knew we'd have a wonderful show, but I have to admit that over the last couple of weeks you have completely surpassed my already high expectations. Thank you, so much, for all of your hard work and long nights and dedication. You are all so talented, all of you, cast and crew, and"—he shouts this next line over his shoulder down to the orchestra pit and Mr. Iverson, who has arrived in a tuxedo to complete his metamorphosis from musical director/rehearsal pianist to conductor—"persons of the orchestra." Mr. Iverson smiles and makes a little bow, and the orchestra kids cheer. Mr. Henry continues, "We have something truly special here, thanks to you guys."

"Thanks to you, too, Mr. H.!" someone shouts. I think it is Jeff Cohen, who is playing Judge Turpin. There is a chorus of support from the rest of us regarding this sentiment, and Mr. Henry grins and blushes and finally has to raise his hands in surrender to get us to shut up again. "Okay, okay, I did my part, too," he allows. "But I want you all to know that you are the ones who are really making this happen, and as of now my part is done. I turn *Sweeney* over to you, and I can do this without hesitation because I have such complete and justified faith in my amazing cast and crew."

"And orchestra!" Mr. Iverson shouts out, and we all laugh, in part to counteract the fact that Mr. Henry is starting to get us all a little choked up, himself included. He raises his hands once more and we subside. "This show means a lot to me," he concludes in his now-serious voice, "and I know it means a lot to you, too. Let's run through curtain calls, then we'll do warm-ups, and then we'll open the house. I can't wait for the audience to experience what you've created here. You're going to blow them away."

There is enthusiastic cheering at this, and then the crew goes back to finishing up whatever last things we have to do while Mr. Henry does a few quick curtain-call run-throughs and then turns the cast over to Mr. Iverson for warm-ups. Watching my minions reinforcing tape marks on the floor and reading over tech cues while perfectly synced voices run up and down the scales along with the piano gives me chills, and I give myself one more moment to just appreciate the joy of this whole crazy thing and take in a good full dose of the energy and the excitement and the, yes, I'm saying it again, awesomeness. God, I love this so much. And as I think those words, I am suddenly overwhelmed by them, and I have to fight back the tears that suddenly want to spill from my eyes. *It's not the last time you'll ever get to feel this*, I swear to myself. *It's not. I promise.*

I promise.

I pull myself together and run through my preshow checklist again. It doesn't matter what happens later. Not right now. Right now, the only truth is the old standby: the show must go on. I know how this works, and the knowing and the doing bring me back to calmness and purpose and happiness in fulfilling my piece of the whole.

Warm-ups end, and the cast and the musicians hurry backstage, and the ushers head for the doors with their armloads of programs, and the house is opened.

I settle myself off stage left, headset in place, listening to the murmurs from the lighting booth and the chattering voices floating in from the lobby and the squeaks and grunts of the old auditorium seats and all the other sounds of the slowly gathering audience. We've been informed that it's a full house tonight, standing room only. There are three more performances scheduled, but apparently people did not want to wait. I certainly don't blame them; I wouldn't want to wait either.

When Mr. Henry calls five minutes, I feel Ryan's presence next to me before I see him standing there.

"Hey," I whisper. "All set? You look great." Which he does, of course. He is the sexiest Sweeney Todd ever.

"Almost," he says. "I just have to do one thing."

He puts one hand on the wall behind me, and before I can even start to wonder what thing he's talking about his other hand is under my chin and there's not even time enough to finish my thought of *oh my God he better damn well be about to kiss me this time* before his mouth is on mine and the kissing is actually happening.

My whole brain just goes away. For however many seconds it lasts, there are just the kiss and my ecstatic nerve endings in every imaginable location and his mouth is soft and warm and I want to kiss him harder but I'm afraid of messing up his makeup, and so I just let him kiss me carefully yet thoroughly in the backstage preshow dimness. There's still not much thinking going on. Just feeling. Lots of feeling. I am nothing but the physical sensations of where our lips meet and where his hand is still gently touching my face and where my blood is racing forcefully through all of my veins in response to my suddenly very, very poundy heart.

He pulls back, eyes smiling. My mouth opens but I can't make words come out yet. I just stare back at him, which makes his mouth twist up into one of those Ryan Halsey grins which makes me glad I'm still sitting down on my nice sturdy stool.

"Break a leg," he says softly.

"Yeah," I manage, barely. "You too."

He winks and then disappears into the darker backstage regions to get in position for the top of the show. I stare at the place where he was standing for several more seconds before I hear Liz on the headset trying to get my attention. "Cyn? You there? Everything okay?"

I force myself to focus. Mostly I just want to sit here and replay the last minute in my mind a few million times, but there is no time for that nonsense now. *Later,* I promise my brain. And my heart. *All you want.*

"Yes, sorry!" I say into the headset mic. "All set here. You guys good?"

"Lighting booth set," she says back. "Break a femur!"

I wish her the same and take a deep breath and struggle back to my calm and centered tech-director inner balance just as Mr. Henry calls places.

Later, I tell myself one more time. But I don't try to make myself stop smiling.

The houselights go halfway down, and then Mr. Henry

walks out on stage to give the cell phone and flash photography speech, and then he walks down the side steps, and although I can't see this part, I know he is walking up the aisle to take his reserved seat in the eighth row. Then the lights go down completely, and Mr. Iverson raises his baton, and then the overture begins.

And finally, the curtain goes up.

From the first soft notes of "The Ballad of Sweeney Todd," the magic of the performance is in full and powerful force. The silence and stillness of the audience is absolute; no one whispers, no one shifts in their seat, no one even coughs. The music and the voices of the opening number slowly build, line by line, moment by moment. Various principals and chorus members sing their parts from assorted positions across the stage, until the music swells and Ryan strides out on stage to join the others and add his voice to the rest. I feel the impact of this moment on everyone in the theater. Everything is amazing, and Ryan is the most amazing of all, and the show is off and running and we're all making it happen together and I am once again blissfully, gratefully lost in the musical-theater magic and for the next 2.5 hours, nothing else exists at all.

During intermission, I give the chair one last inspection. It gets carried onstage for the first time during the opening number of act 2, so the audience hasn't seen it yet. In that first song, after the chair gets delivered, Sweeney makes some "minor adjustments" to it, and then he and Mrs. Lovett test out the added special features by sending some lashed-together books down through the trapdoor into the bake house. The setup sometimes gets a laugh, and I'm excited for it, but of course what I really can't wait for is the first time Sweeney sends a person down through the trapdoor. That's when the chair will be in full effect, with the lights and flames and everything. "Break a leg, chair," I whisper to it, patting it gently on the arm. Then Mr. Henry calls places for the second act, and I head back to my position.

The setup scene does get a laugh, which is great because I know it will make the horror of the first real onstage chair-death that much more effective in comparison. And then "Johanna (Quartet)" begins, lovely and tragic, and Claude seats himself in the chair as Ryan and Jerome (who plays Anthony, the young sailor) sing their lines. And then Ryan drags the razor across Claude's throat, still singing, and the lights dim and the trapdoor opens and the audience gasps audibly as the red flame-lights burst forth to bathe Sweeney and the blood-spattered razor in hellish splendor, and his victim tumbles dying and terrified down into the depths.

I can hear them react again when the second killing happens, even though this time, of course, they're expecting it. (Sweeney's third killing is thwarted when his next customer shows up with a little girl in tow, and so he has to actually give the guy a shave and leave him alive.) Through the final sequence of the show, which includes the last and most significant murders, the chair and lights and music and the cast combine again and again to work their magic and transport the audience every single time. Jessica gives me a thumbs-up from her own perch stage right, and I grin back at her, relieved and proud and happy and grateful that everything worked the way I'd planned and hoped and desperately wished it would.

I am crying a little by the end. Part of it is the story, and part of it is still my lingering pride at the audience's reaction to the chair scenes, and part of it is the huge release of the first night being just about over, and part of it is that I know bad things are going to start happening very soon.

The final notes fade, and the audience leaps to their feet almost as one. *Almost* as one; I am pretty certain that the first three standers by like a fraction of a second are Mr. Gabriel, Principal Kingston, and Ms. Královna. They are sitting together, a couple of rows behind Mr. Henry. The curtain calls begin: chorus, then minor roles, and then the leads. Principal Kingston gives a loud wolf whistle when Danielle, who plays Johanna, comes out, which is a little creepy. And they all — demons and humans alike — scream for Gina/Mrs. Lovett. But when Ryan walks out on stage, the roar from the audience is absolutely deafening. They love him. As they should. I am so proud of him, and of the whole group of us, and I lean out to see that other teachers are patting Mr. Henry heartily on the back, and even from here I can see that his eyes are glistening in the semidarkness.

The cast does a group bow, then points at the orchestra, and Mr. Iverson bows with arms spread to include the students who are still playing curtain-call music and so can't actually bow themselves. Then the cast bows again.

And then they break into groups and point again, some backstage left, some backstage right, and some up at the lighting booth. The crew looks around at one another; this is not a standard part of the curtain call. I gesture them to go ahead. Why not? After a second I get off my perch to join them. We dart up onto the upper platform and bow together.

And then they all step back and leave me standing there a couple of feet in front of them, on my own, next to the chair, and Tom and Liz flash the lights and swing the trapdoor open, and Ryan yells, "Let's hear it for the backstage crew and their fearless leader, Cyn Rothschild!"

And this is perhaps the coolest thing that has ever happened to me. Mary Chang never got to bow at the end of the show. I'm blushing and laughing and Ryan catches my eye and winks again, and what with the cheering and the recognition and the still-tingly aftermath of that preshow kiss, this may be one of the happiest moments of my entire life.

The cheering goes on and on, and everyone is shouting and clapping, and the cast and crew take bow after bow, and then suddenly the whole world seems to shift. I am still looking out at the auditorium, but there is another version of it superimposed on top of the real one — it is kind of a twisted reflection of the familiar school setting combined with something like the arena from that creature battle scene in *Star Wars: Attack of the Clones* and the colors of everything are starting to run together and the happy shouts of the audience have started to become screams of terror.

Backpack. Oh, God. I start toward the platform stairs but before I get two steps someone slams into me and together we go tumbling down through the trapdoor.

We fetch up on the mattress in a tangle, and it takes me a second to realize it's Ryan. My first crazy thought is: *How the hell did he get up the stairs so fast?*

My second is: *I'm tangled up with Ryan Halsey on a mattress.* I have dreamed about this moment, oh, so many times, although this is not exactly how I have imagined it. I have to fight back a hysterical giggle.

My third is, as I notice how he is not trying to get up, how he is in fact attempting to keep me down under him: *He tackled me deliberately. He is trying to stop me.*

Suddenly the other thoughts don't matter anymore. I glare up at him furiously.

"No," he says. "Don't do it, Cyn. Please."

I throw myself sideways, twisting away from him and off the mattress and stagger out the door of the pie shop. I don't look back to see if he's coming after me. I run for the prop table, nearly smacking my head on it as I lunge down for my bag and dig out the protractor and the textbook. Everyone is still screaming, but it is hard to see what's happening, because the colors are still running together and starting to swirl around and, although I am probably the only one who can see this part, there is a flood of deep red underlying everything else.

Because . . . what I am seeing down underneath the real world is the demon world. Where lots of demons are.

Where Mr. Gabriel is about to take Annie.

Where I am about to go, too.

Oh, God.

The redness is bleeding into the other colors, and

everything together is making this giant swirling vortex, kind of like a slow tornado funnel turned on its side.

I look to tenth-row-center and our own three demons are still there, and they seem to be arguing, but they are also changing. Their human forms are stretching horribly upward, becoming elongated and way less human and then really not human at all. As I watch, they expand into terrifying enormous things with some kind of ghostlike spirit-tentacles reaching out from the center where their faces used to be. Everyone else is struggling to get as far away from the vortex as possible; those three fling themselves into it.

I see Annie, who I somehow didn't guess would be sitting right next to Mr. Gabriel (*stupid*), just as one of the tentacles loops around her. She looks shocked and confused and afraid, and she screams as she's pulled in and down after Mr. Gabriel. A second later I see Danielle, also screaming, her eyes and mouth huge in her white, white face, her hands clawing at the dirty carpet, being pulled in as well. By Kingston? Which makes the inappropriate whistling during Danielle's curtain call suddenly seem way less creepy in comparison to what he is doing now.

I shove the textbook as far as it will go down the back of my pants (uncomfortable but practical) and wrap the fingers of my right hand through the middle of the protractor and then I jump off the stage and go running toward the vortex. The fact that I am terrified and really, really don't want to do this is lost in the central line of thought streaming steadily through my brain, that I need to go with them, I need to be there, I need to get down there if I'm going to save Annie. I hurl myself at the center but I only fall forward and smash into the broken auditorium chair behind it. I get up and throw myself at it again, but it still won't work, it's not working, it won't *take* me and I don't have a way to get in and I have to get in and I think my forehead is bleeding and they're getting away and it can't all be for nothing, it can't, it can't, the demoness was a liar and she's just running away with the rest of them and this is it I'm losing her I'll never see Annie again.

I look back in panic toward the stage and instantly lock eyes with Ryan, who is trying to push his way toward me through the throng. And then something circles my waist and I look down to see a tendril-tentacle that somehow I can tell belongs to Ms. Královna. It tightens and I yelp and I can feel the edge of the textbook, caught between me and the demoness's boa constrictor–like grip, gouging at the skin of my back and I can barely breathe as she drags me painfully forward and down and down and—

and then stops.

I'm at the brink of the vortex, and *now* it wants me. Now it's trying to suck me down, and the tentacle around me is pulling and pulling but Ryan has hold of my wrist and he is pulling me back.

"Let me go!" I scream at him. I have to go, I have to go now, or it's going to be too late. "Let me go, you *promised!*"

"I don't care!" he shouts back. "I can't let you do it!" He forces himself closer and grabs my other wrist, too, trying to hold on. I see him brace his legs against a pair of seats, anchoring himself in place, but I still don't really get how he has the strength to hold me there against the demoness's opposing effort. They're both strong, pulling in their opposite directions, and I am the rope in the worst game of tug-of-war *ever*, and it feels entirely possible they might very soon literally tear me apart.

His face is very close to mine now, and he can talk without shouting but he's still kind of shouting because he's angry and sad and scared but I think angry most of all. "You can't really believe I'm just going to stand here and watch you get sucked down by some messed-up demon vortex into hell knowing that you probably won't ever come back!"

"I have to! Annie's already down there!"

The demoness suddenly wrenches me toward her with new urgency and I slide backward a few feet toward the vortex, my right wrist pulling free of Ryan's grip. He immediately clamps his newly freed hand next to the other, both of them now crushing my left wrist in desperate overlapping circles, his thumbs pressing together white with the force of his effort.

"*Fuck* Annie!" he screams at me. "She chose her own fate, and I'm not letting you go down there after her. I don't care what you think you want, Cynthia Rothschild! Fuck her, and fuck you, too! I'm falling in love with you, goddammit—" And his voice breaks there and he closes his eyes for a second and then opens them again, and he is trying to hold on to me that way, too, staring into my eyes and not letting me look away. "I don't care what I promised, I just don't care, we don't have a deal, deal *over*, canceled, I am *not* doing this, I am not letting you go."

He's killing me.

I'm in physical agony from the impatient and increasingly

insistent yanking on my midsection from the other side of the vortex, but of course it's not just that. It's because this is what I have always wanted, always, more than anything, more than the moon: for someone to love me, like this, like in a story, fiercely and completely, and yeah I *know* it's crazy and ridiculous and we're only sixteen and barely know each other even after all of this but then all of this is exactly the kind of experience that accelerates emotional connection, and we both know in this moment that there is something real and true between us. There really is. It's like musical-theater love, condensed and intense and with music and power, and I look at him standing there, still in full makeup, his mouth set in a determined line, fingers digging into the skin of my wrist, fighting to make me stay, to not disappear, to stay, with him, and screw the cost and screw the consequences.

And oh, I want to.

My mind is broadcasting emergency renditions of every applicable musical-theater song at full volume, trying to drown me out with "I Will Never Leave You" from *Side Show* and "All I Ask of You" from *The Phantom of the Opera* and "Stay with Me" from *Into the Woods* (damn you, Sondheim) and all the nerve endings in my entire body are trying to squeeze themselves into my wrist at the point of contact with Ryan's hands and I know that if they could they would jump ship entirely because I am not following the script I am making the wrong choice and taking the stupid path and going against the music and screwing up the ending.

I'm sorry, I tell them.

I want to stay.

Oh, God, do I want to stay.

But I can't.

"Ryan," I say, and I'm crying, and it hurts to say his name because I'm afraid it's the last time I'm ever going to get to say it to him, "I'm so sorry."

I stab him in the side with the corner of the protractor as hard as I can.

He jerks backward in surprise and pain, losing his grip, and in that instant I fly backward and down into the vortex. Ryan's angry, horrified, wounded eyes are the last thing I see before the swirling darkness takes me in completely and everything goes black and I am gone.

Chapter | 16

There is darkness, and falling, and pain.

My brain isn't speaking to me anymore, and there is no more music, and everything is black and there is nothing to see except the lingering afterimage of Ryan's eyes. I don't want to see them, but closing my own eyes doesn't make them go away, and so apparently there is nothing I can really do about that.

The tendril of the demoness is still around me, a different black in the blackness, and I understand instinctively that if she were to let go of me now, I would be trapped here in this nothingness forever.

Which would totally, totally suck.

I try to use that, to remind myself that as afraid as I am of what is about to happen, there are always worse things.

It doesn't really make me feel any better.

My head is stinging, and when I touch it I can feel what is probably blood; I think I gashed my forehead on the seats while trying to throw myself into the vortex those first few times. The more I think about it, the more it seems to be hurting, and then I realize that it's not just my head. The quality of the blackness is changing, becoming different, thicker, *harder,* somehow, and it's like a fine web of pain has begun to settle over the entire surface of my skin. My heart is beating faster and faster and I am starting to get even more afraid. Because the darkness around me now feels like something else, something sharper, like instead of air or nothing or whatever it was before, it is starting to be made of sandpaper or jagged rocks, scratching and piercing. I open my mouth to scream because now it's more like knives, and I can't get enough breath to scream but I can feel my nerve endings screaming and then suddenly the darkness is filled with light and there is air and I do suck enough in to start to scream but something forces itself into my mouth and I can't make any sound and then I crash to the — ground? — and something is holding me down and silent and I try to thrash my way free but I can hardly move at all.

Slowly I start to realize that the knives are gone. And that leads to the ability to start to think again, and to remember where I was on my way to, and that the fact that I am no longer moving or falling might mean that I have arrived there.

As soon as I think this I stop fighting, and then the thing holding me down lets me go. As it slides free of my mouth I get a glimpse of ghostly tendril and realize it was the demoness. And I try to think of why she would do that, and I realize it must have been important for me to be quiet and still. So I stay quiet and still. But I listen, and I look, and I try to get my bearings.

This is harder than I expect. I'm not moving, but everything around me still feels shifty and unstable. Flickery. It's like watching several channels of TV on the same screen at the same time.

One channel shows a vast barren plane surrounded by enormous spiky towering forms that could be mountains or giant stalagmites (stalactites? I can never remember which is which, up or down) or some kind of unnatural structures that just resemble those other things. Another channel looks for all the world like a New York City street, except that all the buildings are taller than they should be and tilted and the street is about ten times wider and there aren't any hot-dog vendors or taxis and the surface of the blacktop occasionally undulates like something is pushing up against it from below. Another looks like a boiling orange sea, and another looks like an alien football stadium, where the seats are filled with moving shapes that hurt my eyes and the cheap sections are so far up that I can't actually even see them.

It's like all of these things together and so not really any of them, but the one constant is a group of figures facing a central structure that alternately looks like an enormous judge's bench, a concert stage, a satanic temple, and the Washington Monument. Each of the figures is a demon, which I can tell because of the red auras above them but also because of how their shapes are wrong and terrifying and too big and with too many parts. And also because superimposed or lurking underneath or something I can still see the human aspects of Mr. Gabriel and Principal Kingston and Ms. Královna among them.

And each of the demons is accompanied by a smaller figure, and those don't change at all.

And one of them is Aaron and one of them is Danielle and one of them is Annie.

The humans are standing very still. I think they are in some kind of stasis or something, because none of them are showing any kind of expression. I am not super close to them, in my position tucked away behind what is sometimes a rock and sometimes a burning bush and sometimes a weird, alien blue thing that is still somehow entirely recognizable as almost being a street-side mailbox, but I am close enough to see their faces. I am also, I realize slowly, as I am still trying to process the unstable environment around me, able to hear that the demons are still arguing.

It's like when they say the word for *super-roach* and I can understand that's what they mean but I can also hear that the actual syllables being spoken are not anything close to human, let alone English, speech.

The gist of things seems to be that Gabriel and Kingston are *pissed*.

Good old Ms. Královna did exactly what she promised, apparently. She created the vortex before Kingston and Gabriel had a chance to stage their final, massive soul-sucking massacre in the auditorium and drain the life force out of everyone at once. The two men had their deal, of course, which included the sharing of the final spoils before heading back for the final battle, but they'd forgotten to account for the possible actions of Ms. K. Once the gateway was open, they had to go through. She dragged them away, and now they aren't nearly as strong as they'd planned to be. Which, of course, is just fine with her. But they are still, they assure her, strong enough to defeat her. Blah, blah, blah, lots of evil feather-fluffing and posturing. I don't understand most of what they actually say, there are too many demon words in there that don't seem to have human meanings, but I definitely get the overall picture.

The demoness just smiles at them and radiates self-satisfaction.

Have I mentioned that she is my favorite demon ever?

There is a klaxon sound, loud and long and piercing, and the arguing ceases instantly. All the demons turn their attention to that central structure, which now seems to be occupied by another demon, or maybe more than one — it's hard to look directly at it. They are apparently ready to get down to business.

Which means that pretty soon I am going to have to stop crouching here behind my rock-mailbox-fiery-foliage-whatever and do what I came here to do.

I'd been feeling kind of okay once the pain stopped and I was distracted by trying to figure out the lay of the land and stuff. But now my terror is back with a vengeance. My legs don't seem to want to hold me up anymore all of a sudden. I pull back from my peeking position and sit down hard on the ground. Something pokes me painfully in the back, and I remember that I'd stuffed the textbook down the back of my pants when everything started happening in the auditorium. I also remember that I've still got my right hand clenched tightly around the protractor.

Except it's not a protractor anymore. It looks more like an Alaskan ulu knife, with a bone handle I can curl my hand around and a very wicked-looking curved blade.

I reach back with my other hand and pull out the textbook, which of course is no longer a textbook, either. It's not as impressive as the ulu knife, though. It's just kind of a flat rectangle of some kind of flexible plasticky material, and it still has the biology cover art on the front of it. The back, though, now sports a strap that's connected to the plastic at both ends with some slack in the middle, which is very convenient. I loop my arm through it and slide it up around my shoulder. Much easier than trying to keep it stuffed in my pants.

Okay. So: magic protractor/ulu knife? Check.

Magic shieldy thing that is hopefully more impressive in function than form? Check.

That was a really short checklist. I wish I had more things to count. I miss my prop table.

I should probably keep an eye on what's happening. I should probably have a plan. I don't really have a plan. I know I need to use the ulu-protractor to sever the connection between Mr. Gabriel and Annie, and then I guess I will need to use the bio textbook/shield to stop Mr. Gabriel from killing us. But the demoness said I will only get to use it once, which seems kind of insufficient given that I can't imagine he will give up after one attempt.

Plus, there are a whole bunch of other demons here. There are maybe twenty or so in the row of what I take to be the contenders. And then there are unfathomable multitudes in the audience. I can really only see those clearly sometimes, depending on what form the arena is taking at any given moment. But I have no doubt they are always there, whether I can see them or not, and if any of them see me, that might be bad. What had Ms. Královna said? Meat and prey. I am meat and prey to them. I should probably try very hard to find a way to carry out my tasks without drawing too much attention to myself.

So that's kind of a plan, right? Save Annie, remain inconspicuous.

I get up into an awkward crouch again and peek back around my rock-mailbox-burning-bush.

All of the demon contenders are in a neat line now, facing whoever or whatever that central authority figure or figures may be. I think they are presenting their human consorts, proving they've met the requirements of the competition. They step forward one at a time, and I feel more than hear a deafening roar from the audience in response. There is a pause, and then a decisive movement from the center, and the roar becomes a million times what it was and I have to fight not to cower behind my rock.

The demons turn and move outward, toward the edges of what has become a fixed great circular arena. What had been the central structure has now somehow moved itself to be far to one end and slightly above one edge of the circle. The demons set their humans against the enclosing wall, appearing to tether them there with some of their own tendril-energy material. Then they turn toward the center. There is another klaxon. And then . . . well, then, of course, all hell breaks loose.

The demons launch themselves toward the center of the arena and, necessarily, one another. They have all taken mostly fixed forms now, all different, but all about equally horrifying. Principal Kingston resembles what I can only think of as some kind of bear-lion hybrid with eight enormous spider legs sprouting awkwardly from a matted, filthy, furry abdomen. Ms. Královna seems to have a nautical theme going on: she has real tentacles now, plus a series of spiky fins, several long tendrils that look like sea anemone or jellyfish stingers, and a long eel-like head with rows and rows of very sharp-looking teeth. Mr. Gabriel looks a lot like the Minotaur from Greek mythology—giant bull's head with sweeping horns curving up into cruelly sharp points, barrelly fur-covered chest, flashing red eyes, even a shiny golden nose ring—only with gargantuan black wings and a lower half that morphs gradually into some kind of monstrous bird, with hooked talons bigger than my head. His huge, muscular arms are almost human-looking, except for the giant clawlike hands at the end of them. I can't help wondering whether the Minotaur thing is a nod to Annie's one-time obsession with mythology or just a weird coincidence.

The demoness's head swivels toward me, and as we make eye contact I feel her take hold of me, like she's reached right into the essence of what I am, the swirly cocktail of molecules and atoms and particles and whatever else that combine to make me *me,* and stretched it, pulling it thin and wide and wrapping it around herself like a blanket.

Bed hog, I think incoherently, and then what she's taken — no, not *taken,* because it's still connected to me, so maybe *borrowed* — what she's borrowed, what's she's using, the part of me that she's pulled over to where she is, settles into her like a second skin.

"Oh," I say out loud as I stagger forward and land hard on my knees. That's . . . really unpleasant. The umbrella analogy was *so* way off. I feel — diminished. Weak.

Vulnerable.

I fall forward onto my hands, head down.

"Okay," I tell myself out loud. "It's okay. You're okay." Because I have to pull it together here, right now. I give myself a few seconds to breathe, in and out, there you go, totally fine, and then I make myself start to straighten back up.

This is harder than I would like, and I stop once I get back to my knees. I give myself another few seconds, breathing, getting used to this new different feeling of being *less* than I was before. Temporarily, I remind myself. Just for now. Except now is probably exactly the time when it would be highly beneficial to be at full power.

Well, not much I can do about that at the moment. I have to work with what I've got. One more deep breath and then I get all the way back up to my feet and raise my head.

The demons are going at one another like maniacs.

They all have weapons of some sort, either semi-familiar weapon-type things like axes and knives, or else parts of their demon bodies that kind of extend into claws and hooks and things like that. The weapons — all of them, external and body-part — are glowing red at various intensities. I watch for a minute, and I think I finally get how this is going to work.

Scary as the demons have all become physically, the real fighting is being done with their demony magic energy. *That* is what Gabriel and Kingston were feeding with the souls of the high school kids, and it's also why my roachy goodness is so valuable to Ms. Královna. Because if the demons were just fighting physically, my resistance would be next to useless. But they're not. They're using their demon essence. The same stuff that gives off the red aura that Mr. Gabriel made me able to see. I see it now, in what they're all using to smite one another with.

And I see something else, too. The more intense the red aura on the weapon, the more the other demon seems to feel it, and suffer . . . but then the more diminished the attacker seems to be, energy-wise, immediately after. I think they've only got a finite amount of the stuff to work with, and the harder the hit, the less they have left to hit with the next time. Or to defend themselves with against the others. Which, again, puts the demoness in a very good position, since she can use my resistance to bolster her own defenses. And so she can hit harder, and suffer less damage. It's really frickin' brilliant. She's totally going to win.

Right. So she's all set, and I should get to work.

The initial shock of having a great swath of my own personal energy shifted over to someone else has eased a little, but I still feel shaky and weak. Which sucks, given that I am surrounded by terrifying creatures who are going to want to kill me if they notice me. Which so far they have not, since I am very small compared to everything else around me, and they are all focused on the general massacre happening in the center of the arena at the moment. Which means I should get going while they remain thus distracted.

I turn to scan the edges of the circle, to find where Gabriel left my best friend.

I see Aaron first, who seems just as happy to be here as he expected to be. He's cheering for his demoness and screaming insults at the other demons and to all appearances having the time of his life.

It only takes me a second more to find Annie, and what I see makes it hard to keep my hard-won upright position.

She's screaming. She's screaming and terrified and, in stark contrast to Aaron's insane joy, staring frantically around her in absolute and completely bewildered horror. I had half expected to have to drag her away against her will once I cut the cord to the librarian, but I can see that this is not going to be necessary. Whatever delusions she'd let herself believe in, whatever romanticized fairy-tale scenario she had bought into, I think her eyes are fully open to her awful situation now.

I can't stand to see her like this. It was almost better when she was delusional. At least then she wasn't so scared.

So go save her, you idiot.

I start to run. It's a stumbly run, because I am still not feeling anything like my personal physical best here, but it's still faster than walking. I keep to the edges of the arena, since obviously running into the middle of the demony fray is not an option. But I really, really wish the arena were not quite so enormous. Especially because I have suddenly remembered that I have to sever Annie's connection to Mr. Gabriel ASAP not just to get it done and over with, but because if one of the other demons manages to kill him before I get to her, then Annie is going to die right along with him.

Oh, crap.

I cannot let that happen. Not now, not when I'm here and I've come so far and the end is finally in sight.

I force my legs to run a little faster.

I am about halfway around when I feel something fast and sharp and agonizing slice through my shoulder.

One of the audience demons has noticed me. It's green and reptilian and gigantic, and one of its long, snaky appendages is wrapping itself around my ankle while another goes for my arm. Each one has long, needle-thin spikes at various intervals along the surface, and one of these is red with blood from my shoulder. I scream and try to jerk away, which only succeeds in tumbling me to the ground, since the thing still has a firm grip on my ankle. It begins to drag me toward where the main bulk of it is, and I stare in helpless horror as a second mouth opens lower down on its scaly abdomen, opening wide to show me all of the many long and pointy teeth it is about to rip me apart with. I scream again and without thinking I slice at the tentacle with the ulu-protractor, praying to God and Sondheim and all that is holy and good that the demoness hadn't said anything about only getting to use the protractor once, too.

Both of the demon's mouths scream in pain and surprise, and the tentacle loosens around my ankle and I scramble back to my feet and take off, away, not looking back to see if it is still coming. I don't think it can; I think the noncompeting demons have to stay out of the arena proper. I hope this is enforced with some kind of absolute, impossible-to-break prevention magic, a demonic Invisible Fence perimeter, because if it's just that they have to pay a hefty fine or something for breaking the rules, I am probably totally screwed.

But nothing new grabs me or slices through me and I keep running. And when I've covered about another quarter of the distance, Annie sees me.

"*CYN!*" she screams, and I can only pray again that Gabriel and Kingston are both too busy or too far away to have heard her.

Shut up! I scream back at her in my mind, still running. I can't hold a finger to my lips to make the international *shh* sign because that is really hard to do when you're running as fast as you can and anyway I'm afraid I might cut my nose off with the protractor.

She can't seem to shut up, though, and she screams my name twice more before she dissolves into wordless sobbing shrieks. Despite myself, I turn my head to see if anyone has noticed. And I stumble to a stop.

Kingston is looking right at me from across the arena.

He looks from me to Annie and then back, still fending off another demon with several of his spider legs. And then he looks in another direction, and I follow to see what he is looking at, and it is Mr. Gabriel.

Mr. Gabriel is not looking at me. Or at Kingston or Annie. He's facing away from us entirely, in the final throes of slaughtering a demon that looks kind of like a giant scorpion crossed with a Venus flytrap and a dandelion.

Kingston looks back at me and smiles a terrible lion-bear smile. And my heart shrivels into a tiny knot and sinks into the depths of my toes, and I wait for him to call some warning to the librarian.

And then he turns to the demon he was still half fighting and gets back to it.

I stand there for a second, not getting it. Until I remember that Principal Kingston and Mr. Gabriel are not actually friends. In fact, they are enemies. They had a truce, but now it is over. That terrible smile was not because he was about to screw me and Annie. It was because I am about to screw Mr. Gabriel.

Annie screams my name again, spurring me back into motion and making me want to punch her in the face. *"Shut up, dammit!"* I scream, out loud this time, but I don't think she can hear me. I don't think she's capable of much in the way of rational sensory input right now at all.

I glance again at Mr. Gabriel, just in time to see him deliver the killing blow to his plant-scorpion adversary. His energy weapons seem to be his long, clawlike hands, and as he stands over the other demon's dead body, screaming up at the sky in savage triumph, he raises his hands above his head and I see that the red glow gathered there around them is growing stronger. And so apparently every demon you kill gives up its remaining energy to you, sort of *Highlander*-style. In the midst of everything, I can't help wondering if anyone else I know has even seen that movie and would get that reference. I bet Ryan has. The thought of him is like being kicked in the heart, and I realize I have wasted several precious seconds in my own head, and meanwhile Mr. Gabriel is done with his victim and is casting around for a new one. There aren't very many left.

I throw everything I have left into a desperate burst of speed. *Don't see me, please don't see me, please don't see me* I beg the librarian in my head, but I don't turn back around to find out if he's seen me or not. I just keep running and running and running until Annie is there in front of me. And then I stagger to a stop and she collapses into my arms.

I shove her backward, away from me. No time for that, and anyway I'm still undecided whether I want to hug her and never let go or stick with my original desire to punch her in the face. I ignore her newly bewildered expression and find the tendril of the librarian's demon energy that has her fixed to where she's standing. It's looped around both of her legs like manacles, anchoring her to the ground. She has clearly tried already to free herself; the skin around her ankles is red and angry and torn. She's bleeding a little on one side, and the bit of Mr. Gabriel's tether that touches her there seems to be pressing itself deeper against the wound. In fact — I stare, and have to fight back a wave of nausea. The tendril is lined with tiny . . . tongues. Lots of them. They are moving eagerly against her damaged ankle, literally drinking in her pain and fear and blood.

And through the semitransparent substance of the tendril itself, I can see a darker thread of Mr. Gabriel's demonic essence, so deep a red it's almost black, and somehow I know that's what I need to destroy. It runs up and into Annie like a vein, carrying his terrible poison into her soul. She may be seeing things for what they really are now, but they're still connected more than just physically. He's still linked to her.

But not for long.

I drop to my knees beside her and swing my hand up and then down, slicing neatly through the librarian's final hold on my best friend as easily as if his horrible demon-energy-binding were nothing but a piece of banana bread and I had the mother of all Ginsu knives to cut it with.

Mr. Gabriel's scream of pain and horror and fury and surprise hits me from behind with actual physical force and knocks me over at the same time as it drowns out all the other sound in the arena.

For a second everything stops; the other demons freeze midfight, the audience goes quiet, and they all seem to be searching around for the source of the disturbance. I scramble to turn around, but I'm still on the ground when Mr. Gabriel stops screaming and whips his head around toward where he'd left his bride-to-be.

And he sees me, and he knows what I have done.

His terrible red eyes flash blindingly and he roars his horrible roar again. And then he comes for me. The rest of the demons — there are only a few still alive among the combatants — burst back into motion and sound, continuing their own efforts, but I can't spare them much attention. My eyes are locked on the evil librarian's. I can't seem to look away; he's got me pinned there like the bug that I am. Vaguely, I feel Annie pulling at me and screaming, and I see that the demoness is drawing her stingers from Principal Kingston's carcass and turning to throw herself after Mr. G.

He only has eyes for me, though. He's coming hard and fast, insane with rage and absolutely terrifying.

I can't move. I can only sit there and watch as he raises his impossible claw-hand, preparing for the strike he is already visualizing in his mind, even though he is still relatively far away, and I think of my biology textbook/shield, still looped around my shoulder, and wonder whose astoundingly stupid idea it was to make it only work once. Was I supposed to negotiate that point during the deal-making process? Did the demoness expect me to talk her up to a three-strikes kind of scenario? Three is a much more reasonable number.

I do still have the ulu-protractor, but using it as a weapon against him would be like pricking King Kong in the toe with the point of a safety pin. He'd barely feel it, and in the meantime he'd be ripping through me with his claw-hands and tearing my insides out like spaghetti.

Well, you've got to do something, my brain says reasonably, *and he's getting close now, so make a choice and carry it out. It's not like you've got all that many options to choose from.*

This is very true. In fact, I think I've only got about two: get my textbook/shield up in time to catch his blow, or die horribly.

I like when choices are easy like that.

Annie is still screaming and trying to pull me away; she's behind me on the ground, pulling me backward, and this is good, that's a good place for her, because I don't want her to get in the way.

I'm still half sitting, half lying on the ground, my legs splayed out before me, but I don't feel pinned anymore. I feel patient and calm. I am just waiting for my cue. I make sure my shield is positioned appropriately on my upper arm, biology-side out. Timing is everything, and I have to get this exactly right.

The librarian staggers suddenly; this is because the demoness has thrown herself forward and is clinging to his back, crushing one of his wings and flaying him with her stingers. As I watch, she opens her mouth and bites deeply into his shoulder with her eel-teeth.

Mr. Gabriel keeps coming. Without Annie he's lost everything, and I don't know if he still thinks he can win and have his dreamed-of future of eternal demonic romance, or if he just wants to get to kill me before he dies, but either way he's not stopping to deal with Ms. Královna. He's growling and roaring, and I think there are some words mixed in there with the animal sounds, and I think some of them are *mine* and *no* and *kill* and *bitch*.

He's coming, coming closer, and I'm waiting, and everything else just falls away. I'm listening for the call in my headset, waiting for the conductor's baton to drop, and I'm ready. And then the moment comes. With a final scream of rage and pain and loss, he swings his claw-hand down to rip me open, but it is all happening as I have rehearsed it in my mind and I turn and raise up my shield and at the moment of contact there is a blinding flash of light and I have to turn my head from the brightness and the power of it. I can't see, but somehow I can still tell that Mr. Gabriel is thrown violently backward. And as my sight comes slowly back, I see the demoness atop him, driving her stingers into him again and again and again.

There is that *Highlander* moment again, but this time it is Ms. Královna who absorbs her victim's energy. She screams her own scream of triumph, and then the klaxon sounds again, and the battle is over.

Aaron is jumping around at the end of his tether like an overexcited dog, visibly beside himself with happiness. He's gazing lovingly at his bloody, exhausted, exhilarated fish-featured demoness with the same naked *want* as when she was in human form. Perhaps more. She spares him a tolerant, fond smile, which is particularly disturbing with her long eel's mouth, and I swear he almost loses consciousness from bliss.

I finally turn around to look at Annie. She's sitting behind me, still crying, but at least the screaming has stopped.

And honestly, I think she's allowed to cry a bit after everything she's been through. I think she's allowed to cry a lot.

I scootch back to sit beside her, and put my arms around her, and she collapses against me into helpless sobs.

"It's okay," I tell her, smoothing my hand over her hair in that way that you do when someone is sobbing into your chest. "It's over now."

And I know that I'm right, and I also know that *over* has a lot of meanings for her right now, and that part of her is still probably mourning the loss of her sexy librarian fiancé.

And that's all okay, too. Because she will still be fine in the end, because all heartbreaks heal in time, and life goes on, and we still have another year of high school to survive. And I'll help her get through it, because that's what best friends do. And I can do that, because I'm still here, and not dead.

Somehow, I have managed to make it through this relatively intact.

And more than anything else I'm feeling right now — residual terror and pain and relief and exhaustion and revulsion and mild yet somewhat amused contempt for Aaron and anxiety about the rest of what I promised the demoness and uncertainty about how I'm going to make things right with Ryan and everything, everything else — mostly, I'm just so happy to have my best friend back at last.

Chapter | 17

After a while, Annie whispers against my now very tear-dampened shirt, "Can we go home now?"

That's a good question. I would like the answer to be yes.

The demoness is doing what I'm guessing are some kind of official demony things over by the judge's bench/head table/satanic temple. There is probably some serious paperwork or something when a new demon ruler takes over, I would imagine.

I'm definitely antsy to get out of here. Both because, you know, it's a demon world and we do not belong here and there are dead demon remains everywhere, but also because I'm starting to worry about all of the audience demons, who are no longer distracted by the fighting now that the fighting is over. They have left us alone so far, but I keep hearing the demoness saying meat and prey in my head. After all of this,

I do not want to be eaten by some random demon who just wanted a postshow snack.

I am trying to figure out how to get Ms. Královna's attention, planning to give her a little *check, please* gesture and hope that she takes my meaning, when she turns away from the official whatevers and starts walking over to us. *Walking* is a loose term; she's sort of half swimming, half balancing on her tentacles, but it's the same general idea. Aaron is glued to her side, still radiating ecstasy like a space heater of joy.

"I have something that belongs to you," she says without preamble, and all at once I feel that part of me she'd pulled into her come snapping back to where it belongs. Instantly I feel tons better.

"Thanks," I say. "Glad to have all of me together in one place again." And I am. Very glad. I might not have been aware of my whole roach thing before Mr. Gabriel came along, but it's clear that not having it makes a big difference. It's a part of me, like it or not. And actually I realize that I do like it. Because, hey, without it, I would almost certainly be dead right now, and Annie would be Mr. Gabriel's tormented demon bride.

"I suppose you may take that other one back with you as well," Ms. Královna says, and for a second I have no idea what she is talking about. She gestures impatiently to a section of the wall, and I see Danielle lying there, apparently unconscious. I had completely forgotten about her.

"Is that Danielle Hornick?" Annie says in a voice that suggests she doesn't see how it can be but that clearly anything is possible at this point.

"Yeah," I tell her, and then to the demoness, "Um, yes. Thank you." A thought occurs to me, and I glance around, trying to see what happened to the other human consorts. At least some of them are probably still alive, like Danielle is, unless they were linked in the same special demon-deputy way that Annie was. "What about —?"

She seems to know what I am thinking. "Those others are not your concern."

"But — can't they come back with us, too? I can't just leave them . . ."

"That was never part of the deal. I'm giving you this other one from your school. As a gift. Be satisfied with that."

"But —"

"Do you want me to say that you can't have her either?"

"No," I say at once. I remember how she took the first deal off the table during our initial negotiations. I hate this, but I know there's nothing I can do. I have to save who I can. "Can you send the three of us back now, then? Please?"

She is all business again. "Yes. My schedule is already completely booked, and I still have things to . . . do, here." She glances aside at Aaron when she says this, with a frighteningly predatory expression. He beams back at her.

"I, uh, hope you guys are very happy together," I manage.

"Oh, yes," she says, smiling widely. "We will be."

She caresses the side of his jaw with one of her tentacle tips, leaving a faint trail of slime, and he closes his eyes in apparent rapture.

There is an awkward pause for the rest of us, which I break

by saying, "So how does this work, then? Do we have to do that vortex thing again?"

"Not exactly," she says. "The gateway to the library still exists, and I can send you that way. It won't be as bad."

"Thank God," Annie mutters. I agree with this statement wholeheartedly.

And it turns out to be true. It's not fun, but it's nothing like the knives and agony of the vortex. We all hold hands — or rather, Annie and I each hold one of Danielle's hands, since she is still unconscious, and then join our free hands together to close the circle — and then the demoness makes a hole in the air and pushes us into it. As it closes up behind us, I hear her voice faintly but very clearly inside my head.

"See you again soon, Cynthia."

And then there is a very disorienting space of nothingness until we all slam heavily down onto the floor of the high-school library's back office.

"Ow," says Danielle, coming groggily awake. She mutters something else that sounds like it wants to be "What the hell?"

"You're okay," I tell her. "It's a long story but you'll feel better tomorrow."

"Mmnnnnnhh?"

I sigh and make Annie help me drag Danielle to her feet. "Come on," I say, "we'll help you get home."

I have no idea how much time has passed.

It's still dark out when we reach the main entrance of the school, but that could mean it's later the same night or six nights from when we left or maybe six years, for all I know. I decide not to worry too much about that right now. I've apparently become really good at compartmentalizing my problems over the past few weeks.

My cell phone is still in my backpack, which I last saw under the prop table, and Annie's is God-knows-where at this point, but Danielle has hers (I make a mental note to be appalled later that she was carrying her cell phone in her pocket *during the show*) and I use it to call us a cab. I wake her back up enough to get her address. It takes both me and Annie to help her to the house, and I have no idea what to tell her parents, but that turns out not to matter. They fling the door open and yank her inside as soon as they see who it is. I hear snatches of phrases like *so worried* and *after the incident at the school* and *thank God you're safe* and then they slam the door.

Annie is barely conscious herself at this point, and as much as I want to talk about what Danielle's parents may have been referring to, I realize that now is not the time. Back in the cab, I let her doze with her head on my shoulder until we get to her house. Her parents have a similar reaction, although they, at least, actually acknowledge my presence.

"Thank God you girls are okay," Mrs. Gibson says. "We heard about what happened, and they said they couldn't account for everyone and we didn't know . . ." She trails off, holding Annie tight against her. "Well, you're here now. That's all that matters."

"Can you get home all right?" Mr. Gibson asks me, and I'm touched by his concern, especially since he knows I only live a few blocks away and he clearly wants to focus on Annie right now.

"Yes, Mr. Gibson. I'm fine. Thanks. I'll check on Annie tomorrow, if that's all right."

He nods and walks me distractedly to the door.

"Take care, Cyn," he says.

The cab driver lets me off at my own house, finally, and I pay him for all three stops with money I took from Danielle's wallet (also inexplicably in her costume pocket) and head up the porch steps.

After the receptions we got at the other houses, I'm not surprised that my dad pulls the door open as soon as I reach for the doorknob. I am a little surprised to see my mom standing behind him, but I guess that's only because I'm so not used to her ever being there when I come home.

He grabs me and then does that thing where he hugs me tight enough to suffocate me and then holds me at arm's length to look me over for signs of damage. "Are you all right?"

"Yes, I'm fine. Can I come all the way inside, please?"

"Oh. Of course. Come on." He lets me by and then closes the door behind me.

I sink down onto the edge of the couch.

"What happened to your forehead?" my mother says, reaching out to almost but not quite touch it.

"Oh. I don't—I don't know. I think I fell against a chair." Which is definitely a very lame explanation, but they just look at each other and nod.

"They said—they said there was some kind of chemical leak at the school following the performance," my dad says, and even now I'm kind of amazed that he remembered there *was* a performance. "People hallucinating, a lot of people missing . . ."

He pauses, then goes on. "They said to try not to worry, that kids may have wandered off under the effects of the hallucinations, or maybe passed out somewhere, but that they were out looking and we should all just stay home so we'd be here when you made it back." He sits down beside me and hugs me again. "I'm so glad you're okay."

I wonder who started the chemical leak/hallucinogen story. It's a good one — covers a lot of ground, and explains away a lot of really hard to explain things.

"Did — did anyone get hurt? I mean, really hurt?"

My parents look at each other again. "Some teachers are missing," my dad says, "but they could still turn up, just like you kids are still turning up. A lot of people were hurt in the confusion, but minor things, mostly, I think. Do you — do you know if all of your friends are okay?"

My dad remembering to ask about my friends is even more amazing than him remembering about the show. "I know Annie is okay. I don't know about Diane or Leticia or — or Ryan."

"Diane's mother called a few hours ago," my mother says. "She and Leticia are both fine. They were worried about you, of course. I'll call to let them know you're all right." She gets up and heads to the kitchen.

"I don't know what happened to my cell phone," I say. "I think it might still be at school. Somewhere."

"Don't worry about that now, honey. We'll sort that all out tomorrow."

I nod, but that wasn't all that I meant. "I need to call Ryan. To see if he's okay. What — what time is it?"

"It's late. But don't worry about that, either. I don't think anyone will mind a late phone call if it's to tell someone else you're alive."

It's the first time he's acknowledged that there was a chance I might have been not-alive. We both seem to realize it at the same time, and we sit there for a moment, just looking at each other, not saying anything. We can hear my mom's voice speaking softly on the landline in the kitchen, but I can't quite make out what she's saying.

"Go ahead and use my office phone," he says.

I head down the hall to his office and dial Ryan's number, which I have memorized in the course of staring at it over and over in my contacts list since he first gave it to me. It rings until it goes to voice mail. I hang up without leaving a message.

I try his home number next (I have to look that one up). His mother answers after one ring, which strikes me as a bad sign.

"Hello?"

"Mrs. Halsey? It's —" I realize suddenly that she might have no idea who I am. "It's Cynthia Rothschild, from — from school. From the show. I'm a friend of Ryan's. Is he —?"

"Oh, hello, Cynthia. Ryan's mentioned you, of course. I'm sure he'll be glad to know you're all right."

Something that had been crushing my heart like an iron band suddenly loosens. "So he's okay? He's there?"

"He's okay," she says. "He's not here. He's at the hospital with Jorge. Jorge's all right, too, but he's got a bad sprain or maybe a fracture. They're waiting on X-rays now. Ryan's just keeping him company."

"Can you tell him I'm okay? And that I lost my cell? I tried calling his, but . . ."

"He lost his, too. But I'll tell him. Don't worry. Thank you so much for calling, Cynthia. I'm so glad you're all right. And of course Ryan will be, too."

We hang up, and I stand there in the dark for another minute. My relief at knowing he's okay and my surprise and pleasure at the fact that he actually mentioned me to his mother at some point are fighting with my disappointment that I couldn't talk to him. I don't even know if he tried to contact me. He didn't call the house, obviously; my parents would have said so.

I don't even know what I would say to him. "I'm sorry, I had to, please forgive me"? Part of me tries to suggest that Ryan should be the one apologizing, that we had a deal, that he shouldn't have tried to stop me. But that part of me is an idiot. I can't be mad at him for not wanting me to go. I can't be mad at him for telling me he was falling in love with me.

But I can't really be sorry for what I did, either. I'm sorry I had to hurt him, but I'm not sorry I went after Annie.

Will it matter that I kept my part of the deal? That I came back?

I hope so.

I go to see Annie late the next morning. She's still in bed, but her parents send me right back to her room anyway.

"Hey," she says weakly when I knock on the doorframe. She's propped up against some pillows, a book lying unopened beside her. Above the blankets, I can see that she's wearing pink pajamas with little cats on them.

It hits me all over again how much I've missed her.

"Can I come in?"

She rolls her eyes at me. "Of course, you freak. Get over here."

I close the door behind me and go over to sit on the edge of her bed. For a moment we just look at each other. I'm not sure what to say, or how to begin. But before I can even try, she reaches over and grabs my hand.

"I don't even know how to try to tell you how sorry I am," she says, looking into my eyes like she wants me to be able to see right through them, directly into her mind and heart. "Or how grateful. Grateful is not even close to the right word for what I'm feeling, Cyn. I can't even—" She laughs awkwardly, but even this faint shadow of her normal Annie laugh is like music to my soul. "How do you thank someone for going to hell and back to save you from—from yourself?"

"I don't think it was technically hell," I say. "I mean, not *the* hell, at least. Maybe *a* hell."

She punches me in the thigh with the hand that's still holding mine. "It was hellish enough, whatever it was." She shakes her head. "Don't try to make light of this, Cyn. I can't."

"Okay," I say. I can't make light of it either, really. "But I'm sorry, too."

She stares. "For what?"

"For not saving you sooner. For not being able to—to talk sense into you before it got too late." These are not really the things I'm trying to say. I don't know what I'm trying to say, exactly. "For letting you disappear like that."

"It's not your fault, Cyn. Jesus. You tried! I remember — a lot of it's weird, kind of fuzzy and not-real, but I remember. I remember thinking you just couldn't understand, but of course I was kind of, uh, not quite myself, I guess."

"Do you — do you miss him?"

She stares harder.

"I mean, what you thought he was. The part that you wanted to believe in. The last time I saw you with him, in the library . . . you looked so happy."

She's quiet for a minute. "A little," she says at last. "Not really him, of course. Not who he was underneath. But that feeling — I miss feeling that way. I miss having someone, loving someone. Being loved. I mean, I know it wasn't real, but it *felt* real. Losing that . . . hurts. Even though I know it wasn't true. None of it was true. But my heart doesn't seem to really get it."

"I'm sorry, Annie."

She shrugs halfheartedly and tries to smile, although it's not very convincing. "Hey, everyone goes through breakups, right? I'll survive. I just — I wish I could have it for real, you know? With an actual human boy. Who wouldn't want to turn me into some kind of monster."

"You can. You will!"

She shrugs again. "Maybe."

I grasp her hand a little tighter. There's something else I need to ask her, and it takes me a minute to work up to it.

"How much of what you said was true?" I ask quietly. "About how people see you, how you feel . . . ?"

She looks down, and I wait.

"Some of it," she says. "I mean, I wouldn't have chosen any of what happened if I'd been in my right mind, obviously. But what I said about feeling trapped, about not being . . . not wanting to be that person that everyone thinks I am . . . that's true."

"Why didn't you ever tell me?"

She bites her lip, still not looking at me. "I don't think I really ever admitted it to myself before. It didn't seem possible that things could ever be different, and so I didn't let myself really think of how much I wished they could." She sighs, and it's as though I can see her settling back into accepting this, putting on her old beliefs like some uncomfortable dress she hates but feels like she has to wear anyway.

"Hey," I say. She still doesn't look up, so I poke her with my free hand. She glances at me from under her lashes but still won't quite meet my eyes.

"Things can be different," I tell her. "Christ, Annie, I don't think either of us could possibly go back to being exactly who we were before even if we wanted to."

She appears to think about this for a minute. "That's probably at least a little bit true," she admits finally.

"It's a lot true, you moron. Um, are you *aware* of what has been going on over the past few weeks? Allow me to recap for you: *Crazy impossible things* have happened. *Demons* invaded our school and one of them tried to steal you away to be his terrible child bride. The world has things in it that we never knew were there. We know things that most people don't even come close to suspecting. We have been through things that most people could never, ever believe. We went to hell and back, dammit! We are so not the same people we were before. We can be — we can be whatever we want to be now."

As I say this, I realize I believe it. Not that I didn't like who I was before. But there's no way I'm just going to cast aside the things I know about myself now, the discovery of what I'm capable of, of what I can do. I *want* to be this new person, the one who has made it through all of this alive, and is still remarkably mentally sound despite it all.

"Annie," I go on, very seriously. "You cut class, like, every day by the end. *All* of them. You are quite obviously no longer the sweet, rule-abiding girl I knew before. That ship has *sailed,* my friend."

She laughs again, and this time it's almost her real laugh. But there's a tinge of fear to it as well.

"I still love you, though," I tell her. "You can be different and still yourself and I will still love you, no matter what."

Now she meets my eyes, and I see that I have hit on at least part of what the fear was about. She doesn't say anything, but she holds my hand a little more tightly.

"Maybe once we get back to school we can work on finding you some of that adventure you're looking for," I add.

"Uh, no. Or at least, not quite yet. I think I've hit my adventure quota for the time being." Then she smiles, just a little. "Maybe in the spring."

"Deal," I say.

"In the meantime," she says, "speaking of adventures, I seem to remember some progress being made on the Ryan

Halsey front before I, um, kind of lost track of what was happening."

Now it's my turn to look away. "Yeah. I don't quite know where things stand there, exactly. He did tell me that he was falling in love with me—"

She sits bolt upright. "*What?*"

"But then I stabbed him with a magic protractor and we haven't spoken since."

Her mouth opens and then closes without saying anything. After a moment she tries again. "You might have to explain that a little."

I explain. I tell her the whole story of what she missed, leaving out the part where Ryan tried to convince me that maybe we should just let Annie go, but keeping the part where he tried to stop me from going through the vortex. I just made it more about how he'd suddenly realized he loved me—more in the moment, less premeditated. I stand by my continually evolving belief that not everyone needs to know everything.

Just like neither of them needs to know about the rest of my deal with the demoness. Some things get to stay secrets, I think.

I focus a lot on the details of that kiss, which I think successfully distracts us both from some of the other, less-pleasant details.

"Well, when are you going to call him?" Annie demands when I am done.

"I already called him! He never called back!"

She waves this away. "He was at the hospital. You don't even know if his mother gave him the message."

"He could have called me anytime on his own, if he really wanted to. For all he knows, I'm dead!"

"I'm sure he knows you're not dead. Otherwise he definitely would have called your house by now."

I think about this. "So, he would have called if he thought I might be dead, but since I'm still alive, he doesn't want to talk to me?"

Annie gives me an exasperated look that I don't think I quite deserve. "Since he knows you're still alive, he doesn't have to call to find out if you're dead. But you were the one who stabbed him. I think that leaves the ball in your court."

"But last night —"

She shakes her head. "Last night didn't count. That was the call to find out if *he* was alive. Now that you know he's alive, you have to call again, with different motives."

That . . . sort of makes a weird kind of sense. But I still don't feel ready to act on it.

Annie's mom pokes her head in to say that she thinks Annie should probably go back to resting. It's still not clear exactly what they think happened to her, but the official story has included reassurances that the effects of the chemicals were not long lasting or harmful, other than the initial hallucinations, and so a few days of rest should be all anyone needs who wasn't actually injured in the immediate fallout.

I promise I'll come back to see her again soon, and make my way back home.

✳   ✳   ✳

The school is closed for a few days, so they can repair the damage to the auditorium and make sure there are no further signs of the (imaginary) chemicals that were somehow released into the school that night. All the students have been accounted for, with only various minor injuries. All the teachers, too, with (of course) three notable exceptions: the new principal, the new Italian teacher, and the still-kind-of-new librarian.

I go back on the first day it's open. Annie stays home; she's still sort of reeling from the whole experience, and I don't blame her for wanting to take a little more time to recover. Leticia stays home, too, since her mom is, understandably, even more freaked about this than she was when Principal Morse died. Diane texts me (on my new phone) to say she was going to come in but actually woke up feeling kind of sick, so she's just going to lie on the couch and watch bad TV and I should call her later and let her know how the first day back was.

It's a Monday, so no Italian, which is good. I don't think I'm ready for that. I keep almost texting Ryan, assuming he must have gotten a new phone by now, too, but I don't. I don't know what to say, exactly, but I know that texting is a woefully inadequate way to try to express even the slightest fraction of it. I want to believe that he hasn't texted me for the same reasons.

Overall, otherwise, things seem like they might actually be okay.

A lot of kids are still absent, but on the whole, the ones who are there seem pretty much back to normal. No one is wandering aimlessly down the halls, or at least, no one other than the stoners who used to do that anyway, long before Mr. Gabriel ever showed up. And although I make a point of looking closely at every unfamiliar substitute teacher, I don't see any red auras anywhere.

They're still working on the auditorium, but Mr. Henry stops me in the hall to say that we're going to do another weekend of *Sweeney* once they're done fixing everything up again. Miraculously, none of the sets or costumes were damaged, and he thinks with a week or so of rehearsal time we'll be back up to speed and ready to wow more audiences. Because while what happened afterward was weird and terrible and scary, of course it was, everyone still agrees that the show itself was amazing.

I'm glad to hear this, although, of course, it only makes me think that much more about Ryan.

I'm at my locker after lunch when something makes me turn around, and there he is.

He turns the corner with his friends, Jorge limping along on crutches surrounded by girls trying to carry his books and offer him various baked goods, and the other guys in their group joking and laughing and pushing one another like nothing ever happened.

And suddenly it *is* like nothing ever happened, like the past few weeks were just a dream.

He seems so far away to me, like I'm seeing him through the same hopeless window I always used to, wanting to cross over and get to know him for real, wanting to be a part of his world, and vice versa, and feeling like it could never, ever happen. *I've lost him,* I think. I screwed it up and now he's back to being that other Ryan Halsey, the one who's forever out of my league, who I'll never get to kiss again or sit with in dim closets or talk to or share extraordinary experiences with of any kind, ever again.

They come toward me, the whole group, in slow motion, like old times, and when Ryan's head turns and he sees me there and our eyes meet, I instantly, like old times, look away before I can help it. Old stupid habits, rushing back, like nothing ever changed at all. Like I never changed at all.

My eyes fall from his quickly, but not fast enough to miss the way his face hardens in response. By the time I catch myself and look back, he's facing straight ahead, walking on by. Like I just sealed some new deal, set the course of things to come.

No, I think suddenly. *No no no no no.*

This is not how this is going to go down. I mean, are you *kidding* me?

I went to a goddamn demon world with nothing but a magic protractor and a shield made from a biology textbook. I fought giant terrifying demons and saved my best friend from eternal romantically induced horror at the hands of an evil librarian. I struck a deal for my would-be boyfriend's life *and* the lives of everyone else in the school and still owe the demoness two more favors in return, two more trips to her world and all the horrors and dangers and terrible shifty plant-animal-alien landscapes and creatures that will be waiting there to try to make me meat or prey or both. And yes, okay, I also stabbed said would-be boyfriend in the side with said magic protractor just after he told me that he was falling in love with me, but I was doing what had to be done, and I am damned if I'm going to let him walk past me after all of that. I'm still capable of doing what needs to be done. I'm going to do it right now.

I lunge forward and tackle him, carrying him all the way across the hallway to slam into the lockers on the other side. *YES!* my legs cry happily, released to chase their destiny at last. Ryan opens his mouth but before he can get out whatever exclamation of shock or surprise he's about to express, I pin his arms against the wall and lean in and kiss him deeply and passionately right there in the middle of everyone. It's just what I used to dream about all through Italian class while staring at the back-right side of his beautifully shaped head. But I don't have to dream about it anymore. I can do it. I'm doing it right now.

After a moment of initial rigid surprise, his mouth smiles against my own. And he kisses me back.

My nerve endings are singing tiny musical-theater songs of joy throughout my entire body, and I let them, because if this isn't exactly the right kind of moment for that sort of thing, I don't know what is.

Vaguely I am aware that somewhere beyond the immediate scope of my blissfully distracted mind and mouth and heart (and loins), students are hooting and staring and calling out encouragement, and perhaps at some point I would have cared about these things, but not today. I release Ryan's hands, and one of them immediately comes up to grab the back of my head and pull me closer.

One of mine immediately goes down to grab the back

of his pants. *No, just the* outside *of his pants,* nerve endings, *STOP BEING SO GREEDY,* and somewhere far off I think I hear the non-dulcet tones of the humorless once-again-Acting-Principal Levine shouting at us to break it up, threatening all kinds of detentions and suspensions for our completely inappropriate behavior.

But he is no match for my nerve endings, nor for the music that I can hear all around us now, swelling to a melodramatic crescendo of soaring notes and a chorus of voices singing in perfect four-part harmony. It's the act 2 finale, baby, and I'm writing my own happy ending.

Ryan pulls me even tighter against him, still with the kissing (*oh my God* the kissing), and I kiss him back for all that I am worth.

Acknowledgments

I am very grateful to the many people who helped me and this novel along the way. To start with: everyone in the Vermont College of Fine Arts MFA in Writing for Children and Young Adults program (where this story began) for general and overwhelming awesomeness. Among them I would above all like to thank my wise, talented, and beloved advisors Uma Krishnaswami, Cynthia Leitich Smith, Tim Wynne-Jones, and Margaret Bechard, and my fellow Thunder Badgers — especially roommate extraordinaire and very good friend and writer Margaret Crocker. Thanks also to everyone at Kindling Words who laughed in the right places when I read little pieces of this story out loud on certain candlelit Saturday nights. I am also grateful to Dana Klinek for sharing high-school stories with me, as well as for greatly appreciated friendship and weekday conversations that sometimes make me feel like I'm in high school again (in the best of ways), and to Jenny Weiss and Kristin Cartee for being who they are and for ongoing and much-needed across-the-board encouragement and counsel. Extra super special heartfelt thanks go to Spencer Schedler and Bridey Flynn, who read drafts and gave invaluable advice and support in pretty much every conceivable way.

On the musical theater front: Thank you to my parents for letting me get involved in children's and community theater growing up and for sending me to theater camp for all those summers, and also to everyone who ever cast me in a play or in the chorus of a musical. Thanks also to all my Tottenville High School friends — Stephanie Comora Santoriello and Jennifer Gurian Rosenkrantz and all the rest of you crazy kids — including the casts and crews of Soph/Fresh, Junior, and Senior Sing (Junior Sing Rules!) and the spring musicals, and all the teachers who gave their time and energy to advise, direct, and support those endeavors. I'm especially looking at you, Rob Herbert, and remembering Bob Gresh with love. From college, thanks to the Cornell Savoyards, Risley Theater, Gateway Theater, and most of all my dear and multitalented friends Pedro Arroyo, Carrie Fox, Alan Florendo, Jessica Hillman-McCord, and Matt Winberg. Most recently, thanks to the Village Light Opera Group of New York City and all the dedicated people involved in that organization.

Enormous thanks as always to my amazing agent, Jodi Reamer, for guidance, hand-holding, late-night e-mails, and all-around kick-ass excellence, and to my wonderful editor, Sarah Ketchersid, for endless patience, enthusiasm, smart questions and suggestions, and for getting my sense of humor and letting me keep my nontraditional punctuation, at least some of the time.

Finally, eternal gratitude to all the (100 percent non-evil) librarians and other library staffers I have known and worked with and been helped and inspired by over the years. I don't know where I would be without you!